Christine Green trained as a nurse at the Hampstead General Hospital, North London. She has worked in District Nursing and Health Visiting, and she lives in Northampton with her husband, two children and two dogs.

Death in the Country introduces the sparky new police duo of Chief Inspector Connor O'Neill and Detective Sergeant Fran Wilson – 'Satisfyingly gruesome triple murder mystery with new cop duo: he, boozy Irishman; she, the new girl on the beat. More please' *Telegraph*

Christine Green's previous crime novels, featuring feisty private eye Kate Kinsella, have been highly praised:

'An excellent first novel . . . Comes through with flying colours' *Weekend Telegraph*

'Green's writing has all the requisite crackle and tension, and she has given Kinsella a partner from heaven – the gloriously weird Hubert Humberstone, local undertaker. May their double act run and run' *Evening Standard*

'Prime nastiness explored with a light, civilised, endearing touch' *Sunday Times*

'Green's considerable talent to observe and amuse' *Guardian*

Death in
the Country

Christine Green

HEADLINE

First published in Great Britain in 1993
by Macmillan London Limited

First published in paperback in 1994
by HEADLINE BOOK PUBLISHING

10 9 8 7 6 5 4 3 2 1

ISBN 0 7472 4497 9

Printed and bound in Great Britain by
Cox & Wyman Ltd, Reading, Berks

HEADLINE BOOK PUBLISHING
A division of Hodder Headline PLC
338 Euston Road
London NW1 3BH

Death in
the Country

Chapter One

Two dead piglets, one stillborn lamb.

Jessie Harrington parted her bedroom window curtains, removed a circle of condensation with one hand, and stared out on to the farmyard. By the stone wall sat the black plastic bag containing the dead animals. She had placed the stillborn lamb carefully on top of the piglets in the bag the night before. They were to be food for the hounds at the Eastone Regis hunt. She would be glad when the collection was made, dead animals attracted vermin.

Downstairs, this time from the kitchen window, she stared out momentarily at the grey sky. Upstairs, downstairs, what did it matter? The sky was still grey, it would probably rain again today. Maybe even snow. It was early April and it had been a long hard winter.

She made tea in her big white pottery teapot, put three sausages on a low heat on the Aga, and sat down to watch for the kennel man to arrive. Sometimes he shared breakfast with them.

Jessie was glad of the company, any company; even the kennel man, whose name was Charlie Sutton and who had only two topics of conversation – the hounds and real ale. Sometimes, though, she could persuade him, with an extra sausage and an extra rasher or two, to talk about members of the hunt. It seemed to Jessie that hunt members lived exciting lives, having affairs, making lots of money effortlessly, holidays abroad, new clothes, going to hunt balls, while she spent her life – no, that wasn't true, she didn't spend her life. It was spent for her. She worked her life away. The only dancing she ever did was a quick-step through mud several times a day. The only entertaining she did was the occasional fry-up for Charlie and sometimes when the vet called she'd have just baked a fruit cake and he'd enjoy a slice. As for holidays, she'd had a honeymoon in Torquay ten years previously and nothing since. Nothing, unless you counted the yearly day trip she went on with the Women's Institute.

As Jessie saw her husband come out of the pig shed she turned over the sausages and poured out his tea. She heard him approach the kitchen door, heard the noise of him removing his Wellington boots, and the latch lift sharply before he entered the kitchen.

'Smells good,' he said. 'Charlie been yet?'

Jessie shook her head. 'He's late. Usually he comes here first. Perhaps his truck is playing up again.'

Tom didn't answer but went to the kitchen sink to wash his hands. He dried them carefully on the roller towel then sat down at the kitchen table which Jessie always kept covered with a tablecloth. Today she had put on her second-best embroidered one, just in case Charlie stayed for breakfast.

'You're not having any breakfast,' said Tom as she put a plate of sausages, bacon, and eggs in front of him. It wasn't a question. She hadn't eaten breakfast for years. Not since . . . Not since it had been cooked for her on her honeymoon.

Later on, mid-morning, when Tom was out, she'd have some toast. Her not eating much riled Tom. Not that anyone else would notice his irritation. But she knew by the way his lips tightened and his eyes, the colour of clouds on the worst of a February day, seemed to darken slightly. As if her not eating much was a slight against him.

They sat opposite each other. He ate hungrily, looking down at his plate. Not looking at her. Jessie sipped hot sweet tea and fingered the corner of the tablecloth. Smiling to herself, she thought, If I had to choose between him and my second-best tablecloth – I'd choose the tablecloth.

It was then she heard the sound of Charlie's truck coming slowly up the hill.

'There's Charlie,' said Tom. He always stated the obvious. Jessie stood by the back door under the porch and watched as Charlie's truck drove up and parked outside the pig shed. Their collie dog Jethro ran up, tail wagging. Dogs seemed to like Charlie.

'You staying for breakfast, Charlie?' she shouted.

'Morning, missus,' he shouted back. 'Be over in a minute.'

Jessie paused for a moment to watch him bend down and pat the dog and take from his pocket the titbit he normally kept there. Then she went into the kitchen to make another pot of tea and cut fresh bread.

When Charlie appeared a minute or two later at the kitchen door Jessie knew something was wrong. He hadn't bothered to take off his muddy boots and his cheeks seemed to have lost their healthy redness. Suddenly he was piglet-pink and his eyes were bluer and glistening . . .

'Charlie – what's wrong? What's the matter?'

'I'll be all right. Just a bit of a shock, that's all. Didn't expect it, you see. Thought I'd cut down on the number of black bags, fill up one more before I used another . . .'

'Come in, for Gawd's sake,' said Tom looking up reluctantly from his plate. 'And close the door. Good money I pay to heat this place, I don't want it all escaping.'

'Come in, Charlie, and sit down,' said Jessie, giving Tom a warning look. 'I'll make you a cup of tea and then you can tell us.'

She guided him to a chair at the table and Tom noticed for the first time something was wrong.

'What's up with you?'

'Nothing's wrong wi' me,' said Charlie. 'It's what you been doing that worries me.'

Tom pushed his now empty plate away. 'What's that supposed to mean?'

Charlie shrugged. 'It'll be a police matter . . .'

'What will?' interrupted Jessie, pausing with teapot in mid-air.

'You better put down that teapot, me duck,' said Charlie, 'before you scald yourself.'

'Come on, Charlie, get it off your chest,' said Tom.

Charlie looked from Tom to Jessie as if seeing them for the first time. A doubting sort of look. A bit fearful. Apart from the clock ticking on the mantelpiece all was quiet. They all waited. Charlie for courage, Tom and Jessie intrigued but not obviously worried.

'In the black bag,' began Charlie. 'I emptied it out and there it was . . . it was a shock I can tell—'

'What was a bloody shock?' interrupted Tom angrily.

'The arm,' said Charlie. 'The human arm. Chopped off. The fingers all white and waxy.'

Jessie sank into a chair. Tom let out a slow whistle. No one said a word.

The same morning, just a little later, Alison Lowick was on early morning farm duty at Higham Merrils College of Agriculture. It was college policy that students took turns with the more unpleasant jobs, thus equipping them for the rigours of farm life. Collecting dead animals and mucking out were part of the daily routine. Alison didn't mind the dirty jobs but she hated dead things, hated touching them, hated the smell. The smell seemed to stay in her nose all day.

The other student, Phillippa Hargrave, had been assigned to feed the chickens. Alison, late as usual, was to join her.

It began to rain. Alison told herself she was a summer person and once the summer came the mud would go and she'd start enjoying the course. This was her first year. She'd applied to do equestrian studies but there were no vacancies and so she had been slotted into the farm management course. Phillippa, too, was a first-year student, but she had a head start. She came from an old farming family, landowners. She was used to dead animals. She rode with the hunt.

The chicken shed was dark and noisy. Even though the lights were on it was shadowy inside and there were chickens everywhere, pecking and clucking. Alison could see Phillippa bending down at one of the nesting boxes.

'Hi, Phillippa,' she called.

Phillippa stood up. 'Present for you,' she shouted back as she lifted something high above her head. A dead chicken landed at Alison's feet.

'Bitch,' Alison muttered as she looked down at the corpse. She watched as a few interested chickens came to investigate. She bent down to touch it. It was still warm. Screwing up her courage she picked the hen up and carried it out at arm's length, as though somehow it might wake up and peck her.

'Wait for me,' called Phillippa in her usual tone of expensively acquired bossiness.

Alison ignored her, walked quickly to the stone round that served as the animals' temporary mortuary, and opened the large black refuse bag.

She didn't scream, for at first she failed to recognize what was in the bag. When she did realize, she dropped the bag and the chicken.

'Alison!' said Phillippa from behind her. It was an irate use of her name as though she'd been caught fighting in the school playground. It did have a calming effect, though. Alison turned to face her.

'Look!' she managed to say.

'For goodness sake,' said Phillippa irritated. She retrieved the bag from the ground and looked inside.

'Wow,' she breathed slowly.

Alison felt her own shock justified when she saw that even beneath her mid-winter Tenerife tan Phillippa had paled.

Both girls stared into the bag again as if to confirm that their eyes hadn't deceived them. But it was true. A severed arm, hand uppermost, lay with the fingers grotesquely raised as if in some sort of salute.

Chapter Two

Fran Wilson's first day as a detective sergeant had started at eight. It was now nine and she sat in the staff canteen, alone amongst the empty tables, drinking her third cup of tea and longing for a cigarette. She'd given up now for six weeks. It didn't get easier, it got harder.

She stared out of the second-floor windows on to Fowchester's main road. The transfer had been swift, too swift for her to adjust properly. She'd been a detective constable in Birmingham and yet when her promotion came through it was decided that a more rural location would suit her talents. It was a way of getting rid of her, of course. She'd mentioned once her mother had kept goats. That, perhaps, had been the cause of her downfall. Stop kidding yourself, Fran, she told herself. The real reason she'd been offered a sideways move was because she had shopped her policeman boyfriend. And lost other friends into the bargain. Telling the truth didn't come cheap. She supposed being sent to Fowchester was the British equivalent of a sojourn in outer Siberia.

And now she'd moved into a terraced cottage at the far end of the main street and learned that Fowchester was called Fowster by the locals and her cottage, so quaint from the outside, was full of mould, and damp, rattling windows, and her tenancy was shared by a mouse. That, and the loss of nicotine to her blood-stream, made her wonder if being made a sergeant was worth all the struggle.

Fowchester was yet another staging post on the Watling Street built by the Romans and not much seemed to have happened to it since. Apart from the flat-racing circuit the only reason to stop in the town was for a drink at one of the pubs. It was that sort of town; a one supermarket, four pub, two Indian restaurant, one Chinese, one large church, two video shop sort of place . . .

'WDS Wilson,' a voice called from the doorway, 'the superintendent will see you now. Ground floor, second on the right.'

The owner of the voice had gone in a flash of blue uniform.

As Fran walked downstairs she told herself not to be irritated that some police forces still differentiated males and females. She was now a detective sergeant and she was going to be a good one. A bag man – or would they call her a bag woman? What did it matter? All she really wanted was a cigarette.

The introductions didn't take long. Except that Superintendent Ringstead called her Francesca which she hated and she virtually stopped him mid-sentence to tell him so.

'And this is your mentor and guide Chief Inspector Connor O'Neill,' announced the Super in a loud voice that was almost a shout.

Fran tried not to look him up and down too obviously. At least he wasn't fat and pompous like Superintendent Ringstead. O'Neill smiled pleasantly enough, shook her hand firmly, and said, 'You've chosen a grand day to start.'

She wondered if by 'grand' he meant it wasn't snowing. Fran supposed he was in his early thirties. For a man with an Irish name he didn't have a broad face or the squareness of head Fran associated with the Irish. His was a lean face with worn overtones. His nose was slightly too large, but he had a strong jaw, good teeth, and greenish eyes that seemed a bit distant, as if he'd switched off his receiver. What did surprise her was his clothes – cavalry-twill trousers, green and white checked shirt, and moss-green V-necked sweater. The senior detectives in Birmingham had always worn smart suits and succeeded in looking like a team of estate agents. Fran thought him quite attractive – for a boss.

As they walked through the corridors of the station one or two comments drifted intentionally her way.

'He's 'armless enough, love.'

This was followed by a muted guffaw.

'Going to give him a hand, are you?' someone muttered as they approached O'Neill's office.

'What's going on, sir?' asked Fran once O'Neill had shut the door.

'You'll not be needing the "sir",' said O'Neill, 'just

call me boss. They'll be having a little joke at your expense. A wind-up. Nothing malicious, you understand. But all will become clear soon enough.'

Fran hoped so. O'Neill stared at her for a moment, but he seemed to be looking into the middle distance, not really at her at all. Then just as Fran was sure he wasn't seeing her he would refocus and give her a direct and unblinking gaze. Unnerving, thought Fran, as she looked away.

'You'll be sharing the room with me,' said O'Neill eventually. 'That's your desk. I've put you near the window. The light's better there. You can watch the world go by.'

'Will I have time?' asked Fran as she looked over at the small desk that looked out towards the main road. On her desk sat a typewriter, a telephone, and a half-dead spider plant. She thought it strange she should have her back towards O'Neill's desk.

'You'll have to make time, especially when this case is over,' he said, an open palm indicating that she should sit down. Fran swivelled her chair round to face him.

'A detective who doesn't sit and think is like a dog chasing its tail – a complete waste of time and effort.'

Fran nodded, wondering if he always went in for homespun philosophizing this early in the morning. She was trying to place his accent, Irish, but not obviously so, low and soft, so that you had to listen carefully.

'I'll be having only two rules,' O'Neill was saying with a brief smile. 'Apart from complete loyalty, that is. The first one is that CID don't go around looking like detectives in sombre suits. We go dressed to mingle and not be noticed. Dark suits might just as well be uniform. We want people to talk to us. To tell us all their little criminal secrets.'

He paused and smiled again as Fran looked down at her severe navy skirt and jacket.

'And the second rule?' asked Fran.

'Not exactly a rule,' said O'Neill. 'More a convention, really, just stick to me like toffee and we'll get on fine. But for now we're on a brand-new case. You'll be needing wellies and a change of clothes. I keep some gear here but I expect you'll be needing to go home.'

'Well, yes,' said Fran, feeling that somehow she'd managed to fall short on her very first day.

'I'll drive you,' he said.

'Now?'

'It is a murder case.'

Fran opened her mouth slightly, then closed it again. No doubt he would explain. The Fowchester police force seemed not so much laid back as laid out. But it was, after all, a murder case. Her first one as a detective sergeant, and – she didn't want to admit it to O'Neill – her first one ever.

In Birmingham she'd been confined to rapes, domestic violence, and female shoplifters. And once she'd had friends. Here she knew no one. She'd had a busy week moving in but she'd only spoken to people on the phone. Face-to-face contact had been reserved for the newsagent, who had a brown shiny face, was called

Aziz, and said 'Cheers' a great deal, and the woman who worked in the bakery and called her 'my duck' or 'my love'. She'd already become a good customer. Each day she'd bought a fresh cream cake. Compensation for not smoking.

O'Neill remained silent as they drove along Fowchester's main road to where it narrowed and to where a row of terraced cottages ended and open countryside began. He wouldn't allow her to drive until he knew her better. Driving with a stranger was, O'Neill thought, more trusting than sex with a woman you'd just met.

She wasn't as he'd imagined. The name Francesca had conjured up visions of a tall leggy blonde, imperious perhaps, ambitious and sexy. Fran was short, with hazel eyes, dark brown hair worn in a long bob that bounced as she moved, and high firm breasts that didn't. On the whole she was a bit skinny for O'Neill's taste, he preferred the more buxom, obvious type; but all in all, he thought, she was too pretty to be a detective – and she smelt pretty good too. He'd have to be very careful. He couldn't afford to get involved again. . .

He sat in the car and watched as his new DS emerged from her cottage. She wore black low-heeled leather boots with jeans tucked into them and a navy-blue anorak. Now she looked about eighteen. He wondered if he could turn her into a good detective. He'd have a damn good try, of course. But he knew deep down that although he enjoyed the teaching aspect of his job, what he really wanted was to impress her, and the members of the force who doubted him.

This time he couldn't afford to fail. His job was definitely on the line.

'Sorry I took so long,' she said, getting into the car. 'Most of my things are still in boxes.'

'I don't think our corpse will complain.'

'Who's the victim?' asked Fran.

'No idea,' said O'Neill. 'Finding out will be all part of the fun.'

Fran stared straight ahead as they drove down country lanes that were now green and fresh-looking with blue flowers growing from the stone walls of cottages and trees beginning to blossom. And still the promise of snow in the grey clouds.

In a way, not knowing who the victim was was quite comforting. She could cope with dead bodies. They couldn't suffer any more. The living could. And it was grief-stricken relatives that frightened her, or at least her reaction to them.

'This is it,' said O'Neill, making a sudden left turn. 'Harrington Farm.'

He drove slowly along the gravel track and at the end Fran could see the greystone farmhouse and outbuildings that seemed to be in a state of near collapse. A collie dog ran along by the car wagging his tail excitedly and a woman appeared from a side door and waved to them.

As they walked the short distance between the car and the kitchen door mud gathered on their boots and splashed on to Fran's jeans.

'Come in,' said the woman. 'Leave your boots in the porch.'

O'Neill winked at Fran as he pulled off his boots.

The white teapot was once more on the table and whilst waiting for the police Jessie Harrington had spent her time making scones.

'How are you, Mr O'Neill? Sit down the both of you. Haven't seen you in ages,' said Jessie as she poured tea into her best china cups.

'I'm fine, Jessie,' answered O'Neill. 'This is Fran Wilson, my new detective sergeant. She's from Birmingham.'

'Hello,' said Jessie, giving Fran a brief smile. 'Good shops in Birmingham. I've been once or twice, Tom's never been though.'

'How is Tom?' asked O'Neill.

'Miserable as ever. He won't change now, will he? It's part of his nature. Most farmers seem miserable, it must be the weather.' Then she added quietly as if it were an afterthought: 'And the money, of course.'

Fran sat upright on the kitchen chair. She hadn't expected to take off her boots and her tights had developed a hole in the toe. Nor had she expected all this domestic chit-chat. Surely this was supposed to be a murder enquiry? Jessie Harrington seemed more excited than distressed. She was tall and thin with a few silver hairs mingling with scraped back fair hair. Fran guessed she was about forty and, by the way she looked so appreciatively at O'Neill and the way she spoke about her husband, she was not happily married.

Looking across at O'Neill Fran tried to express her unease by frowning and shrugging slightly.

'Have a scone,' he said, thrusting the plate towards

her, 'could be a while before we get lunch.'

She took the scone and bit into it. Cream squelched out from all sides and she had to lick it from her fingers. O'Neill noticed. 'Grand scones, aren't they,' he said to no one in particular, but as Jessie looked at him he smiled.

'Now then, Jessie,' he said, 'you'll be wanting to tell us all about it.'

'Well I would, Mr O'Neill. It was a bit of a shock to us all. Even Tom was struck dumb. Poor Charlie though, he got the fright of his life.'

'Charlie Sutton from the hunt kennels?'

'Yes, that's him. It upset him so much he wouldn't eat his breakfast.'

'What about Tom?'

'Oh, he'd just finished his.'

Fran coughed. She was afraid she was going to laugh. O'Neill looked at her sharply.

'Where is it now, Jessie?'

'Charlie said to leave it where it was. It's in the black bag by the pig shed. Tom had a look at it but I didn't want to. I think Charlie thought we put it there.'

'Why would he think that?'

'I don't know. I suppose because he found it on our farm.'

O'Neill nodded. Fran tried to force down the rest of her scone. Was this really what a murder investigation in the country consisted of? A body referred to as 'it', tea, scones, and social niceties that bordered on the obscene in the circumstances? Just because she hadn't been on a murder case before didn't mean she was ignorant of the general theory. She couldn't keep quiet any longer. New or not, she had to say something.

'Isn't it about time we looked at the body?' she said.

It was Jessie Harrington who answered her.

'There's no body, dear. Fancy not telling you that. Shame on you, Mr O'Neill. There's only an arm. Well, I think there's a hand too, but as I said I haven't seen it yet. Tom will be in any minute, he'll take you to see it.'

Fran felt her face grow hot. She glared angrily at O'Neill. He responded by looking pleased with himself.

'Don't be looking at me like that,' he said. 'An arm's as good a place to start as any on a murder hunt.'

At that moment a thickset man with an equally thickset miserable face walked into the kitchen. He hadn't removed his boots but stood on the matting by the kitchen door. He wore what looked like an old army greatcoat which he removed and hung on a hook on the wall. Underneath he wore grey dungarees, mud-splattered to the knees, and a green-padded waistcoat.

'Morning,' he said. 'It's snowing.'

'So it is,' said Jessie, and they all stood for a moment watching the wide flakes begin to cloud their view from the window.

'Won't be much,' said Tom.

Fran guessed, judging by the downcast turn of his mouth, that that was probably the most optimistic thing he'd ever said.

'Come to see our bit of corpse, have you?' Tom asked, still standing by the door but looking at the teapot. 'Bit of a shock that. It might not have been found, you know. Charlie was trying to save on rubbish bags.'

'You point us in the right direction, Tom,' said O'Neill, 'and we'll have a look round. Scene of crimes will want to have a look too – bag it up, label it, search every nook and cranny, and cordon off the area.'

'Just out there by the wall near the pig shed,' he answered, jerking a thumb at the door. 'Hope they won't be long, my pigs will need feeding again soon.'

'They'll be as quick as they can,' said O'Neill. 'Come on, Wilson, we'll be away. We can't be enjoying ourselves all day.'

Fran stood up silently, hoping no one saw her bare toe or guessed how irritated she felt and walked to the door. Tom stood aside but he neither smiled nor said a word. Jessie murmured, 'Nice to see you both,' and then added in a whisper to O'Neill, 'Take no notice of Tom. He's just a rude old bugger.'

'We'll be back, Jessie,' said O'Neill, patting her shoulder as if in consolation for being married to a man like Tom. 'Your scones are the best in the county. Probably tomorrow.'

Jessie smiled and her eyes shone. Fran saw in her face how pretty she must have been before harsh wind and sun had damaged her skin. And being married to Tom had damaged her soul.

As O'Neill and Fran walked heads down against the snow and towards the barns they could hear the sounds of raised voices and then angrier tones: 'You stupid bitch,' followed by 'Bastard,' and then even worse.

'Country living,' said O'Neill thoughtfully, 'should be reserved for the Irish. Only they know how to do it properly.'

By the time they reached the wall near the pig shed Fran's face was wet and her hair shed extra rivulets of cold slush into her eyes. Then just as abruptly the snow changed to rain and O'Neill was opening the black plastic bag for her to peer inside.

'Well, what do you think?' he asked.

Chapter Three

The rain, now falling fast, sounded noisy against the black plastic. Fran looked inside. She wasn't shocked because she'd known what to expect, but even so she was surprised, because although she knew it was an arm, it had a sort of unreal waxiness. It was hard to believe that it had once belonged to a human being.

'All right if I touch it?' she asked O'Neill as she crouched down to get a closer look.

'Better not,' he said, 'without gloves. Male or female?'

'I've got gloves,' said Fran, digging deep into her anorak pocket and pulling out a pair of rubber gloves. One up to me, she thought, as though somehow she was in a competition.

Once the rubber gloves were on she inspected the arm, examining it whilst at the same time trying not to handle it too much.

'Male. It's quite big,' she answered slowly, 'and the hand is wide, no rings, no nail varnish. Nails short, large spatulate thumb, long fingers . . .'

'Anything else?'

'It's hairy.'

O'Neill took a cursory glance himself but said nothing. Fran was cool, he had to admit. He wasn't squeamish about most sights but smells could turn his stomach and the bag held smells that were impossible to describe.

'I'll ring scene of crimes. You can have a preliminary look round – tracks, footprints, scraps of material, more bits of body – anything.'

O'Neill walked off towards the car. What are minions for? thought Fran as she stepped backwards in the mud trying to keep in her own footprints so that she didn't ruin any potential clues. It was unlikely she would ruin anything other than her boots because the whole area around the bag and the shed was as churned as liquid chocolate. She squatted down for a closer look at the ground and as she did so the collie dog came bounding up and placed both muddy paws on her knees. Hastily she stood up before she toppled over.

'Off you go, dog,' she said, and then more loudly 'Home!' but the dog ignored her, tail still wagging, friendly, expectant, and in the way.

'Anything?' asked O'Neill when he returned only moments later.

Fran shrugged. 'I couldn't get rid of the dog but I don't think we'll get any good prints, the ground's too wet and churned-up.'

O'Neill turned to the dog, whose tail still wagged enthusiastically.

'Home, Jethro – now!' he said firmly as he pointed towards the farmhouse. Jethro ran off instantly.

'There's a lot of unasked questions here,' said O'Neill as they watched the dog running off. 'I hope you're making a mental note.'

Fran thought his tone pompous and she wondered if it was deliberate. Was he trying to irritate her or what?

'Come on, Wilson,' said O'Neill abruptly, 'we're getting soaked. Let's get back to the car.'

As they walked, heads down, trying to avoid treading in the bigger puddles, Fran said, 'Talking of unasked questions, boss, was there a reason you didn't ask the Harringtons many questions?'

O'Neill smiled. 'Think we're slow here, do you? I've found that those who tell the truth need time to think about what's happened. To let it sink in if you like. Those that tell lies need time to fabricate them. It's lies that trap people, the more elaborate, the more damning. Tomorrow we'll be back and tongues will loosen. Yours too I hope.'

'What's that supposed to mean?'

'It means that when we go on interviews I expect you to make a contribution and not spend your time worrying about being without your boots and having a hole in your tights.'

Fran bit back a retort. What was the point? She had a sudden longing for a cigarette for she had the strongest suspicion she was going to hate this job. And was O'Neill beginning to show his true colours? Perhaps she'd been thrust upon him and he resented not having someone more experienced. Or perhaps it was simply that she was female.

As O'Neill drove away from Harrington Farm he

said, 'I can be irritable at times. You'll have to be a bit thick-skinned.'

'I'll try,' said Fran.

There was silence then and instead of being filled with enthusiasm for her first murder case Fran wondered why she'd ever agreed to come to the middle of nowhere and be friendless into the bargain. Unless she made friends within the force she knew that making friends outside would be impossible. Once people knew your job they expected you to fit a certain pattern – humourless, strait-laced, verging on the tough and butch. That was one of the reasons Fran had wanted to be a detective. She'd thought that not having to wear a uniform would liberate her in some way. It hadn't of course.

O'Neill drove the car fast towards the village of Higham Merrils. Fran Wilson was unsettling him. Somehow on an investigation like this he felt he should only have to think about himself and solving the case. At the moment he felt he had to be responsible for her. Which of course he was. But with another man he could relax more. Failure didn't seem so crucial. But he hadn't failed yet and she seemed bright enough.

'There's another one,' he said absently.

Fran looked at him sharply, thinking she had missed some part of his observation.

'What?'

'There's another arm,' explained O'Neill. 'At the College of Agriculture. Found by a student this morning. We're on our way there now.'

'Thanks for telling me,' said Fran.

He couldn't tell if she was being sarcastic or not.

'Found in a black bag,' he continued, 'all ready for the kennel man.'

'Has anyone been reported missing?'

O'Neill shook his head. 'Not yet,' he said slowly. 'Not yet.'

Even in the rain Higham Merrils College had charm. Of local grey stone, it stood like a manor house against a backdrop of fields, and on the hill above it nestled a small farm. A few sheep grazed in the rain on the upward slope of the field and the sky although grey was big and expansive. Strange, Fran thought, how much bigger the sky seemed in the country.

'This place does a bit of everything,' said O'Neill as he drove through the entrance and parked by the mock-medieval front door. 'Produces free-range eggs, ice cream, plants, milk, even has a few hives, and I'm told the bees give very good honey. It takes students from all over the country and from the Eastern bloc as well.'

'Looks quiet for so much activity,' observed Fran. Apart from the sheep and a slight swaying of the daffodils and tulips in the flowerbeds, nothing moved.

Inside had a dark, quiet, church-like atmosphere. The floor was quarry tiled and the walls were of dark brown wood panelling with the occasional painting of Highland cows and large sheep. A grandfather clock ticked steadily in one corner and on a pseudo-medieval coffee-table piles of *Farmer's Weekly* and *The Dairy*

Farmer had been neatly arranged next to a vase of daffodils.

A receptionist sat at a typewriter in the hall itself opposite the front door. She looked up and smiled as they walked in. She was, Fran supposed, in her late thirties. She wore a buttoned to the neck cream blouse, a beige skirt that showed quite a lot of knee beneath the desk, and tiny pearl earrings. Her make-up was minimal except that her nails sported a cyanotic purple nail varnish and they were either false or she didn't in fact do much typing.

'Hello, Connor,' she said, smiling broadly in obvious delight, 'nice to see you again – even if it is under such awful circumstances. The students are all a bit upset, as you can imagine.'

O'Neill stood in front of her desk, also smiling and looking into her eyes as if for that moment the odd dismembered limb was a mere excuse for seeing her again. 'You're looking well, Kay. Life at Higham Merrils must be suiting you.'

Kay smiled again in response. 'You're looking well, too,' she said slowly.

Fran watched this exchange warily. So this was her new boss! A rural Don Juan. Or had Don Juan always been rural? She couldn't remember. Anyway, not only did O'Neill seem to know everyone, he obviously knew some of the populace very well indeed. Fran coughed, which wasn't too difficult as her lungs were still rejecting a few years' worth of nicotine and tar. She felt the need to assert the fact that she was in attendance and as yet she hadn't been introduced.

'It's all right, Wilson,' he said, turning his head

towards the sound of her cough. 'I'm just coming. Kay and I are old friends. You can have a look round the farm if you like. We'll set up an incident room here. I'll tell the Principal—'

'He's not here, Connor,' interrupted Kay, 'he's on holiday in Wales.'

'The deputy, then,' said O'Neill. 'Where could we use? We'll need access to phone lines of course. I'll arrange for a computer to be brought in.'

'There's a classroom that's just been redecorated, you could use that. I'll make a few arrangements if you want.'

'Great. You're an angel, Kay.'

Fran was by now on her way out. Why she should feel like a rejected other woman she didn't know. She'd only just met O'Neill but he'd managed to make her feel about as welcome as a crop of warts and with no cure in sight.

At the back of the main building were the classrooms, modern low buildings with wide windows, and as she walked past Fran could see the students copying notes from the blackboard. It all seemed pretty dull: 'The Modern Tractor' in one classroom and 'Increasing Milk Yield' in another. She looked upwards towards the farm wondering just how muddy it would be. She was cold now, the steady rain had begun to seep through her jacket and she felt increasingly at a loss. A complete body would have been more satisfying somehow, a limb here and there was, it seemed to Fran, an insult – the murderer having a little game at police expense.

To get to the farm's land Fran had to climb over a

stile and then walk up a narrow track between two fields with sheep grazing either side. There were several young lambs, none of whom seemed to mind the weather, and by the time Fran reached the farm itself she could see patches of blue sky appearing and the rain abated to a mere fine spray. Her spirits lifted with the improvement in the weather. Perhaps she would be the one to find the rest of the body. Or if not that, maybe she would find a clue and O'Neill would be impressed. She'd been warned that being a DS was one of the harder jobs in the police force, no real power but several bosses watching you to see if you'd make the grade; and being female you had to prove yourself over and over again.

The farm itself was fronted by a cottage-style farmhouse that was probably once quite picturesque, but now the brickwork had begun to crumble and it appeared to be held up in parts by a straggling lattice-work of creeping ivy. Behind the farmhouse Fran could see several barns and to her right a row of greenhouses. There was no one around. She walked on towards the barns and was just about to look inside when a man came out. He stood for a moment watching her suspiciously, one arm propped on the door lintel as if barring her entry. He was tall, rough-looking, middle-aged, wearing a black donkey jacket and black mud-caked Wellingtons.

'What do yer want?' he asked gruffly.

'Police. Detective Sergeant Wilson.' She flashed her warrant card at him. He wasn't impressed, she could tell.

'You come about the arm?'

'That's it,' said Fran.

'Good,' he said. 'Every bugger's seen it as an excuse to clear off. I'll be glad when it's off the premises. You taking it away?'

'Not me personally. But I'd like to see it.'

'It ain't pretty.'

'Would you show me where it is please?'

He lowered his arm. 'Come on, I'll show you.'

She followed him behind the barns to a stone round tucked into a corner by a low wall.

'It's in there,' he said, pointing to the squat half-chimney. 'I've got work to do now. I'll be in with the pigs if you want me.'

And then he was gone, walking quickly, his wellington boots making squelchy noises in the mud.

Fran looked at the ground and the pattern of footprints that ended in the stone receptacle. Probably half the college had trekked up here, she thought, but to be strictly accurate the mud and gravel had ensured that there were no perfect footprints, just parts – like the body.

'Found anything yet, Wilson?' came O'Neill's voice from behind her.

'That was quick,' said Fran turning round to face him. 'I thought you'd be in for a long session with – the deputy.'

If O'Neill noticed her meaningful pause he didn't respond but looked over her shoulder and said, 'He was teaching. A staff member's off sick. I'll catch him later. Have you found anything?'

Fran shook her head. O'Neill's eyes scanned the ground.

'Looks like a battalion has marched up here,' he said irritably, as though somehow she were responsible.

'Well, I suppose it is of interest in a place like this.'

'Don't like the country much, do you?' he said giving her a quizzical glance.

Fran smiled, 'Not when it rains. I quite like sheep though. Nice gentle relaxing creatures—'

'Now then, Wilson,' he interrupted. 'Stop shilly-shallying and look in the bag.'

'I'm not squeamish,' said Fran. 'I'm ready when you are.'

O'Neill smiled faintly. 'Fair enough, but my stomach doesn't appreciate protracted waits for its shocks. It likes them over and done with.'

'You're the boss – boss,' said Fran as she knelt down to open the bag. She stared for a moment at the contents. 'It's . . . it's . . .'

'Yes, Wilson. It's an arm and I expect it's just like the last one. There's no need to go dramatic on me.'

'I'll start again,' she said. 'It's a small hand, longish fingernails – one broken, no rings but a mark where one used to be, short forearm – not hairy.'

O'Neill looked over her shoulder to confirm her findings. But as the smell hit his stomach he stood up abruptly.

'What's wrong with you, Wilson? Haven't you got a sense of smell?'

She turned to him. 'Yes, it's just my iron self-control. I think of smells I like and then concentrate on those.'

'Well, it obviously works. Lucky you. You can stay here until we get the manpower to cordon this lot off.'

Fran noticed O'Neill had paled slightly and he appeared not to have noticed the differences. She would have to spell it out.

'There's something else, boss, about the arm.'

'Yes?'

'It's female.'

'Are you sure?'

'Positive,' said Fran. 'It's definitely female.'

'Just stay here, Wilson. I'll call scene of crimes, get them here first, and get the incident room up and running.'

Fran watched as O'Neill walked away. The patch of blue sky had disappeared and the rain fell more heavily. She would have loved a cigarette – just one puff.

O'Neill was relieved to be away from that sight and the smell. His stomach lurched again. He swallowed hard and tried to think about the first day of the cricket season. He couldn't. The only thing that crossed his mind was the nasty thought that the female arm in his patch could belong to someone he knew.

Chapter Four

Tom was mad, not angry mad, barking mad. Jessie was quite sure of that. She'd had a terrible night. Tom had always been the jealous type and the finding of an arm on their land seemed to have unhinged him even further. His general idea was that someone Jessie knew had put the arm there to incriminate him in some way, or that the arm belonged to a rival for Jessie's favours. Fat chance, thought Jessie, but she denied all allegations with the seriousness that Tom obviously believed they were worth.

She'd been interrogated most of the night until, at last, Tom had slumped backwards in bed full of whisky and evil suspicions and snored his way towards dawn.

Jessie had watched him for some time, stretched out on his back, his mouth open displaying his dental caries and flaccid, coated tongue. She spent some minutes gazing at his tongue wishing that it could spring into action and choke him. That's the stuff dreams are made of, thought Jessie. One day, though, she'd have her revenge.

At six she went downstairs to the kitchen and pulled

back the red gingham curtains. Once she'd thought they were cheerful but they were now faded and not red but pink. Faded like me, she thought. Then she put on the fat sausages that Tom insisted on seven days a week and watched as they spat and sizzled and slowly changed colour. Not that Tom was in any way fussy about his food, as long as it was always the same. Roast on Sunday, cold on Monday, steak and kidney Tuesday, cottage pie Wednesday, gammon Thursday, fish and chips Friday, and steak and onions Saturday. It was no wonder that she'd long ago lost her appetite. In the first year of marriage she'd tried to be a little adventurous – lasagne, spaghetti, curry.

'I'm not eating this foreign muck,' he'd say. 'I keep you. All you have to do is cook the food I like.'

And so she did just that, without variation. She rarely ate with him. She watched him eat. Sometimes on Saturday night she'd deliberately overcook his steak hoping he'd choke. Of course he never had.

At six fifteen she heard him moving about upstairs.

'Why didn't you wake me?' he asked as he came into the kitchen. 'Half the bloody day's gone already.'

'Police will be here later,' she said. 'Try and be civil to them.'

'It's you they'll want to talk to,' said Tom slyly.

Jessie let that remark pass. Tom obviously wanted to start up again last night's row, a rehash like Monday's dinner.

'Got your best dress on, I see,' he said, his mouth half full of sausage.

'Second best and five years old,' retorted Jessie,

34

'and don't speak with your mouth full.'

Tom raised his backside from the chair and Jessie half expected he'd try to land her one. But he'd have to be quick to catch her. She was used to ducking and diving and anyway she had the frying pan in her hand. He sat down again, probably because he thought the police might catch them fighting – or was it the frying pan that deterred him? No matter what the reason, Jessie felt a change in her attitude. It was hard to describe the feeling – more resolved somehow. To do what? That was the question and as yet Jessie didn't have an answer.

The police came at nine thirty. She heard the car, its wheels crunching up the gravel path, and by the time Detective Chief Inspector O'Neill had got out and walked to the kitchen door the tea was just made and a fruit cake and plates were being arranged on the table.

Jessie was disappointed that the woman detective was with him. She was pretty but not the sort you expected to be a policewoman. She'd seemed ill at ease yesterday as if she had never set foot in a farmhouse before.

'Good morning, Jessie. That fruit cake looks wonderful, nearly as good as you,' said O'Neill as he walked into the kitchen.

'Sit down, Mr O'Neill and . . .' She waved her hand at Fran.

'Fran.'

'Oh yes,' said Jessie.

'Tom busy, is he?' asked O'Neill.

'Shall I call him?'

'Not yet, Jessie. I'd like to talk to you first.'

Jessie stood to pour the tea. 'Help yourself to fruit cake. Vet's special, I call that. He's very partial to my fruit cake.'

O'Neill cut a slice for Fran, one for Jessie, and an even larger piece for himself.

'Tuck in, Wilson,' he said before he bit into the cake. 'It will do you good.'

After a few bites and muttering 'delicious' once or twice he said, 'Now then, young Jessie. You'll be wanting to tell me about the night before last.'

She smiled delightedly at the 'young'. 'Of course, Mr O'Neill, but there's not much to tell. Tom went to the village for a drink, he came home . . . well, I'm not sure exactly when. I went to bed about half-past ten. I didn't hear him come in. In the morning I got up at the usual time to cook breakfast. Tom was already up and out working.'

'And the dog?'

'Jethro?'

'The same.'

'He was in his kennel.'

'The whole night?'

'Yes.'

O'Neill smiled at her encouragingly. 'And he didn't bark?'

'Not that I heard.'

'Not even when Tom came in?'

'No. I've said.'

Jessie had begun to look uncomfortable.

'Any questions you'd like to ask, Wilson?'

For a moment Fran's mind went a complete blank. She had been surprised that Jessie was lying. For she was sure she was. But what lie exactly?

'Did Tom drive to the village?' asked Fran.

'Course he did. It's about three miles.'

'Which village?'

'Clopstock. He likes the pub there. Beer's slightly cheaper. Tom would do anything to save a few pennies.'

'And how much was he likely to drink of this economical beer?'

'What's that supposed to mean?' Jessie looked towards O'Neill.

O'Neill nodded and smiled as if confirming that Fran's questions were to be answered.

'About how much beer?' said Fran. 'Two pints, four, six?'

'I don't know. How would I know? I wasn't there, was I?'

'Did he stay till closing time?'

'I told you I don't know what time he came in.'

'Does he usually?'

Jessie took a sip of tea before answering. 'Yes,' she said reluctantly, 'he usually stays till closing.'

'And is he always or usually drunk when he returns?'

'Now look. . . I never said he was drunk. . . I—'

'It's all right, Jessie,' said Fran softly, 'you didn't need to.'

Jessie looked straight at O'Neill with a 'help me'

expression. Spots of colour had appeared in her cheeks.

O'Neill said gently, 'I should give Tom a call now, Jessie. He'll be able to tell us what time he got in.'

Jessie opened the kitchen door, her relief at Tom now being the object of their attention obvious.

'Tom,' she called loudly, 'Tom! You're wanted.'

Tom came immediately, as though he had been lurking somewhere near by just waiting to be called. He removed his boots in the porch, nodded at O'Neill, and walked over to the sink to wash his hands. Even though he washed them thoroughly, as he dried them on the white roller towel smeary marks appeared.

'Come and sit down, Tom,' said O'Neill. 'Your wife's fruit cake is very good.'

'I don't eat cake,' he said. 'She makes it for the vet and Charlie, of course.'

Once Tom had sat down and had his tea poured, liberally sugared and then stirred by Jessie, O'Neill said, 'Well, Tom, I'm sure you'd like to tell us about the night before last. You were out for the evening, I believe.'

'That's right. I went to the pub.'

'Which one?'

'The Plough at Clopstock. I drink there quite often.'

'Beer's cheap there, is it Tom?'

'I wouldn't say cheap. It's cheaper than some places.'

'And what time did you get home?'

'What time was it, Jessie?'

She shrugged. 'Not sure.'

'You accused me of waking you up, you ought to know.'

'Well, I don't know, I don't remember.'

Tom's eyes darkened and his mouth set in a hard line but he said nothing as he stared into his tea cup.

Soothingly O'Neill said: 'We don't need an exact time, Tom. Just after closing was it you left? About five minutes to drive home, so that would make it . . .'

''Bout twelve.'

'Why so late?'

'I never said I was driving, did I? I walked. Got in about twelve.'

'I see,' said O'Neill. 'Jessie thought you went by car.'

'Well, I didn't. Steering's not too good.'

'And the van?' asked O'Neill.

'Needs new tyres. Can't afford that sort of thing at the moment.'

'So you walked?'

'I walked,' said Tom firmly.

O'Neill took out a notebook and pen.

'I'll just write that down, Tom. Wilson, any questions?'

Fran smiled at Tom. 'Just one or two.'

He shrugged as if to say he couldn't care less.

'What time did you arrive at the Plough?'

'Eightish. That would be right, wouldn't it, Jess?'

Jessie nodded but didn't answer.

'And you left at closing. Eleven fifteen or thereabouts?'

'That's it.'

'So in that time you would have drunk say four or five pints?'

'I wasn't plastered if that's what you're trying to say. I could walk a straight line. I walked home.'

'Were you fit to drive?'

'Of course. . .' Tom paused. He was about to fall into her trap. 'Of course I wasn't,' he said. 'That's why I walked.'

'And you heard nothing in the night?'

'Not a thing.'

'Jethro didn't bark?'

'If he did I didn't hear him.'

'And the dead?'

'What?' Tom's eyes widened in surprised confusion and he swallowed quickly as if that would aid his thinking.

'The dead animals.'

'Oh, yeah. The animals. What about them?'

'Who put them in the black bag?'

'Jessie. That's her job. She always does the rubbish.' Jessie nodded as if in agreement.

Fran turned to her then and asked, 'When exactly did you put the animals in the bag?'

'I don't remember the time,' said Jessie, 'but last night I put the lamb in the bag, one piglet was from last week on Friday, the other on Saturday. They don't all die together, you know. We don't always have anything to be collected.'

'Just as well,' muttered Tom.

'There were just the three animals in the bag, then?'

Before Jessie could answer Tom said, 'Should have

been just the two piglets only madam was too lazy to put the lamb in the field overnight.'

It was Fran's turn to be surprised. 'Could you explain that to me?'

Tom could scarcely hide his contempt and he grinned showing yellowing broken teeth.

'For the foxes, see. Then they don't bother the living. My wife would rather they were boiled in a pot for the hounds.'

Jessie looked away. She pretended that was the reason. A dead lamb didn't care one way or the other. But Charlie had to have a reason to come and he was company after all.

'I think we're a bit more sorted now,' said O'Neill. 'We'll leave it there, Wilson. There's just one more thing I want to ask . . .'

He paused as he glanced at the Harringtons. A long pause that Fran could tell made them uncomfortable.

'Who do you think he is?' he asked eventually. 'The chap who used to own the arm?'

Tom gave a short laugh. 'Don't know, mate. Could be anyone.'

'Hardly anyone,' said O'Neill. 'But we'll find out soon enough. Do you know of any missing men around here?'

They both shook their heads. Then Jessie frowned as if remembering.

'Well. . . there's that farmer on the border. Melksham. . . I think, Frank Melksham. . . Yes, that's his name. His wife used to come to the WI. He's missing. . .'

'Don't be daft, woman,' interrupted Tom. 'It can't be him. He's been gone for years!'

O'Neill remembered now. He'd heard about Frank Melksham. The farm had been making a loss and one day he just walked out. He left a note for his wife and had never been seen since. Well, no, that wasn't quite true. He had been seen once.

'Come on, Wilson,' said O'Neill as he lifted the latch of the kitchen door. 'Let's be away now. We'll be back, of course, Tom. In the mean time I'd be grateful if you could rack your brains for any more information. Missing people. People you haven't seen or heard of for a while.'

'What do you mean, *people*, Mr O'Neill?' asked Jessie, looking worried.

O'Neill paused before answering. 'There's a woman's arm been found too. Any ideas who she might be?'

Jessie shook her head and Fran noticed that she trembled slightly as Tom put an arm round her.

'She wouldn't know, would she,' he said, 'she doesn't go out much. Let's hope he's not a bleeding maniac.'

'You keep an eye out for us then, Tom,' said O'Neill, 'and make sure you lock up at night.'

'I will,' said Tom. 'I will.'

The couple stood and watched as Fran and O'Neill put their boots on. Jessie's face had paled and she didn't smile as they left. When they'd arrived she had seemed pleased to see them. Now, as they were going, Fran noticed the anxious expression on her face, an expression she'd seen many times before. In women whose fear of their husband had suddenly increased.

Chapter Five

The next day the newly redecorated classroom at Higham Merrils College of Agriculture had been transformed into an incident room. Fran had to admit the activity did look impressive. Extra manpower had been drafted in and O'Neill spent time explaining the different roles everyone would take and that as Superintendent Ringstead was on sick leave with a twisted kneecap sustained on a squash court the night before he would be in overall charge.

'See those two over there,' said O'Neill, pointing to two young men working with a computer in one corner of the room, 'they're statement readers and collators. One of them writes questionnaires for the door knockers – PDFs.'

'PDFs?'

'You're not knowing much, are you?' said O'Neill good-naturedly in a broad Irish accent. 'Personal Descriptive Forms. And that chap at the desk in front is the office manager, he's Inspector Preston, Pete. He's responsible for general management of the enquiry.'

'Where does that leave us?' asked Fran, wondering as she watched all the activity if there would be anything left for her to do.

'Us?' repeated O'Neill. 'That leaves us free to do all the tearing about the countryside following leads. All the exciting bits, in fact.'

'Have forensic come up with anything yet?' asked Fran.

'Nothing so far, but quite soon the Home Office pathologist should have some news for us.'

'No more body found?'

O'Neill shook his head. 'Not so far, Wilson, but I thought today we'd spend our time having a look round the college and speaking to a few people. The two girls who found the female arm, for instance. I would be more than interested to know when exactly that arm was disposed of.'

'I see,' said Fran, not quite sure of the correct response.

'Well, I'm glad you do, Wilson, because this case has to be solved quickly. You know how murder enquiries work – six weeks, a quarter of a million spent – solve it or forget it – that's how the Home Office works.'

The interview for the two girls had been arranged for 10 a.m. in the refectory. At five to ten O'Neill and Fran left the incident room, turned into a glass-covered walkway which seemed to encircle the middle section of classrooms, and followed the signs leading to the refectory. As they approached two girls were also walking towards them.

'Yours is the short plain one, Wilson,' whispered O'Neill. 'I'll take the one in the riding boots with the aristocratic looks.'

'Thought you might,' murmured Fran.

O'Neill strode ahead, put an arm round both girls, and said: 'Good of you to come, ladies. I'm Detective Chief Inspector Connor O'Neill and this is my sidekick – Detective Sergeant Fran Wilson.'

The shorter girl giggled somewhat nervously but Fran could see that O'Neill's choice cast him a meaningful sidelong glance, a look that, if Fran was right, was as lecherous as a wolf whistle and about as subtle.

'Now then you must be Alison,' O'Neill was saying, 'DS Wilson will have a chat with you. I'll be talking to you, Phillippa.' With that, Alison was very gently pushed in Fran's direction.

The refectory was a vast room, high-ceilinged, with wood-panelled walls, high windows, and rows of empty, beige formica tables. Dominating the furthest wall and hanging less than true was a large portrait of a black-haired woman with a tight perm and an equally tight green ballgown. Watery sunshine streaked the portrait and somehow nature's intervention lent it an aura of importance that Fran didn't think it deserved.

From the kitchen area behind the serving hatch came sounds of pans being set down, of chopping and frying and the muted voices of the cooks, and an all-pervading smell of cauliflower and stew.

O'Neill, already leading his sexy interviewee to a corner table, half turned and thumbed at a side table that he deemed suitable for Fran.

'We'll sit here,' said Fran, smiling at Alison, trying

not to let her irritation at her boss's behaviour show.

Alison sat down but twisted round to check Phillippa's whereabouts as if she needed reassurance of her presence.

'Just a few details first, Alison,' said Fran, taking out a notebook and pen from her shoulderbag.

'I haven't got anything to tell you,' said Alison, folding her arms defensively across her chest. 'I don't know why I'm being questioned. I only opened the bag to put the dead chicken in – and there it was.'

Fran merely smiled, turned the pages of the notebook, wrote the date, noted the exact time by her wristwatch, and sat for a moment with pen poised.

'Full name, please,' she said softly.

Alison ran a hand through her cropped fair hair and then pushed up the sleeve of her navy sweatshirt.

'It's Alison Mary Lowick,' she said, as she pushed up the other sleeve and then sat with one arm on the table and the other hand resting on the arm, but not really resting, more holding it down. As if she were very nervous.

'Address?'

'I live here,' said Alison.

'Your parents' address?'

'Why do you want that? I only found . . . it . . . If they find out . . . well . . . I mean they'll be worried, won't they?'

'It's only for our records, Alison. Purely routine. Though of course they might read about it in the papers.'

Alison's grey eyes flickered once more in Phillippa's

direction but she mumbled their address and then sat once more with her arms folded.

'You seem a little nervous, Alison. Is there anything wrong?'

'I'm not nervous,' said Alison. 'I've done nothing wrong. It was just bad luck finding it, that's all.'

'Tell me about the morning in question. What did you do – from the beginning, from the time you got up?'

Alison frowned and then sighed like a harassed shop assistant forced to believe in the dictum of the customer always being right. 'It was the same as most mornings,' she said slowly, 'I got up about eight, had a shower, got dressed, and walked up to the farm. We have to muck out and things, do all the dirty jobs.'

'No breakfast?'

'I don't eat breakfast. I can't face it and it's fattening.'

'Would you like some tea or coffee, Alison, as you haven't had breakfast?'

'No thanks. I've gone off tea and coffee lately.'

'OK. Tell me what happened next.'

'I went to find Phillippa. She was in the chicken shed. She threw a dead chicken at me.'

'Why?'

'I don't know why. She's like that, I suppose.'

'I meant,' said Fran, 'why did you go to find Phillippa?'

Alison blinked rapidly and looked away. 'I just wanted some company, I suppose.'

It was a lie, Fran knew. 'Is Phillippa a special friend of yours?'

Silence for a moment. 'Not exactly. I quite like her though. She's bossy but sort of. . .'

'Dependable?' suggested Fran.

'Yes, that's it.' Alison smiled for the first time, her small roundish face suddenly pretty.

'Tell me about finding the arm,' said Fran.

The expression on Alison's face changed immediately. She looked as if she was in pain.

'I opened the bag to put the chicken in and there it was. I dropped the chicken. It was horrible. . . the hand seemed to be waving.'

'And then? Did you scream?'

'I can't remember. I think I just shouted for Phillippa.'

'What happened then?'

'I was sick.'

'There on the spot?'

'No, I ran to be sick in the bushes. And. . . oh no. . .'

Before Fran could stop her Alison had stood up, her chair clattering to the floor as she made a bolt for the door. As Fran followed her out she was aware that O'Neill was also on his feet and fast behind her.

Alison made her way to the nearest lavatory, knelt on the cold stone floor and retched into the china lavatory bowl, the maker's name doubtless level with her eyes and imprinted on her memory for ever.

The lavatory door was unlocked and Fran could only watch and listen as the retching continued. She felt nauseous and ashamed that she couldn't offer any help. She couldn't bear people being sick – bleeding, yes, even mangled, but vomiting made her feel downright ill. Not that O'Neill noticed.

'What on earth did you say to her to get this response?'

'I didn't say anything. . . I. . .'

Alison retched again and at the sound of it Fran put out a hand to steady herself against the wall.

'Oh, hell!' she heard O'Neill say before he disappeared. It seemed ages before he came back. Her knees were beginning to buckle and mercifully in her pre-fainting stage her hearing had faded so that she could no longer hear Alison who, between heaves, had begun to ask for God's assistance.

The chair came just in time. Fran was aware of her head being thrust down to meet her ankles and a pressure on her neck keeping it there. When her head was finally allowed up both O'Neill and Alison were there watching her. Did she imagine their disdain or was that merely the effect of the temporary loss of blood to her brain?

'I'm all right now,' said Alison, speaking directly into Fran's face. 'It's passed off.'

'Oh, that's good,' Fran managed to utter.

'I think I'd better take you home, Wilson,' said O'Neill, 'you look terrible, you're as pale as an old maid's knee.'

Fran was still wondering why an old maid's knee should be pale when she felt O'Neill lifting one elbow and hauling her to her feet.

'I was getting quite fond of this loo,' she said, as the white tiles shimmered and winked at her. 'But in a few minutes I'll be fine. I'd rather not go home if you don't mind, boss.'

'We'll go next door, then. I know just the cure for you.'

He turned to Alison. 'Off you go, you'll be needing a lie down now. I'll catch up with you later.'

Alison shot Fran a glance as if it was her doing she'd probably have to be interviewed again but even so she managed a tight smile for O'Neill as she left.

Next door turned out to be the Bird in Hand, which had just opened and was heavy on the brassware but low on customers. A log fire had been lit but it was smoking furiously with only a hint of the full firepower to come.

'Sit there, Wilson,' said O'Neill pointing to the table nearest the smoking logs. 'I'll be fetching you the cure.'

The cure came in the form of a double Irish whiskey.

'As smooth and gentle as mother's milk,' said O'Neill, although Fran found it hard to tell which drink he meant because O'Neill himself was gazing into a pint of draught Guinness at the time.

Fran soon realized that even a single whiskey on an empty well-churned stomach, was too much. But gradually she noticed that O'Neill had settled back into his chair and the logs had stopped smoking and started spiking bright orange flames instead and the Bird in Hand suddenly became the warmest, friendliest place on earth.

'It's a great little pub this,' said O'Neill. 'Don't you agree?'

'I do,' said Fran. She would have agreed with almost anything after a double whiskey at 11 a.m.

'Tell me all about yourself, Wilson. Like what makes a pretty girl become a detective and why you left a mecca of sanity in Birmingham to come here, to hunting, shooting, fishing land.'

Although Fran couldn't stop herself being vaguely flattered at being called pretty she resented his patronizing tone and his questions. 'I'd love another drink,' she said. 'I could get to like Irish whiskey at this time of the morning.'

'It's good any time,' said O'Neill. 'But I hope you won't be needing it that often. Just leave me to do the interviews this afternoon.'

He left then to fetch more drinks and as Fran watched him at the bar chatting to the barmaid she wondered why he was in Fowchester. Had he, like her, been relegated to a third-division town because his face didn't fit in the first division. Or perhaps his mother had kept goats too. She'd ask when he came back.

'Boss,' she said as he sat down. 'Did your mother keep goats?'

He raised the refilled glass to his lips and savoured another mouthful before he spoke. He seemed not one whit surprised at the question.

'Not goats. She was a stray cat person. Why are you asking?'

'In Ireland?'

'No, Wilson, in Kilburn, West Kilburn. It wasn't a

great success. They were often out at night, screeching, and the neighbours complained. Why is it you're wanting to know?'

'I just wondered, boss, if we had anything in common.'

'Like goats?'

'Yes.'

'You could ask me questions outright, Wilson. I'd be more than happy to tell you.'

Before she had time to formulate one, O'Neill said, 'I'm thirty-five, keen on cricket, football, women, good Irish whiskey, and draught Guinness. I go to confession once a week and repeat the same sins the following week. I'm not sure if He's listening but I give it my best shot. I'm a widower, no children, and before you ask my wife committed suicide two years ago. I became Chief Inspector because the selection board thought it was about time ethnic minorities had a chance in Fowchester. And it gave them the opportunity to make a public statement that not all Irish Catholics were bombers, gun-runners, or any other form of fanatical patriot. Combined with the fact I managed to convince the board that I was more British than Irish – I was a safe sort of choice. The ethical ethnic choice if you like.' Then he added quietly, 'I probably got the pity vote as well.'

Fran stared at him for a moment not quite knowing what to say. She didn't want to question about his wife's death. Didn't in fact want to see her boss in a vulnerable light. Now she knew, there was always the danger she would start to worry about him. She resolved not to pry into his private life. If and when he wanted her to know the details he would tell her. Somehow, though, she hoped he never would.

'And your mother took in strays,' she said lightly.

O'Neill laughed, a laugh as deep and rich as his glass of Guinness. 'Wilson, I don't know what you're talking about but you're damn good for the crack.'

They fell silent then for a while, Fran trying to dredge up something innocuous to say but not succeeding. It was O'Neill who spoke first.

'Now then, Wilson,' he said. 'My job could be on the line with this one. The Chief Super was well against my appointment. In his opinion anyone born five miles outside Fowchester is either a spy or a pervert. I'm in the latter category. And since I've not remarried he views me as a rampant male whose choice in women is. . .'

'Catholic?'

'Quite,' said O'Neill. 'You're sharp with a drink inside you. I'll have to keep you well topped-up.'

Now that O'Neill seemed more light-hearted, Fran recognized that her relief was due as much to the effect of alcohol as to his mood. She was definitely a little drunk. The sober side of drunk, she convinced herself. She could still function – just – if her head would stop spinning and her stomach stop exercising itself.

'Well, Wilson. Time to get back to work,' said O'Neill as he drained his pint glass. 'Forward!' he said, slapping a fist into the palm of his hand as if rousing himself to action, and then, remembering Fran, held out a hand to help her to her feet.

The cool air outside made her sway a little but as O'Neill strode off she walked in a perfect straight line behind him. No one would ever know she'd had a medicinal drink.

The incident room quietened as they entered. The allocations sergeant moved from his desk and approached O'Neill.

'Forensic rang, Chief. They want you to ring back. We've got maps now of both scenes and photographs. The PDFs are ready for you to look at. I think we've done a good job on those, covered most questions.'

'Missing persons?'

'No new ones in so far. We've got someone at Scotland Yard checking HOLMES for names.'

Fran asked: 'Sherlock come up with anything?'

Both men looked at her pityingly as if she didn't know that HOLMES stood for Home Office Large and Major Enquiry Systems.

She shrugged. 'It was only a joke.'

A look passed between them of masculine solidarity in the face of female stupidity but O'Neill managed a condescending smile as he said, 'You can type up Alison Lowick's informal, Wilson. See if you can find a reason for such a strong reaction. There must be a reason. The girl's country born. She should be hardy.'

'Definitely,' murmured Fran.

Fran had never quite mastered typing. Even getting the paper in straight posed a problem, usually the typescript was at an odd angle. And she made lots of mistakes, partly, she supposed, because she saw typing as a form of office work, and one of the reasons she had joined the police was to avoid sitting at a desk. She had, of course, learned since that office work formed a major part of police work. It didn't make her like it more.

She typed for some time slowly and quite accurately and while she did so she remembered those tiny snippets of chit-chat that don't find their way into reports: 'Tea or coffee?' And the reply: 'I've gone off tea and coffee.'

Fran's great-grandmother, who was so old she should have had a medal for stoicism, was so knowing that she knew the first sign of pregnancy was a sudden turning away from old favourites like tea and coffee. So Alison Lowick, aged seventeen, was perhaps pregnant. Was that why she wanted to meet up with Phillippa? Because Phillippa was older, dependable, and would know what to do?

O'Neill greeted the news with a shrug.

'Hardly likely to be having any bearing on the case. And I don't want you getting involved. Social workers are available for that sort of thing and we won't be interviewing them again this afternoon. We've had a preliminary report on the body parts.'

'What did it say?' asked Fran as O'Neill continued to sort through papers on his desk.

'Well, Wilson,' he said, looking up and smiling. 'I'll be telling you all about it in the car.'

Chapter Six

O'Neill drove out of the village before he spoke again. Fran had sunk into the leather seat of the gold-coloured Mercedes that was very elderly but obviously pampered. The drive was smooth and the late sunlight on the wide horizon made her squint. Fran soon felt the need to close her eyes and with the quietness of the engine she began to feel drowsy. Shaking her head to keep herself awake she said, 'You were going to tell me about the forensic report, boss.'

'I was indeed,' said O'Neill slowly, 'I was indeed.'

She wanted to say, 'Well, hurry up then,' but she didn't. She closed her eyes again and waited.

'You're not going to sleep, are you, Wilson?'

'I'd like to.'

'Well don't. I need your—'

'Rapier-sharp mind.'

'No, Wilson. I was going to say thoughts, just thoughts.'

'Try me then,' said Fran, opening one eye and then closing it against the glare.

'Arm number one,' began O'Neill, 'hereafter known

as specimen A, belonged to a white male, bone age fifty to fifty-five, healthy skin and fingernails, no bruising, no old fractures, no evidence of ever having worn a ring, skin on palm of hands roughened. Soil under nails still waiting to be analysed. Tallish, so I'm told, because of the length of the forearm, but that's guesswork. He may have had long arms and short legs but it's more likely that he was tall. Dark haired, in all probability, so the pathologist tells me, by the amount and colour of the hair on the forearm. Also the palm of his hand was thickened and calloused – not a pen pusher.'

'I'm impressed,' said Fran, now wide awake.

'Any questions?'

Fran thought for a moment. 'Blood group?'

'O, Rhesus positive. Very, very common.'

'Fingerprints?'

'They have been taken but that's a no-hoper unless he's already on file or unless we get a good match from somewhere that would give us a positive association.'

'What about the soil under the nails?'

'Now that's a real possibility, but it'll take time.'

O'Neill stayed silent whilst he negotiated a few sharp bends but once he was on a flat stretch of road he said, 'There's something else. . .' He paused. 'It does rather complicate things.'

'What's that?'

'The arm had been frozen. Chopped off with an axe or a cleaver, then frozen.'

'What does that mean, exactly?' asked Fran.

'Mean? It means we'll not be knowing how he died, and, much more to the point, when he died.'

'But surely. . .'

'There's nothing sure about this case, Wilson. The pathologist says properly wrapped, even in a domestic freezer, it could have been kept in good condition – indefinitely.'

'I thought that even in a freezer there would be some deterioration.'

'There is, Wilson. But only in the taste!'

Fran winced. 'Is he sure it's been frozen? I mean if it had defrosted how would he know?'

'Oh, he's sure all right. He found crystals – ice crystal artefacts, he called them.'

They had driven another mile or so with O'Neill in a gloomy silence which made Fran reluctant to ask any more questions. But after a while she said quietly, 'And the other arm?'

'Specimen B,' said O'Neill slowly. 'Female, white, marks of ring on ring finger, healthy nails and skin, no marks, bruises, or old fractures. Of medium height, that's a guess, and probably of medium build judging by the layers of fat. Skin tone fairish, could be blonde or brunette but not excessively dark. She may have scratched her murderer, there was a smidgeon of skin under the nails. Again, a report on that will take time. Aged between thirty-five and forty. Probably not a manual worker because the skin of her hand was soft. And this time, Wilson, we're dealing with fresh not frozen. Judging by the amount of decomposition the pathologist thinks she was dead about four days. The severing of the arm was done quite cleanly with an axe or a cleaver. Any ideas?'

'You've got a fantastic memory, boss,' said Fran, genuinely impressed.

'One of my better points,' said O'Neill, pleased that his DS had even noticed he was almost word perfect. He'd worked hard on memorizing the telephoned report. Now perhaps he could relax and think about cricket and how the county would do this year, and if the weather would be good, how the draught Guinness would taste on a warm summer's day, and the gentle murmur of the crowd and sheer delight of it all, even when play was slow and however slow, the boredom was such a pleasure. . .

'Boss?'

'Yes,' he said sharply.

'You did ask for ideas.'

'Yes again. Well?'

'It's only that I've got an idea that the car behind us wants to get past and you're hogging the middle of the road.'

O'Neill slowed and steered to the side of the road, to be rewarded as the car drove past with a shout of, 'Stupid sod!' through the open window and a two-finger insult.

'Take his number, Wilson.'

'Are we going after him?' asked Fran in surprise.

'Not today. I *was* hogging the road but on another occasion it might be him in the wrong. Then I'll have him – the little bastard!'

Fran smiled. She might just get to like this job after all.

The road had become single track and O'Neill turned to her. 'Be watching out for the turning, it's easy to miss. There is a sign but it's a bit back from the road.'

'Where are we going?'

'Home Farm – the Melksham place.'

Fran remembered the name. The farmer in financial trouble who had done a runner five years before.

'You don't think it's him, do you?'

'Just be looking for the sign, Wilson.'

Fran scanned the bushes that enclosed the track, they were overgrown and spiked against the car as they passed.

'There, just there,' she indicated. 'On the left, there's a gap.'

A sign saying Home Farm hung on a tall wooden frame. A smattering of dirt had dulled the gold paint of the lettering and as they passed by a breeze caught the sign and the supporting chains clinked, as if, thought Fran, in recognition or warning that someone had passed by.

O'Neill drove on; occasionally between the bushes Fran caught a glimpse of pastures beyond and green shoots.

'What's that growing?'

'Rape,' said O'Neill. 'Harmless unless you can't stand the smell or the brilliance of its colour. Don't expect they have much rape in Birmingham.'

'Only the real thing,' said Fran, 'but there are fields surrounding the city. I just didn't recognize it before it became yellow.'

'There's the farmhouse,' said O'Neill pointing

ahead, as he rounded a slight bend.

Fran was surprised it was so large and majestic. The walls had been whitewashed and the windows glinted slightly in the sunlight. There was a well-shaved lawn in front and Fran guessed the mud was kept to the back of the house. The barns on the left as they passed by were empty and deserted.

O'Neill parked at the side of the house and sat for a moment as if waiting for some response to their presence from inside. When there was none he said, 'We'll try the front door.'

Loud knocking and shouting – 'Open up, it's the police' – had no effect.

After a while Fran said, 'It's no use. There's no one in.'

'No one alive, anyway,' mumbled O'Neill.

'Do you want me to pick the lock?' asked Fran. 'It's my speciality.'

'Pick bolts as well, do you? We'd need a battering ram.'

'It may not be bolted,' said Fran, and at that moment the door opened.

The woman who stood in the doorway wore a short denim skirt and black sweatshirt with 'All Mine' emblazoned across the front. Her hair could only be described as a feminine crew cut and had been streaked with yellow as bright as summer rape. Fran guessed her to be in her late thirties though looking younger.

O'Neill hadn't at first recognized her. He still wasn't sure.

'Sheila Melksham?' he said uncertainly. 'Is it you or should I be looking for your mother?'

She laughed. 'Come on, Mr O'Neill, you know it's me. I've only lost a bit of weight. . .'

'Now there's an understatement if ever I heard one. You're looking ten years younger.'

'Stop giving me the blarney and come on in. I do have company but he won't mind.'

Sheila Melksham led them through a warren of doors to the back kitchen. Cans of paint stood on a table, newspapers were spread over the floor, and paint-splattered white sheets covered all cupboards and appliances. A stepladder had been placed in the middle of the room as if the person who put it there couldn't quite decide where it was needed. She shrugged at the sight of the kitchen and spread her hands.

'Terrible mess, isn't it? All the rooms are in a bit of a state.'

'What's brought this on?' asked O'Neill. 'And by the way this is DS Wilson, a refugee from Birmingham.'

Sheila nodded at Fran. 'I've been left a bit of money and we thought we'd redecorate the place. Steve Holcot, my boyfriend, said he'd do all the hard graft so that's what we're doing.'

At that moment the 'hard grafter' walked in. A young Adonis with tight blue jeans, a neat crew cut (no doubt to match Sheila's), and a well-set face that matched his well-set body. No wonder Mrs Melksham looked ten years younger.

'Steve,' said Sheila, 'this is Detective Chief Inspector

O'Neill and Detective Sergeant Wilson. Do you remember I told you how the police were so good to me when Frank disappeared?' She turned towards O'Neill. 'You were just an inspector then,' she said smiling. 'I heard you'd got promotion.'

Steve moved closer to stand by Sheila's side. He managed a smile of dazzling charm in Fran's direction and she smiled back.

'You haven't asked why we're here, Sheila,' said O'Neill.

'I was half expecting you,' said Sheila. 'It's about the arm that's been found. Charlie the kennel man told me. I suppose you think it's Frank?'

'What do you think?'

'Could be,' said Sheila. 'I can only hope.'

'Do you know where he's been living?'

Sheila shook her head. 'I've had one letter in five years and of course the one he left me. It was late in the first year after he left.'

'What did the letter say?'

'Not much. Just said I could keep the farm and the debts and good luck. That's what I've had really. I tried to sell the farm but there were no takers and then I did bed and breakfast for a while. Now we're thinking of making it into a proper hotel, aren't we, Steve?'

Steve smiled good-naturedly.

O'Neill persevered.

'Any post code? Anything at all?'

'Why don't you all sit down,' said Sheila, 'and I'll have a look for the letter. Steve will make you a hot drink.'

Whilst Sheila rummaged upstairs Steve made a pot of tea. The only comment he made as he did so was to say, 'She's a wonderful woman. She's had a rough life, you know. But I'm looking after her now.'

Fran guessed he was about twenty-six. And she couldn't deny it, she felt envious.

'Did you know Frank Melksham?' asked Fran.

'No. I only moved here two years ago. I've only heard gossip and of course what Sheila has told me about him.'

'And that was?'

'Nothing good.'

Fran was just about to ask another question when O'Neill, who had perched on the stepladder, asked, 'What about Andy?'

'He's OK. He helps out here in his spare time. Works at the cottage hospital as a porter and lives in Fowchester. At Mrs Jake's place. The big house on the corner. She's got a few lodgers.'

'Who's Andy?' asked Fran, just as Sheila reappeared.

'My son Andy,' she said defensively. 'He's fine. You won't bother him, will you, Mr O'Neill? You know what he's like. He's found himself a girlfriend and he's happy for once in his life. Let sleeping dogs. . . please.'

'I can't promise that, you know I can't. But I'll be tactful. To be sure I'll be like an Irish uncle.'

Fran could see Sheila forcing a smile. For a while there was silence as they drank their tea. Then O'Neill said, 'Did you find the letter, Sheila?'

'No. . . I must have burnt it. I've been getting rid of a few things recently.'

Fran noticed she didn't lie well but O'Neill didn't press her. No doubt he had his reasons. He finished his tea and eased his tall frame from the stepladder. 'If you think of anything, let me know. I'd like to save Andy a visit if I could.'

'Well. . . There is one thing I do remember. . .' She paused, glancing at Steve as if for his approval. 'I met a woman, a few months after Frank left, in the town. She said she thought she saw him at a market in Lincolnshire. She said he looked just like Frank but she wasn't sure. He was selling free-range eggs. She remembers it because the crates of eggs were marked Last Chance Farm. She thought that suited Frank. I snapped at her and said it wasn't him. But I think it was. Lincolnshire's so near that I was scared he'd come back.'

'And he never did?'

'No, I told you. He left here five years ago and I haven't seen him since. I have heard rumours, though. . .'

'Come on, Sheila, tell all,' said O'Neill, smiling.

'Oh, all right then. Just for you. If Frank is alive, though, don't tell him about Steve, will you?'

'My lips are sealed.'

'Good. It was about two years ago I heard the rumour that Frank was living with a woman called Trudi Miller and calling himself Miller. It was someone who knew her, a friend of a friend of her sister. And she also mentioned Last Chance Farm, so it must be true.'

'And this sister of Trudi Miller lives round here?'

'Yes. But I don't know where.'

'Thanks, Sheila, we'll be off now. You've been a great help,' said O'Neill as he walked towards the kitchen door. 'But I may have to come back. You see, someone else has died – a woman.'

'Oh God,' whispered Sheila in obvious surprise. Steve put an arm round her and gave her a little squeeze. 'Don't fret, sweetheart,' he said, 'everything will get sorted.'

She looked up at Steve adoringly. 'I do hope so, darling,' she said, 'I do hope so.'

The mud was at the back of the farmhouse. Fran's boots sank well in and it was as though she was walking through treacle.

'We could have gone out the front way,' said Fran as she tried to walk in O'Neill's footprints, reasoning that the mud would be flattened and less likely to splash. O'Neill turned round and laughed. 'You'll get used to it, Wilson. And I wanted to have a look in the barns.'

There were three barns in fair condition, one derelict, all empty save for a few bales of straw and a couple of pitchforks.

'What did you hope to find?' asked Fran, noticing O'Neill's disappointment.

He shrugged. 'Oh, just the odd axe or cleaver.'

'I did notice something in the house,' said Fran.

'What, exactly?'

'Under the sheets in the kitchen. A freezer. A chest freezer. And I did wonder why they took so long to answer the door.'

'They must have been in bed.'

'She wasn't flushed with spent desire, was she?'

'Well, no, Wilson. What do you think they were up to?'

'I think they were covering up – metaphorically and physically. Most people when they're decorating leave a downstairs room untouched. We were ushered into the kitchen deliberately.'

'What were they covering up, though? Most people on farms have a freezer. Nothing unusual in that.'

'My guess is,' said Fran, 'they were busy covering the floor with newspaper.'

'For what purpose?'

'To hide the bloodstains.'

O'Neill tried not to laugh. Wilson was bright but this time he felt she had taken a turn for the dramatic.

'Anyone who decorates covers the floor before they start,' he said.

'I was just surprised that they used today's newspaper, especially as they hadn't even opened the paint pots. And the day is nearly over and they'd not made a start on the kitchen. Their clothes were spotless too, unless of course they had changed them for some reason.'

O'Neill felt his jaw muscles twitch. He shouldn't feel angry that his DS was using her powers of observation but he did. He bloody did!

Chapter Seven

Home is where the mouse is, Fran told herself as she closed her front door, and then called to her unseen pet that she was home and that he or she shouldn't get too excited. A small piece of cheese, left as a house-warming present in the middle of the kitchen floor, had gone. No doubt her mouse friend was sleeping it off.

Fran tried to stay cheerful but this rather dark, damp-smelling, miserable little house had nothing to recommend it other than being within walking distance of the bakery. Tea-chests of books and pictures and crockery still needed to be unpacked and somehow in the move she'd forgotten the cardinal rule of labelling containers. Some had gone upstairs that should have gone downstairs and she had packed so eccentrically and unpacked so little that a box of kitchen utensils sat in the middle of the front room. Clothes hangers seemed to have reproduced themselves during the day and all varieties from plastic to wooden to handmade cotton-covered filled with lavender jutted from every box. She definitely hadn't got the equivalent amount of clothes to justify the multiplying coat hangers.

Worse than that was the fact the only food in the house was a lump of stale cheese and half a loaf. Fran enjoyed food as only the naturally slim can, more so since she had given up smoking and could now taste it. Once she had enjoyed cooking for friends but even she couldn't manage to make a decent meal without a cupboard full of ingredients. Also, she was a vegetarian and Fowchester shops still seemed to be in the grip of suet dumplings and big fat sausages. O'Neill, it seemed, lived mostly on the food he managed to scavenge on his interviews, and draught Guinness of course.

For a while Fran drank coffee, then she busied herself unpacking until pangs of hunger drove her to make cheese on toast. She ate on the move, wandering first into one room then another. The previous occupant had been somewhat trendy and had rag-rolled most of the walls. Rolled being euphemistic, because surely the person who had done the deed had lurched into action rather than rolled. Great swirls of blueish-white paint, like surf, coated the walls of the front living room so that Fran felt all she needed to hear was a sea-gull to make her feel seasick. The back room cum kitchen had been painted, equally eccentrically, in ragrolled orange and lemon, but that had lost its sparkle, if it had ever had any, under a layer of dust and grease. The furniture – it was part-furnished – was of the 'look what I can make with an orange box' type, and although the sofa, covered with an anchor motif in black on a blue background, looked comfortable, it offered no head support and the only way Fran could tolerate it was to lie full length with her head resting on a cushion.

At ten o'clock she switched on the television and organized herself with a few magazines, which would no doubt give her all sorts of ideas for rejuvenating her new home. With feet up and a cup of coffee to hand Fran relaxed and waited for the TV to warm up. She was hopeful but the television had obviously died during the day. Fran tried cardiac massage by banging it a few times but it was too late for resuscitation.

Well, that's it, she thought, life has definitely taken a turn for the worse. No friends, no telly, no cigarettes, and nothing to eat for breakfast in the morning.

Leaving a few crumbs on a plate for the mouse Fran went upstairs for a bath. The water was cold. She had forgotten to boost the immersion heater.

She lay in bed staring at the walls. At least the last tenant hadn't got round to this room with his rag. Small roses instead scaled the walls. She began counting until her eyes blurred and the bed warmed and she didn't care about anything any more. . .

The phone by the bed rang and rang and rang.

'Yes. What?' she said, eyes tightly closed, holding the receiver away from her ear just wanting to stop the noise and hoping its ringing had all been a terrible mistake. It wasn't. The voice at the other end was O'Neill's.

'Are you with me?' he was saying.

'I'm with you,' answered Fran. 'What's wrong?'

'I'll be round in ten minutes. Were you asleep?'

'I was.'

Fran looked at the alarm clock. It was only eleven fifteen.

'What's happened?'

'Sure I'll be telling you when I get there,' said O'Neill.

Fran splashed her face with cold water, put on jeans and a sweatshirt and an old pair of trainers (she hadn't yet cleaned her boots) and sat anorak in hand on the sofa and waited. She presumed they were going out.

When O'Neill did arrive he said, 'Wouldn't you be going to ask me in now?'

'I thought we'd be going straight out, boss.'

'There's no hurry,' said O'Neill, 'and I'd be loving a cup of coffee.'

Reluctantly Fran showed him through to the kitchen. She felt embarrassed at the state of the house even though it was really no fault of her own. A dim and dismal house, she reasoned, would make him think she too was dim and dismal.

He stood for a moment surveying the house like a disappointed would-be purchaser and making 'tsk tsk' noises.

'It's not that bad,' said Fran defensively.

'Is it all like this?' asked O'Neill.

'More or less.'

'You'll be needing a hand, then.'

'I can manage.'

'You'll not be having much time. I'll come at the weekend and start you off.'

'There's no need. I know what to do.'

'I'll come anyway and supervise.'

Fran took the coffee jar from the cupboard and spooned generous teaspoons into mugs. She couldn't be bothered to argue.

'I expect you're wondering why I've come,' said O'Neill.

'It had crossed my mind.'

'Shortly we'll be on our way to Lincolnshire. The local bobby's just informed us that a local woman has been reported missing – not seen for several days.'

'Is there any reason to think she might be our victim?' Fran asked as she passed him a black coffee, explaining she had no milk.

'Sure there is, Wilson. Her name is Trudi Miller, and guess where she's living – or rather was living, before she disappeared?'

'Last Chance Farm?'

'That's it. So we'll drink this coffee and be off.'

Lincolnshire by night was as dark and flat as the inside of a black beret. O'Neill sang on the journey, his voice low and mellow, Irish folk songs with lyrics that when she caught a word here and there were about love and famine and leaving Ireland.

'When did you leave Ireland, boss?' Fran asked in a rare pause.

O'Neill smiled. 'Ah! Now there's a tale . . .'

'Yes?'

'I've never lived in Ireland. I've been there of course, for holidays. I was born there but I came here as a baby. Kilburn, London, was where I practised being Irish. And I've made a damn fine job of it, don't you think?'

Fran laughed. 'Does that mean you've never kissed the Blarney Stone?'

'I didn't say that, now did I,' said O'Neill. 'Now go back to sleep and let me drive in peace.'

Fran dozed then through the blackness of Lincolnshire until she heard O'Neill say: 'It's up ahead.'

Fran opened her eyes to see a stone cottage, its porch light gleaming in the darkness. A dead-looking tree stood on the left of the house and the shadow of barns to the right. Surrounding the house seemed miles of blackness although out in the distance past the tree Fran could see the twinkling of lights on the horizon.

As they drove up the gravel path a figure came into view. Tall and dark in the light of the porch it took Fran a moment to realize he was a policeman. When she got a closer look at his face she was surprised to see he wore gold-rimmed glasses. They didn't suit him, his nose was bent and squashed as a professional boxer's and his whole face had a flattened look. Yet his voice didn't have the aggressive tone she expected. His voice matched his glasses.

'I'm PC Mike Ecton, sir,' he said as O'Neill got out of the car. 'Hope I haven't got you out here on a fool's errand. Since I phoned I've found out a bit more.'

'Which is?' asked O'Neill.

'Well, sir, for one thing the farm is up for sale and for another she's sold all the chickens.'

'And?'

'Well. . .' said PC Ecton, 'it seems Mrs Miller could well have gone away because she didn't have to worry about the chickens.'

'Is that what the neighbours say?'

'She didn't mix much but I've spoken to her feed supplier and a friend of hers who lives in the village and she said Mrs Miller was thinking of moving to France and perhaps that's where she was, looking for property.'

'Have you had a look round, Constable?'

'I have indeed, sir. I can't see anything much inside, it's too dark.'

'Who left the porch light on?'

'Must have been her. There's no outside switch.'

'Wilson,' said O'Neill, 'pass me my torch. It's in the glove compartment.'

Fran found the torch, a large black rubber one, useful as a truncheon and nearly as heavy. 'Shall I see if there's a way in round the back, boss?'

'Stay where you are, Wilson. We'll all be having a look round,' said O'Neill, taking the torch from her and sounding as peeved as if she had just knocked over his first Guinness of the day.

Fran waited by the car while the two men disappeared round the back of the cottage. Then she walked to the front door and examined the lock. Yale, new, matching the new door. From her anorak pocket she took out the key ring that held a variety of keys and two different-width credit cards. She reasoned if there was a dead woman in the house the murderer would not have been able to bolt the front door, unless, of course, he'd left by the back door. Anyway it was worth a try.

She was still trying when O'Neill and Ecton returned.

'Forget it, Wilson,' said O'Neill. 'We haven't got all night.'

'I'll do it any minute now,' said Fran, disappointed that not only had they come back so soon but that she hadn't managed to show her prowess with locks.

'There's no point,' said O'Neill. 'Back door's open. We found a key under a flowerpot.'

At the back of the cottage the kitchen light was now on.

'Try not to get your fingerprints everywhere, Wilson, and you, Ecton, we don't want to be making the scene of crimes boys work any harder.'

'You're convinced there has been a crime, then?'

'We'll soon be finding out,' said O'Neill. 'Lead on, Wilson.'

Fran walked into the kitchen. At first glance all was neat and tidy, no washing-up still to be done, draining-board empty, likewise the plastic wastebin. A bunch of dried flowers in a pottery vase sat on the scrubbed pine table next to an empty fruit bowl. The cooker sparkled, as did the white cornflower-sprigged wall tiles.

O'Neill and PC Ecton moved ahead and Fran could hear them clumping up the stairs and across floorboards. Fran stayed in the kitchen for a few minutes, looking around, trying to commit it to memory, trying to visualize the woman who lived there.

On the wall nearest the table were two small framed watercolours; one was of a bluebell wood, the other a seaside resort. She stared at them both for a moment and then as she looked away something caught her eye on the floor beneath the table. Kneeling on the floor Fran reached out. Her find was disappointing, just a few scraps of dried flower, brittle pieces of yellow and pink. She glanced from them to the pottery vase on the table. They were probably insignificant but even so she thrust them deep into her anorak pocket.

'What are you doing?' asked O'Neill suddenly appearing at the kitchen door.

'Just looking, boss,' said Fran, 'just looking.'

'Find anything?'

'Not really. . . I—'

'Neither have we,' interrupted O'Neill. 'She's not upstairs; it looks like she was moving out, though. There's just the sitting room and the cellar to check now.'

They walked out of the kitchen along a small hallway, O'Neill and Ecton in front, Fran coming along behind. In the sitting room chintzy chairs sat grouped around a large-screened television set. More watercolours decorated the walls and in the corner of the room a huge yucca plant and a rubber plant grew healthily in large ceramic tubs. All was as neatly organized as the kitchen. As they turned to leave Fran looked back.

'What is it?' asked O'Neill.

'Just a thought, boss,' said Fran as she walked over to the plants and felt the compost carefully with her fingers.

'They're very dry, boss. I shouldn't think they have been watered for several days.'

O'Neill nodded. Why hadn't he thought of that? 'Cellar next,' he said. 'And the barns. Ecton, you take the barns, we'll do the cellar.'

The stone cellar steps were lit by a naked light bulb on the wall at the top. Its forty watts or so meant that the bottom of the steps was practically in darkness.

Fran's special fear was not so much finding a corpse but finding spiders; lurking, predatory, with spindly fast-moving legs and fat well-fed bodies. O'Neill hoped it wouldn't smell bad and PC Ecton, he suspected, was a pragmatist who simply hoped nothing they found this night in the barns or in the cellar would involve too many written reports.

As they descended O'Neill asked, 'Are you all right, Wilson?'

'I'm fine,' said Fran. But she wasn't. 'I'm fine,' she repeated.

O'Neill turned to look at her sharply but said nothing.

Some way down the steps curved and a few more steps led them to a stone-floored vestibule. O'Neill used his torch to pick out paint pots, a wooden ladder, a few cardboard boxes, and a folded trestle table. There seemed to be no other light switch. A closed door faced them: a door with no lock, that as O'Neill swung open, swung closed again. O'Neill opened the door again and with it held open with one hand he found a light switch to the right of the doorway. He propped a paint can by the door and said, 'Let there be light!' as he flicked the switch. The sudden light from a central bulb made them blink.

The body, or what remained of it, lay, legs straightened, on plastic sheeting. The left arm had gone, an empty sleeve of a cream-covered sweater lay raised above the head. A thick pool of garish red replaced the arm and a cleaver had been laid on her chest as if the gruesome task was not yet finished. A tea towel covered her face and over a navy skirt, an apron, covered with primroses the colour of sunshine, had been dotted with blood.

O'Neill lifted a corner of the tea towel.

'She's been strangled,' he said.

'There's no sign of a struggle, is there,' said Fran. At that moment a spider scuttled from somewhere near the body and Fran shuddered and put out a hand to O'Neill.

He frowned. The smell of decomposition, he imagined, hung in the air like some foul dangerous miasma.

'Let's be going upstairs,' he said, 'to ring Scene of Crimes and the doc. You and I could be doing with some medication ourselves.'

PC Ecton met them at the top of the stairs.

'Is she . . . ?' he asked his eyes flicking towards the cellar door.

'Yes,' said O'Neill.

The three of them sat in the Mercedes. O'Neill

offered Ecton a drink from his hip flask but quite properly he refused. 'Not on duty, sir.'

Fran had no such qualms. She had seen the body. The apron and tea towel had upset her. Mrs Trudi Miller had probably been washing up at the time, getting ready for her new life in France, feeling happy and excited. Had she known Frank Miller, alias Melksham, was dead? Or did she just think he had left home, as he'd done before? What made tidy Trudi so dangerous she had to die?

The police surgeon took an hour to arrive. He made no excuses. He was a small, middle-aged man with a thin irritable face and a slight twitch in one eye which gave the impression he was giving you a nod and a wink when he in fact wasn't.

'I'll need a hand,' he said to O'Neill.

He glanced at Fran. 'I'll come,' she said.

O'Neill couldn't hide the relief in his smile. It was easier to put a brave face on things with a female in tow. It had smelled down there. Of cold and damp and blood and decomposing flesh. He'd been glad when Fran had held on to him, it had made him feel stronger. Violent death was always an obscenity, never dignified, a reminder of the fragility of life, of loss and waste and sorrow.

Graham Gretton didn't take long to come to his conclusions. Death by strangulation, arm lopped off by the cleaver and dead a few days, but as the cellar was fairly cold it could have been longer. The body had hardly decomposed at all.

'Manual strangulation?' asked O'Neill, who had

looked at the neck but merely seen bruises as he had been too busy holding his breath against the stench.

'Looks like it. Her larynx has been crushed. There's no evidence that I can find of any recent sexual activity. She's had at least one pregnancy and I don't think she was killed down here. There's some bruising to her back as if she'd been dragged down the cellar steps.'

Graham Gretton turned then half smiled at Fran and winked. Fran was taken aback until she realized his wink was only a tic and not in any way suggestive.

As they were about to leave PC Ecton creaked down the stairs and walked over to the body.

'Mind if I look?' he said.

No one did. He stood staring at the body for a moment with a puzzled frown on his forehead.

'What's wrong?' asked Fran.

He shook his head from side to side. 'I'm quite new here,' he said slowly. 'She looks different. No make-up I suppose.'

'People do look different in death,' said O'Neill.

Ecton stared again at the blueish face and the half opened eyes. 'I'm sure you're right, sir.'

O'Neill too looked at the face once more. The personality that had once animated Trudi Miller's face had gone, leaving in its place mere blankness. She existed now only in the memory of those who knew her. And even that would become misty with time. As if the person you once knew was merely a figment of your own imagination.

Already O'Neill was dreading the moment of telling

the next of kin. The formal identification, the disbelief, the shock. He looked at Wilson. He felt glad she'd be there. He'd be forced outwardly to act like a chief inspector. Inside, though, he felt like a small boy who had become lost in a crowd and knew panic was beginning to set in. However hard you looked, no face was familiar.

He re-covered her face with the tea towel and slowly crossed himself.

Chapter Eight

O'Neill stood for a moment staring at the corpse. Then he said abruptly, 'Let's be having a proper look over the house.'

Graham Gretton, with a slight twitch of his head and his left shoulder, said, 'I'm off. I'm glad to say it's not my problem.'

He picked up his black bag and, with the cheerful wave of a man who knew he was going back to his bed, walked towards the cellar door without a backward glance.

PC Ecton saw his escape too. 'OK if I go, sir? There's not a lot more I can do here, is there? I should have been off at ten . . .'

O'Neill shrugged. 'Sure. Thanks for your help.'

They watched PC Ecton's retreating back. Fran was envious, hungry, and tired. A night's sleep was ebbing away fast and no doubt she'd have to keep going all the next day – all *this* day she corrected herself, it was one thirty a.m.

'Wilson,' said O'Neill, 'if we hurry we'll have time to have a good look round before the SOC boys arrive and want us out of the way.'

'Shouldn't they be here by now?'

'Depends what job they're on. They get called to a large number of burglaries, as well you know. They're only a small team and they have to finish one job first before they start another.'

'Won't they mind us touching things?'

'Sure they will,' said O'Neill. 'But I don't give a damn.'

In the main bedroom, which was painted a subtle peach colour and had a large landscape above the bed, Fran began opening cupboards and searching through drawers, even searching under the bed. The only belongings, it seemed, had already been packed. A large navy-blue suitcase, zipped and bulging, had been placed near the door. A half-packed weekend bag lay open on the bed among a small pile of new underwear and a large make-up bag. The selection of make-up surprised Fran but O'Neill showed no interest when she pointed out how odd she thought it. He merely stood about looking chief inspectorish and thoughtful.

'Wilson,' he said eventually, 'let's start on the suitcases. You're a woman, you might spot something useful.'

'Thanks for noticing,' murmured Fran.

O'Neill heaved the bulging suitcase on to the bed and unzipped it. Fran went to work on the half-packed one.

'Strange there is no handbag,' she said. 'That's where a passport would be.'

'This whole case is strange,' said O'Neill as he pulled out clothes and generally rummaged about.

Fran tried to be more organized. It was in the side-zipped compartment she found the passport.

The face which stared at her was a brunette, thin faced, with a slight smile. Mrs Trudi Miller was described as having no scars, being thirty-five, five foot six, born in Lincoln, and a farmer's wife. In death, with no smile, she looked very different. O'Neill too looked at the passport carefully. Neither spoke for a few moments, then he said, 'Just carry on looking. I want to know what's missing. That's often more important than what you find.'

'Is that Irish logic, boss?'

O'Neill scowled but said nothing. He stared for some time at the open window with its curtains tied back and then at the neatly made bed.

'Killed in the daytime, it seems,' he said slowly.

Fran continued methodically sorting through clothes and finding nothing of any real interest began looking round the room for places she hadn't yet searched. There was nothing in the bottom of the wardrobe but she hadn't yet looked underneath it. Kneeling on the floor she pushed the flat of her hand into the narrow space between carpet and the wardrobe door. There was no room for her hand to sweep the area so she used a metal coat hanger, carefully sweeping backwards and forwards, and she was just about to give up when the hanger came in contact with something other than carpet.

'I've found something, boss.'

O'Neill didn't answer but watched as she manoeuvred the object out. Fran felt a twinge of disappointment at what she had retrieved – a dusty, mangled copy of *Country Lady* magazine. She sat on the bed to read it.

'There's no time for that, Wilson,' said O'Neill. 'Give it to me.'

'No, wait, boss. It's the only interesting item in this room that isn't clothes, apart from the passport of course. Whoever cleared the room missed this.'

'Have you looked in the bathroom yet?' asked O'Neill with his hand out for the magazine. Fran held on to it but O'Neill tugged more forcibly and it was his. He walked over to the window and began flicking through the pages. After a few moments he looked up, 'Well, go on, Wilson. Check the bathroom.'

Reluctantly Fran left the bedroom. She was sure that single copy of *Country Lady* was significant; why keep it otherwise? Or hide it?

The bathroom had sickly yellow walls and a blue-green suite. It was empty save for a roll of toilet paper and a sliver of soap. The bathroom cabinet had been emptied.

When Fran returned to the bedroom O'Neill was holding up the magazine to reveal a cut out portion in the job section.

'This is our best lead so far,' he said. 'She was obviously applying for a job. Where and for whom we'll have to find out from the magazine. I'll be ringing them in the morning.'

Downstairs Fran searched the kitchen drawer. All was neatly arranged: a ball of string, scissors, tacks, pens and pencils, recipes, candles and matches, and two appointment cards, one for the dentist and the other for the gynaecological outpatients' department of the cottage hospital. An appointment a month before that perhaps she had managed to keep.

'I'll be having that,' said O'Neill taking the card from her. 'It may be important.'

Fran went over in her mind the search of the house. Why should the toiletries be missing, and no purse or handbag? Had the arm been carried off in another suitcase along with the toiletries? The tidiness bothered her. As if someone had tidied up after the murder. But why bother?

The scene of crimes trio arrived shortly afterwards, cheerful, raucous even, and seemingly oblivious to the time of night.

'Hello there, Chief,' said the most senior-looking man whose raincoat even Columbo would have rejected. 'This one's a bit of a facer, isn't it? Mind you, my little team is one of the best, as thorough as any SOCs in the Midlands. I've got a feeling we could get lucky.'

'Maybe,' said O'Neill, his spirits sagging under the influence of so much cheerful optimism. 'Just do your best, Alan.'

'OK,' said Alan enthusiastically and then turned to his colleagues to say: 'Come on, lads. Let's get to work.'

The three of them thumped down the cellar steps laughing and chatting as if awaiting them at the bottom was some glorious stag night.

O'Neill, shrugging, said, 'It will take them hours to

do the whole house. We'll go now, Wilson.'

'Just one more look at the kitchen, boss.'

O'Neill shrugged. 'If you must. What bothers you there?'

'I want to look in the fridge.'

'What for?'

'I'm surprised it wasn't left open, that's all. The kitchen seemed so ready for leaving except that the fridge door was closed. If she was going away surely she would have switched it off and opened the door.'

O'Neill didn't look convinced but he followed her into the kitchen and as she opened the fridge door he too peered inside. It was empty, save for two bottles of Bulgarian red wine.

Back in Fowchester, outside Fran's house, O'Neill said, 'We'll be telling the next of kin first thing in the morning. Night time is the worst of times to give people such bad news, mind and body are at their lowest ebb.'

Fran could understand that, her ebb was definitely at an all-time low.

'You'll be making coffee?' asked O'Neill.

'I've no milk.'

'No problem. I've got some whisky.'

'It's late,' said Fran, longing for sleep.

'I'm wide awake. We could discuss the case. For a while anyway.'

'All right,' said Fran, her voice heavy with reluctance. 'Come on in.'

In lamp light the rag-rolled walls looked softer.

O'Neill sprawled on the sofa staring at the walls. Fran sat on a chair opposite and made no attempt to disguise the fact that she was tired. She closed her eyes feigning sleep, hoping O'Neill might take the hint. He didn't.

'Sure it's just like the sea,' he said staring at the walls.

'Galway Bay?'

O'Neill laughed. 'More like Southend,' he said. 'I used to go there as a child. I thought it was the finest place on earth, until I discovered Ireland. They don't call Ireland God's own country for nothing.'

'I've never been,' said Fran. 'The nearest I've got to Ireland was a punch-up at the Irish Centre on a Saturday night. They sent me along as the statutory female officer.'

'Did you get hurt?'

'No, I got pulled out of the action by a drunken Irish man who kissed me passionately.'

'What did you do, Wilson?'

'Kicked him hard in the groin.'

'What did he do?'

'Sank to his knees saying, "Jasus! It was only a kiss." '

'Did you arrest him?'

'No. I told him to say three Hail Marys and not to do it again.'

'You're kidding?'

Fran didn't answer and O'Neill stared at her for a moment and then produced his hip flask.

'You'll be needing a glass,' he said.

For a moment Fran hesitated. Where the hell were her glasses? She made a swift search and found them still wrapped in a cardboard box in a corner by the bookshelf.

'Just a small one,' she said, as she removed the protective newspaper covering and handed him her only pair of crystal glasses.

The whisky hit her stomach hot and scalding and after that came the spreading warmth. A drink or so later Fran began to relax. Going to sleep didn't seem to matter any more but she would have liked just to sit and dream. Whisky in O'Neill seemed to have the opposite effect. He wanted to talk. The Irish like to talk, Fran thought. She'd known Irish girls at college. They liked to talk and laugh into the early hours, going for 'the crack' they called it.

'Now, Wilson, what do you make of it so far?' asked O'Neill watching her steadily.

'The case?'

O'Neill nodded.

'We have two victims,' she began, 'one may have been dead some time – the other was killed very recently. If we assume that Frank Melksham is the first victim and that he was living at Last Chance Farm we could also assume that Trudi Miller found out who had killed him and so she had to die. Or. . .' She faltered.

'Or what?'

'I'm confused, boss. If Frank Melksham was safely in cold storage somewhere and no one any the wiser why bring out the body and start trying to dispose of it? And how can we be absolutely sure the arm does belong to Frank Melksham?'

'Good point, Wilson. Frank is the most likely victim because he disappeared not once but twice, the second time in unusual circumstances, I'll be telling you about that in a minute. He fits the physical description, same blood group, and more importantly he was an almighty bastard with several people saying they would swing for him.'

'Why didn't you tell me all this before?' asked Fran.

O'Neill laughed. 'I like to keep a few things to myself. You're a newcomer, you'll see things with a fresh eye. Familiarity doesn't always breed contempt, it just forms a grey mist. After a while you just stop noticing how odd people are. I'll tell you now about Frank's second disappearance. Sheila Melksham certainly didn't tell all. Knowing of course that I was around and investigating at the time she didn't have to. But still it was strange she didn't go over old ground again.'

'Boss. I'm tired, weary, and confused. Couldn't this wait until tomorrow?'

'Not at all Wilson. Not at all. I'd value your opinion.'

Fran shrugged. The light of enthusiasm shone in O'Neill's eyes. There was no point in arguing. If she'd had a cigarette then she would have smoked it with only the merest wisp of conscience.

'Tell me then before I fall asleep,' she said.

O'Neill smiled at her benignly and lay back on the

sofa as if the telling of the tale was going to take some time.

'It was two years ago, one dark wet November night. There was a darts championship at the Plough in Clopstock. The pub was full. Half-way through the evening Frank Melksham turned up. No one asked where he'd been those three years. Some people had heard the rumours that he was living with a woman in Lincolnshire but no one really gave a toss. Just before closing time, Frank left. He was never seen again. No one reported him missing and although the Lincolnshire police tried to trace him, because his car had been found abandoned in the pub car park, they found nothing. Trudi Miller it seemed was delighted he'd gone, which was why she hadn't notified anyone.'

'I'm surprised she didn't try to find out purely from curiosity,' said Fran, 'and what was so bad about Frank that everybody disliked him?'

O'Neill looked thoughtful. 'I met him a couple of times. He was good-looking, I guess, and on first meeting charming. He was definitely attractive to women, at first anyway. But he liked a drink and his temper was as unpredictable as a pit-bull's and nearly as dangerous. Sheila suffered, and Andy. They never pressed charges though and I do know that one or two of our more hot-headed constables wanted to take him outside. Sure, he even treated his own dog badly. In the end Sheila took the poor creature to the vet's. People round these parts can tolerate a man who ill-treats his wife, but his dog or his animals are another matter entirely. And Frank was a poor farmer. There was some suggestion he sold cows knowing they were infected with BSE but no one could prove it.'

Fran rubbed her eyes as if that would improve her concentration and said, 'You've convinced me that Frank could well be the victim, but why Trudi Miller? And why now?'

'Now don't be asking me such difficult questions, Wilson. We'll be finding that out soon enough.'

'I admire your optimism.'

'I work hard at cultivating it,' said O'Neill. 'You go off to bed now, Wilson, I'll just sit here and think.'

'You're not going home, then?'

'In my state of health?' said O'Neill. 'No, I'll just stay here for a wee nap. Apart from the advertisement where do you think we should start?'

Fran was silent for a moment, then she said: 'The Plough, Clopstock. Something must have happened there. A man can't just disappear, and why abandon his car?'

'Why indeed?' said O'Neill, smiling, and looking more than settled on her sofa.

Fran stood for a moment watching him and wondering why this sort of thing hadn't happened to her before and whether she could insist that he leave? He'd had too much to drink to drive himself home but he could have called a minicab.

'I'll throw you down a blanket,' she said, hoping he noticed the slight tone of disapproval in her voice. He didn't, he just nodded as if it were merely his due.

A short time later, as Fran climbed gratefully into bed, she thought how strange it was that tonight she had a man and a mouse in her home. She hoped the mouse wouldn't be disturbed.

O'Neill couldn't sleep. He'd lived in Fowchester for more than ten years. He knew a few petty criminals, and a few violent ones, but it was a shock to him that the town harboured someone who could kill and then dismember a woman. Partially dismember, he told himself. Had the murderer planned to dispose of the whole body or had he been disturbed in his gruesome task? But who by? And why try to dispose of the limb in such an obvious way? As if trying to be caught. . . a deliberate act. . . perhaps even trying to lay a false trail. . . incriminate someone else.

After a while he thought about the last match of last year's cricket season. It had been a hot day, the cricket had been so satisfyingly dull that he had slept through most of it and woken feeling refreshed but with a sense of loss that another season was over and he had a winter to wait for the next. Frank Melksham had missed two seasons but where had he been hidden? And who would say even if they knew?

It was early the next morning that O'Neill and Fran arrived at the Theodolou house to break the bad news. Trudi's sister Wendy lived in a gracious three-storey house in an equally gracious cul-de-sac. The curtains were still drawn but the middle-storey lights were on and a carriage lamp outside illuminated a black BMW parked in the front drive.

O'Neill lifted the heavy brass knocker and knocked

three times, loudly. His mouth, Fran noticed, was set
in a grimly determined line.

'This is the worst part,' he said. 'I'll never get used
to it.'

After a few moments dull footsteps sounded on the
stairs and then a woman answered the door. She was,
Fran supposed, in her middle thirties and had the
understated but undeniable appearance of someone
who had money. Not so much in what she wore, black
cords and a black sweatshirt, but she had the self-
assurance, a quality of security that Fran was convinced was only really marked in people who didn't
have to worry about the next bill. And she had a
glorious tan that was either acquired on a sun bed or
during a winter holiday in the sun.

'Wendy Theodolou? Police,' said O'Neill. 'May we
come in?'

The smile of acknowledgement that had greeted
them froze on her face. Fear flickered in her eyes.

'What's happened? Is it my sister? Has she had an
accident in the car? I told her to be careful, she was
always going too fast—'

'If we may come inside,' interrupted O'Neill.

'Oh yes, come in, come in – upstairs.'

Wendy Theodolou moved quickly in front of them.
Fran noticed her slim figure and the way her long dark
hair, the colour of her sister's, swished slightly as she
walked up the wide plush-carpeted stairs. She's too
old for a pony tail, thought Fran, but somehow it
suited her.

As they got to the middle-storey room she turned.

'Tell me,' she said, 'please tell me.'

'Is your husband in?' asked O'Neill gently.

'No, no, he's out. He'll be back soon. What's happened?'

'Sit down,' said O'Neill, 'and I'll be telling you.'

Wendy sat down quickly on the edge of a cream-and-gold coloured sofa. O'Neill began to tell her slowly and quietly that in the early hours of the morning they had found a young woman's body at Last Chance Farm. 'We have reason to believe,' he said finally, 'that this person is your sister – Trudi Miller.'

She began to shake then, little tremors as if she had suddenly become very cold. Looking up with tear-filled eyes into O'Neill's face she asked: 'Was it suicide?'

'It wasn't suicide, Mrs Theodolou. It was murder.'

'Murder,' echoed Wendy as if saying the word for the first time. 'Murder.'

'Would you like some brandy or a cup of tea?' asked Fran.

Wendy shook her head. 'Can I see her?'

'Of course,' said O'Neill. 'We'll be wanting you to identify the body. When will your husband be back?'

'Today some time. He's in London – he's in the wine trade. . .' She trailed off. 'I can't believe it. She came here last week, she was going away on holiday – I'm not sure where but she seemed so happy. . .'

This time the tears came and O'Neill stood up and walked to the window and stared out. Fran sat beside Wendy, put an arm around her, and sat silently while she cried for the sister and probably best friend she would never see again.

Eventually the sobbing ceased and when it did Wendy Theodolou rushed from the room with a choked, 'Excuse me.' O'Neill stared at Fran for a moment and he too looked anguished.

'I'll leave her alone for a few minutes,' said Fran. 'Are you OK?'

He nodded. This was only the beginning. He too had experienced the initial shock. Identifying the body would be the confirmation of loss and grief and the start of guilt.

It was at that moment that husband Christopher appeared in the hallway. Fran watched him set down his briefcase and look up at them as they stood at the top of the stairs. If Greek good looks could be measured on a ladder between Onassis and Prince Philip, thought Fran, Chris Theodolou wouldn't even get on the first rung. Something about his build reminded her of a hippopotamus. He was round and rumpy, with dark wavy hair, well dressed in a pale grey suit but with short legs, a sweaty, pudgy face, and sharp ferrety eyes.

'What the hell is going on?' he asked.

If the voice was all there was to the man, thought Fran, he'd win any woman. His voice was incredibly sexy, deep and throaty and with enough accent to make him a little mysterious. She wondered how he had got on with his sister-in-law's boyfriend. Had he been jealous of Frank's good looks and his success with women?

O'Neill, half-way down the stairs, said, 'Detective Chief Inspector O'Neill, Fowchester Police, and DS Wilson. Bad news, I'm afraid, Mr Theodolou. We have reason to believe that your sister-in-law, Mrs Trudi Miller, has been murdered.'

There was a moment's pause before Theodolou said, 'Good God! Does my wife know?'

'I know,' said Wendy as she came out of one of the rooms. Quickly her husband was beside her, a protective arm around her.

'I'm so sorry, darling,' he said. 'So very sorry. And I wasn't here.'

'Where exactly have you been, sir?' asked O'Neill.

'I've been in London for two days on business.'

'What sort of business?'

'I'm in the wine trade – importing.'

O'Neill decided there was no point in prolonging the agony of identification and suggested they left straight away.

The journey to the hospital morgue took only a few minutes but to Fran and O'Neill it seemed longer. No one spoke. It was hard to think of something to say.

The body covered by a sheet of pristine white was ready for identification. As the mortuary assistant pulled back the sheet to uncover the face, Wendy's gasp sounded in the cool air of the mortuary like the last breath of the dying.

O'Neill looked at her sharply. She was smiling.

'It's not her,' she said, 'it's not my sister.'

'Are you sure?' asked O'Neill.

'Oh yes, oh yes. It's definitely not her. That's not Trudi.'

100

Chapter Nine

At Higham Merrils Agricultural College the Principal, Norman Crick, had returned early from his holiday. He'd thought he should make an appearance, that it would be best. It worried him that his usually quiet kingdom had been disturbed in such a way.

He was a man preparing for early retirement in a year's time and many, including his deputy, thought that although he had been good in his day, that day was fast drawing to a close. He had grown absent-minded – some, unkindly and wrongly, said senile. Mostly he was just nervous, occasionally jumpy. He used his little lapses of memory to justify the fact that at nearly sixty he could retire at any time and it couldn't come a day too soon.

'Where's. . . um. . . what's his name?' he asked Kay on his return.

'Your deputy?' she asked.

'Yes, of course. . . Malcolm.'

'He's teaching at the moment. Miss Dunhill is off sick.'

'Oh. I see,' said Norman.

He retreated to his office and sat for a while in his leather upholstered swivel chair staring at the polished antique desk which was all he would miss from his working days. Perhaps he'd suggest it would make an ideal leaving present. On the desk sat a half-week's mail – three circulars and a bank statement. The paucity of his post, he thought, reflected his rapidly diminishing status.

After he'd opened his circulars he carefully put the unopened bank statement in his suit inside pocket and wandered into his private cloakroom and stared into the mirror. He noted sadly the sallowness of his skin, the way the hair poked from his ears in white clumps and failed to grow any more on his balding head. Wrinkles that were once mere lines now seemed wider, like cracks in the earth's crust just waiting for one almighty cave-in.

Why had he bothered to come back? Malcolm Kilsby could easily cope. Malcolm was young, efficient, good-looking – in his prime. And Norman hated him for it. Yes, that wasn't too strong a word for it. He hated the cocky little bastard. Malcolm had usurped him from the moment he came, with his glowing references, his brand-new Range Rover with sparkling new ideas to match. The bees being one of them, and fine profits they'd made too. His efforts and ideas, laudable though they were, only made Norman's previous running of the college seem. . . well. . . pedestrian. And now this. No doubt Malcolm would see murder as yet another entrepreneurial opportunity. Perhaps he'd organize coach trips, agricultural murder weekends, hunt the severed head.

Your trouble, Norman, he told himself, is that you expected a welcome. It seemed that his return, like his departure, was hardly a blip in the running of the college. Even the police hadn't bothered to consult him in any way. It seemed they had created an operations HQ which ran like the college itself, without need of any input from him at all.

It was lunchtime before anyone knocked on his door. It was Malcolm. Malcolm in white designer T-shirt and white shorts and carrying his squash racquet.

'Heard you were back, Norman. Fancy a game?'

'No.'

'Do you good. We do need to catch up on a few things. This murder is creating a bit of a stir as you can imagine.'

Norman watched his deputy bouncing slightly up and down, as though his trainers only served to contain his natural keenness and exuberance. For God's sake, thought Norman, the man was nearly forty!

'If you could spare a moment of your squash time,' Norman said, 'I'd appreciate you telling me exactly what's been going on. Have the police, for instance, found out who he was?'

Malcolm continued to move slightly on the spot, his floppy fair hair lifting a little as he did so, but now a smile, or was it a smirk, played on his lips.

'Haven't you heard?' he asked. But the suggestion was that Norman had forgotten.

'No, I have not,' said Norman coldly. 'Tell me.'

'The first arm was male, found at Harrington Farm,

the second, found here, was female.'

'I see,' said Norman, not giving his deputy the satisfaction of any show of surprise. After a moment's pause he said, 'Thank you, Malcolm. I expect we'll meet up again later this afternoon.'

'Don't forget I'm teaching. I finish at four.'

As Malcolm left, Norman had his hand on the door handle. He kept it there for a long time, squeezing hard.

A little later he rang his friend, the veterinary surgeon Keith Quinton.

'I'm back,' he said, 'I thought it best.'

'Quite right, old son,' said Keith. 'We should meet. Usual place?'

'Fine,' replied Norman. 'About eight?'

'We'll get legless,' said Keith. 'Do us good.'

'Better than armless,' said Norman, feeling relieved when Keith began to laugh.

Norman didn't see Malcolm again that afternoon but Detective Chief Inspector O'Neill and a young pretty detective sergeant paid him a visit. Norman found it difficult. O'Neill had a faraway look in his greenish eyes as though seeing some distant horizon and then, when he suddenly focused, it was as if he saw everything much more clearly. Not that he asked any really difficult questions.

'Did you know Frank Melksham?' he'd asked.

That was easy, he had known him, and like everyone else who knew him he wished he hadn't.

'Yes, I knew Frank.'

'Well?'

'I'd seen him around. Mostly in the pub at Clopstock. He wasn't a friend.'

'Did the man have any friends?' asked O'Neill.

'I'd be hard pressed to name one,' said Norman, 'although I'm sure he had some enemies. A man like him always does.'

'You'll be explaining that,' said O'Neill softly.

Norman hesitated. Melksham was objectionable but on first meetings he could be charming. It was more what was known about him.

'He had a reputation for violence, Chief Inspector, as you well know. Personally he had never done me any harm. I knew of him but I rarely spoke to him. He wasn't a man for casual conversations.'

'When did you last see him?'

'About two years ago in the Plough at Clopstock. I heard he was living in Lincolnshire.'

'Did you speak to him?'

'No. I had nothing to say.'

'Well, that's all for the moment,' said O'Neill. 'We'll keep in touch. Have you any questions, Wilson?'

The woman detective smiled and said quietly, 'Only one. Are you married, Mr Crick?'

Norman swallowed. 'I've been married twenty-five years. Happily, I hasten to add.'

Liar! said a voice in Norman's head. The girl, she was only a girl, had watched him steadily.

'Does your wife know Mrs Melksham?'

'No. Well, she may know her by sight. To pass the time of day with.'

He expected her to say more but she simply smiled and thanked him.

When they had gone Norman rested his elbows on the table and supported his head with his hands. Why? he asked himself. Why now?

Later that afternoon, following two single whiskies, Norman felt able to go home. It was a short drive and as he approached the village and caught sight of his thatched cottage he felt his usual tangle of emotions; pleasure at the sheer beauty of his home and anxiety at what faced him inside. Still, without the whisky, he told himself, he would have felt worse.

Barbara sat in the living room on her favourite chair by the low-mullioned window doing a crossword. The light picked out the silver hairs in her dark curly hair and for a moment Norman was filled with hope. Then she turned to look at him and the scowl was still there.

'Well?' she said.

That word summed up everything she wanted to say. It wasn't meant as a question. It was an unspoken diatribe. It was her way of saying – was it worth losing half a week's holiday? Was it worth going in the first place? No doubt Malcolm had everything under control anyway? How was she going to fill the rest of her week? He didn't think about her one little bit. She couldn't stand being buried alive in this sterile village. Wasn't it about time he thought about her for a change? What exactly were they going to do when he retired? Next year when he retired they wouldn't even be able to afford holidays. He'd always put that stupid college first – et cetera, et cetera.

Norman read her mind like a script. It was just that now they were both word perfect and one of her scowls gave him instant recall. She'd conditioned him like Pavlov's dogs.

'Drink?' asked Norman.

'No doubt you've had some already.'

'No doubt,' said Norman, the thought of more whisky to come emboldening him.

After her initial greeting she hardly spoke again. She did nod for a drink and to ask him if he wanted his salad dressed. At least as they were hardly on speaking terms he could go out without too much argument.

Barbara suffered from depression. No, that wasn't quite true. Norman suffered from it as well. It was as catching as any virus and he was surprised the medical profession hadn't realized that. Barbara had an advantage though, she was treated for hers; anti-depressant pills, sleeping pills, psychotherapy, sympathy – she had the lot. When Norman went to his GP for a spot of the same he was told to relax more and have a whisky at bedtime.

Just before eight Norman stood up and said, 'I'm going to the Plough. Darts match. I could be late.'

Barbara was staring at the TV screen. She didn't look in his direction. She rarely looked at him full in the face.

'Don't disturb me then,' she said.

'God forbid,' muttered Norman under his breath.

Outside the house he breathed deeply. The air was cool and there was a full moon and all around was the smell of damp grass from the first spring mowings. He stood for a while, appreciating the freedom to come.

Norman was never quite sure why he liked the Plough, but he did. It was faded and the decorations were in very dubious taste. Fairy lights hung from genuine oak beams but the beams were all that was genuine. The potted plants were artificial, mostly red poinsettias, the fish were stuffed in glass cases and stared out looking pathetically mournful, even the publican had an artificial eye. The atmosphere, summer and winter, always seemed to Norman to be just post-Christmas – down-beat but tinged with the suggestion that things could be worse.

Keith had got the beer in. Two pints each lined up at their favourite table, near the main bar and within sight of the new barmaid who had big breasts, wore low-cut blouses, and was unfailingly cheerful. The Plough was the only pub they knew that provided such a barmaid. And she had the knack of making them feel like young headstrong boys again.

'Hello, lads,' she'd say. 'Out on the town again?' And somehow they would feel they really were.

'How's it going?' asked Keith. And somehow that one question, that unspoken empathy that exists between two male friends, compensated Norman for his wife's scowl. Keith understood, and as if to prove it he said, 'Sodding awful, I take it. Get the beer down you. We'll have a skinful tonight.'

Keith moved his large frame in the chair trying to get comfortable. His paunch was so large he needed to make constant adjustments to his position. Just like a pregnant woman, thought Norman; but apart from his belly he was a good-looking man, with a wide friendly face and crinkly brown hair. Popular with everyone. He had the knack. Norman wished he had it too.

They drank the first pint in silence, a valedictory drink that signalled the end of sobriety for the evening. After the first drink they could talk.

'Have you heard Trudi Miller is dead?' asked Keith, leaning forward. 'It seems the second arm found belonged to her. At least that's what I heard.'

Norman stared into his second pint of beer.

'What went wrong, Keith? I thought we were safe.'

'We still are, old son. We still are. Just hang on and say nothing. We'll ride this out.'

Norman looked up as the darts team came in noisily and began placing their orders. Then he said slowly, 'Who's the traitor, Keith? Who is the bastard?'

Chapter Ten

The incident room two days later seemed to Fran quiet and subdued. Heads were bent over notes and papers, computer screens were being scanned, but there was no longer an air of expectancy and excitement. If they were farmers she'd have thought BSE was being carried by a plague of rats.

'Why is everyone so quiet?' she whispered to O'Neill, who stood staring out into the grounds, as if the answer to all life's mysteries lay somewhere on the quadrangle lawn.

'It's like this,' he said.

'What is?'

'A murder enquiry. The first few days it's all undiluted enthusiasm – then the rot sets in.'

'So soon?' asked Fran.

'It's only temporary,' said O'Neill with a wry smile. 'A mere post-murder depression. In a day or so this place will be buzzing again.'

'Shall I ring *Country Lady* and find out about the job advert?' Fran asked, sensing that O'Neill's mood wasn't exactly dynamic and whilst other people might

111

have lost their drive Fran still felt the need to keep busy. And she'd noticed that he seemed to have lost interest in what she still thought was an important lead.

He stared at her for a moment as if he'd forgotten all about the magazine, then he said, 'Go ahead, Wilson. I'll be standing here for a while.'

Fran rang the Kensington office of *Country Lady*.

'Please hold,' she was told. She heard a muffled 'It's the police' and then 'the voice' came on the line. A voice that sounded like Prince Charles trying out new false teeth.

'The policy of this company is, and, may I add, always has been, that we only speak face to face with the police and we only divulge information about our advertisements to our clients – verified clients, that is. We do like to keep our house in order. I do hope you understand.'

The voice, who gave her name as Pippa Percival-James, pronounced house as *hice* and even face sounded like *fice*. The sort of voice that always left Fran feeling a bit gibbery as if she had just spoken to an answering machine.

'I do,' Fran managed to say in a voice louder than usual. 'I'll visit your office tomorrow.'

When O'Neill found out about the trip to London he seemed pleased.

'We'll make a day of it. Go slowly, come back slowly. Have lunch out. It could be a grand day. But before that, Wilson, I think we should speak to Andy Melksham at the cottage hospital. And maybe this

112

evening we'll spend a while at the Plough. Something happened on that night two years ago and we're going to be the ones to find out what.'

The cottage hospital, Fran thought, should have been renamed the hospital cottages for there were several small buildings set amongst grass and trees. Reception and the porter's lodge were housed in a small stone construction at the entrance. It was hardly bigger than a bus shelter but the man inside controlled the parking arm and thus wielded considerable power.

'Andy you want,' he said. 'Police, you say. What's he been up to, I wonder . . . ?'

The head porter had a badge to prove it and a navy peaked cap. He also seemed to need to prove he was in charge. Without raising the parking arm he left his post, walked the few steps to the car, and thrust his head through the open window to examine the occupants more closely. He reserved his most thorough stare for O'Neill.

'Chief Inspector,' he said slowly.

Fran could tell he was impressed but she was momentarily taken aback by the continuous movement of his dark eyes. Nystagmus, she knew it was called, but she'd never seen the action quite so closely before.

'He's doing the bins. Round the back. Hope he's not in any trouble, he's a good worker.'

'No trouble at all,' said O'Neill. 'We'll not be keeping him long from his bins.'

Walking back slowly the head porter lifted the parking arm equally slowly and somewhat reluctantly. A

113

gesture, Fran assumed, of his power. As if he were doing them some great favour.

'Straight on, first left, past the admin block, bins are next to the morgue.'

'Many thanks,' said O'Neill.

As they drove on he said: 'I hope he's not playing about with black bags. It might lead us to draw the wrong conclusions.'

'Not a suspect for patricide then?'

'See what you think when you meet him. I think he's harmless.'

Andy wasn't dealing with black bags. He was dealing with huge black square dustbins, throwing in grey bags of hospital waste with a steady swing. He didn't falter as the car approached. Fran could only see his back view, he wore black overalls and Doc Marten boots and his fair hair was close cropped. He was of medium height and he looked strong. And still he didn't pause. O'Neill got out of the car and tapped him on the shoulder. The grey plastic swung for a moment in his hand and then he smiled.

Fran approached them after a moment or two. O'Neill introduced her and Andy removed his leather glove to shake her hand. He was about nineteen or twenty, Fran supposed, and good-looking.

'Just a few questions, Andy,' said O'Neill. Fran noticed how he spoke slowly and clearly, mouthing the words so that Andy could 'see' them.

'Let me finish these bags first,' said Andy. His voice had the slightly nasal intonation of the deaf but not the loud exaggerations of the deaf who had never heard.

They waited the few minutes the rest of the bags took. O'Neill offered to help but Andy shook his head.

'Must use gloves,' he said. 'Hospital rules – Health and Safety.'

When he'd finished Andy took off his gloves, pushed them into the pockets of his overalls and stood waiting expectantly.

'Tell me about the rubbish, Andy,' said O'Neill.

Andy had watched the mouth carefully, now he stared at O'Neill and O'Neill stared back. Fran thought green eyes gave O'Neill an advantage, being an unusual colour interviewees could be unnerved by them, especially if they were lying. Andy wasn't unnerved though.

'What do you want to know?' he asked.

'What's in the grey bags?'

'Just rubbish, paper, cardboard, empty boxes.'

'What about syringes and needles and arms and legs?'

It took a moment for Andy to understand. When he did he smiled.

'They go into the incinerator. That sort of stuff is collected in red bags. Red for danger.'

'About your dad?' said O'Neill abruptly.

'What about him?'

'Is it true he hasn't been seen for two years?'

Andy nodded, but Fran noticed the flicker of fear that the word *dad* caused.

'I haven't seen him, don't want to either. Do you think he's dead?'

O'Neill shrugged in a noncommittal fashion.

'I won't be sorry if he is. I won't. I shall be glad. I

thought about killing him lots of times. I hate him. All my life I've hated him.'

'Tell me about the last time you saw him,' said O'Neill.

Andy concentrated on the question carefully and took his time answering. 'He turned up on the night of the darts match,' he said slowly, 'he left just before closing time. I didn't see him after that.'

'Never?'

'Never,' repeated Andy.

There was silence then until Andy said, 'I've got to do a bit of sweeping round here.'

'You carry on,' said O'Neill, 'we'll talk as you sweep.'

Andy picked up a broom that was propped up against a wall and began methodically brushing to and fro.

'I like sweeping,' he said, 'it's dead soothing.'

Fran started to ask a question but O'Neill looked at her sharply and shook his head. Andy continued to sweep debris into a small pile. After a while he appeared satisfied with his work.

'I like this job,' he said. 'I used to be very nervous. I'm better now. I make extra money doing farm work on my days off. I'm saving up to get married. One day I'll have a farm of my own, being deaf won't matter if I'm my own boss – will it?'

'That's grand, Andy,' said O'Neill. 'It's good to be ambitious. Would you tell us if your dad turned up?'

Andy paused as if he didn't understand. Then when he did he smiled and said nothing.

'If he is dead,' said O'Neill carefully, 'do you know who might have done it?'

Again the pause and then the smile. 'No,' he said. 'And I wouldn't tell you if I did.'

'One last question,' said O'Neill. 'Where were you on Sunday night and Monday morning?'

Looking across at Fran, Andy said, 'With Ali. I was with Ali at her place.'

'She'd say the same, would she?'

'Yes. Course she would.'

O'Neill shrugged. He'd known Andy vaguely for some time. He'd always seemed honest and timid. He'd changed now. He was a man and no longer timid, and he seemed determined. Even perhaps determined enough to kill his father – now – but not two years ago. If in fact Frank Melksham had died two years ago.

O'Neill tapped Andy on the back. 'See you, Andy. Take care.'

In the car Fran said: 'I wanted to ask him a question, you didn't give me a chance.'

O'Neill, smiling, gripped the wheel and watched Andy's retreating back.

'O'Neill's prescription for interviewing people includes lots of silences. Silence makes people uncomfortable, they have to fill the gaps and anyway my old gran used to say, "People can't give you chances, you have to take them." '

'Well,' said Fran, 'my old gran still says, "A tuppenny sod to those who won't give people a chance." '

'Does she indeed?' said O'Neill.

Fran was quiet for a moment and then she said 'Well, no, actually she doesn't. I made it up.'

'Well, good for you, Wilson,' said O'Neill, laughing, 'an Irish woman I'll make of you yet.'

Just for a moment Fran thought he'd said he'd make an 'honest' woman of her. And then she too began to laugh.

'What's so funny?' asked O'Neill.

'Nothing, boss,' said Fran, forcing herself to be serious, 'I was just wondering about his girlfriend.'

'Wondering what?'

'About her name – Ali.'

'Well?'

'Ali – Alison – Mary Lowick – pregnant of this parish.'

O'Neill cursed silently. Fran Wilson was altogether too much of a good thing. Her perfume must have coddled his brain.

'Just a coincidence, Wilson, that's all.'

Even as he said the words O'Neill knew he was kidding himself. And quite suddenly he realized everyone he had spoken to about Frank Melksham had either knowledge or something to hide or a motive to. . .

'This case is all very incestuous, isn't it?' observed Fran.

O'Neill knew exactly what she meant but he didn't reply. Wilson was definitely getting too sure of herself.

Chapter Eleven

At first O'Neill had looked forward to the outing in London. Now he wasn't so sure. A day with Fran Wilson in a different environment might signal a change in their relationship. He didn't really want to get fond of her or rely on her in any way. In fact being with her made him feel uneasy – unless he'd had a drink. Then he felt more relaxed, able to cope.

Sometimes in the evening when he was alone – and he seemed to be alone often these days – he drank to help him sleep. It didn't ward off the nightmares, though. He had the same one most nights: he was running to save Jenny, running and running until he fell. Then, with his ankle broken, beginning the long crawl homewards. Eventually, he would arrive. Hear the engine running, see the closed garage door. Hauling himself on his feet he would begin desperately trying to open it. Banging frantically he would finally collapse knowing he was too late.

Then he would wake, bathed in sweat, and for one sweet second would believe it was only a dream. And then realization came. Jenny was dead. He had been too late in real life.

She'd been dead three years now and it didn't get better, it got worse. They'd been married for seven years. Seven years where their happiness had been marred by infertility – Jenny's. He'd never realized just how much she cared. Selfishly he was glad it wasn't his fault and equally selfishly he had assumed that their marriage itself would be enough. Jenny had mentioned adoption once or twice and he had been noncommittal. He wasn't totally sure he would love his own child yet alone a stranger's. He'd been blind of course. Had immersed himself in his job and failed to notice how quiet she had become, how much weight she'd lost. That day he'd come home later than usual. She'd left his dinner in the oven and herself gassed with carbon monoxide in the car.

At first he'd been numb. Then he was angry. Very angry. How dare she do this to him? There was no note, no explanation, just abandonment. The anger didn't last long but the guilt did. Three years on, he still felt guilty.

O'Neill glanced at the alarm clock and then around the room. They had bought a four-bedroom house to accommodate the three children Jenny had planned on. He used a different bed every night and never slept beyond 5 a.m. His doctor told him it was a mixture of anxiety and depression that woke him so early. In truth he felt neither when he did wake. He felt worse in the evening. He knew the cure for early morning waking anyway, that was to have a woman beside him, to stay until after breakfast. And that was now a rarity.

He showered, shaved, and drank several cups of coffee and stopped thinking about Jenny. Instead he thought about the case and the things he'd undoubtedly missed. In his darkest moments he really did think his promotion had been due to the pity vote. Then he remembered the cases he had solved. Good solid detection work, but those of course had been mostly when Jenny was alive. Since then his performance had been less than sparkling and his brief but varied liaisons had caused quite a stir.

Today though he was going to London and he'd try to enjoy it. He'd take Fran Wilson to a quiet restaurant and perhaps he'd get to know her a little better. He knew his loneliness was contradictory, he wanted friends, shared intimacy, but he was also wary of involvement. As if somehow that could only once again bring him pain.

The office of *Country Lady* magazine was not as he'd imagined. It sat above a Chinese restaurant, with dingy net curtains covering unwashed windows and the smell of cooking wafting up the stairs. The editor, Pippa Percival-James, sat at a desk surrounded on both sides by mounds of paper. She wore some sort of stole around her shoulders, purple and black, fixed with a large butterfly brooch. Her hair was blonde in a page boy style and clung round the cheeks of her rather handsome face.

'Ah! the police,' she said standing up and holding out a well-ringed set of fingers.

She was at least six feet tall but her handshake

seemed to O'Neill to belong to a much smaller woman
– a limp flick of a dry hand through his. He couldn't
help noticing that Fran's hand was held longer than
necessary and Miss Percival-James's eyes lingered on
Fran's face with a certain intensity.

'Now do sit down, both of you. I'll get my assistant
to bring us some tea,' she said with the graciousness
and accent of a matriarch in her country seat. The
assistant was then summoned with a strangled cry of,
'Josephine!'

Josephine promptly scuttled in; a woman of about
five foot, she reminded O'Neill of a startled game bird
who starts to cross the road and then turns back at
the sound of a car approaching. She had a delicate
long neck that seemed to push her head forward and
spindly legs that sported black stockings and a four-
inch pair of high heels. Her dark hair was short with
a quiff-like fringe that came before her.

O'Neill shot a glance at Fran who had her head
down, her hand over her mouth, and was looking at
the floor.

'Yes, Pippa?' asked Josephine eagerly.

'Tea, dear, please.'

'Certainly,' said Josephine, turning immediately and
tottering away.

'She's an odd woman,' said Percival-James as soon
as she had closed the door. 'But I like odd people.
They add flavour to life, don't you think? Marvellously
loyal too. She's been with me since we opened.'

'Which was?' asked O'Neill.

'1988. Not long, I know, but our circulation is

increasing rapidly. There's still a need for domestic help of every kind, you know.'

O'Neill nodded as if he did know. Then from his jacket pocket he produced the copy of *Country Lady* and held it up to show the missing square.

'We'd like to know more about this advert. It's vital to our investigation – murder investigation.'

'Of course. Of course,' she said, 'when Josephine comes back with the tea I'll get her to look through the back numbers for you.'

By the time the tea was drunk Josephine had found the relevant issue. O'Neill read the advert in silence. Without comment he passed it to Fran. It read:

Wanted ASAP. Young woman to help run small-holding. Capable of taking charge during female owner's absence. Must be able to drive and cope with animals and accounts. Isolated rural position. Excellent salary, own room with TV. Apply to Box No. 7869.

'You never met the person who advertised?' asked O'Neill. Miss Percival-James shook her head. 'All done by phone or letter. We merely place the ad.'

O'Neill suddenly realized he had come on a fool's errand. *Country Lady* wouldn't have known who answered the box numbers but they would of course know who placed the advertisement.

'Could you tell me who placed the advert?'

'Josephine will know that.' She smiled at Josephine who, as if programmed to obey even unspoken commands, walked unsteadily towards a well-hidden computer in the corner of the room. After a few minutes work and some obviously abortive attempts at finding the name, she said in a high voice that matched her high heels, 'I've found it. I've found it.'

'Good girl,' muttered Percival-James appreciatively.

'We took the advert from a Mrs Trudi Miller of Last Chance Farm in Lincolnshire. I remember now. She rang me a couple of times.'

'What did she say?' asked O'Neill trying to disguise his impatience.

'Oh, she seemed worried she hadn't had many replies. I suggested she —' Josephine broke off. Percival-James turned to stare at her.

'Carry on,' said O'Neill gently, 'you'll be wanting to help me.'

'Oh I do, I do. It's just that I recommended her to an agency, you see. She said it was really urgent so I told her to contact Super Service, they provide all sorts of domestic help, butlers even. . .'

Josephine trailed off again as she caught sight of her boss's frown.

'Jo, Jo, I'm disappointed in you. You know Super Service doesn't advertise with us. They are not one of our clients. You could have suggested she readvertise with us.'

'Sorry, Pippa,' said Josephine hanging her head so that her quiff trembled.

'Thank you very much for your help, Josephine,' said O'Neill, and she smiled up in time to be rewarded with his most charming smile. 'Now perhaps you could tell us the address of Super Service and we'll be leaving you in peace.'

The address was written on a slip of paper and Josephine handed it to O'Neill with a shy smile.

'Ladies,' he said, giving them both a smile. 'It's been a real pleasure.'

Outside in the street Fran could contain herself no longer.

'Really! That poor woman. There should be a law against you using your charm on innocent persons. She was in a state of shock when you left.'

O'Neill laughed. 'Which one?' he asked.

His laugh was infectious and Fran realized that was the first time she'd heard him really laugh.

'Come on, young Wilson. Let's enjoy ourselves while we've got the chance.'

'I wish you'd call me Fran.'

'Your wish is my command, Fran. You can do your bit with Super Service though. I'll just stand around like the errand boy.'

'Is that a promise?'

'As near as I'll get to one.'

The pub that O'Neill chose was red plush, with dim lights, and busy with suited men buying lasagne, moussaka, and other variations on mince. Fran asked for a white wine which O'Neill obviously thought a disgusting choice. He drank a Guinness chased down with an Irish whisky and managed to get into conversation with a drunk who had an encyclopaedic knowledge of cricket.

'We'll have lunch after a bit more sleuthing,' said O'Neill as they left the pub.

The Super Service office was conveniently situated about half a mile from *Country Lady*. O'Neill strode forward in silence, whilst Fran tried to adjust her steps to his. She would have liked a more leisurely pace, would have liked to pause a bit and soak up the bustling atmosphere. There was a definite comfort in the sight of so many strangers. A little like Birmingham. Not like Fowchester with its tight claustrophobic knot of people, none of whom coughed without exaggerated rumours of their having pneumonia. And if that was true, thought Fran, then more than one person knew how the victims died and why.

Super Service had no qualms about being modern. Beige blinds were closed at the wide ground-floor window but a poster pronounced:

SUPER SERVICE SERVES YOUR EVERY DOMESTIC NEED. WE HAVE THE EXPERTISE. WE PROVIDE THE BEST STAFF FOR THE BEST CLIENTS. BUTLERS. NANNIES. HOUSE-KEEPERS. MAINTENANCE AND MAIDS. IF YOU HAVE A JOB TO OFFER WE HAVE THE RIGHT PERSON. A SUPER PERSON.

'Good morning, madam. How may I help?' asked a young man as Fran approached his desk. He wore a navy suit with a red-striped tie; by his side sat a feminine *doppelgänger*, navy suited but with a red-striped bow instead of a tie. They smiled in unison.

O'Neill hung back.

'I'm Detective Sergeant Wilson, this is Chief Inspector O'Neill. We're trying to trace a woman, Trudi Miller, who came here looking for a housekeeper.'

The young man shrugged. Smiles were obviously reserved for prospective clients and not the police.

'Trudi Miller, doesn't ring any bells with me. What about you, Lucy?'

Lucy did manage a smile, first at O'Neill then at Fran. 'How could I forget?' she said. 'She was extremely fussy. They had to be a certain age, non-smoker, like animals, good at bookkeeping, no ties. She was looking for someone for well over three months. And guess what, in the end she chose a carbon copy of herself.'

'I don't suppose you'd have a photograph?' asked Fran.

'Of Mrs Miller?'

'No. Her employee.'

'Probably still got one in the filing cabinet. I'll have a look.'

O'Neill sat down on a chair in the corner of the office and picked up a magazine. Lucy rummaged for a while in an old filing cabinet behind her. The young man was now beginning to look irritated.

'Here it is,' Lucy said triumphantly as she looked first at O'Neill, who didn't look up, and then at Fran.

Fran took the folder. Attached to the right-hand corner was a passport-size photograph.

'May I keep this?' asked Fran. 'It is very important.'

Lucy looked for confirmation to the young man. He nodded without interest but then said as if in afterthought, 'Do return it to us. Our employees often come back to us and it saves a lot of work if we have everything to hand.'

Fran paused to look at the photograph and the name.

'I don't think Miss Carol Sykes will ever be coming back,' she said slowly.

Chapter Twelve

It was later, sitting in an Italian restaurant called Umberto's, that O'Neill said, 'We'll be eating first. We'll think better on a stomachful of wine and pasta.'

'You might, boss, I'll probably fall asleep.'

'I'll sing to you, Fran, that'll keep you awake.'

Umberto's was one of those restaurants that lulled Fran into believing that she really was in Italy. The soft candlelight, the red-chequered tablecloth, the smell of garlic, the good-natured banter of the staff. And of course the wine.

They were on their second bottle and second course before O'Neill asked to see the photograph.

'I think this is the dead woman,' said Fran as she handed over the folder.

After a long pause O'Neill said, 'Well, I grant you there is a similarity, but I'm not sure.' He continued to stare at the photo. 'People look so different in photos.'

'And in death.'

He looked up sharply and Fran's eyes caught his but he could tell immediately it was an innocent remark. She couldn't have possibly known that he hadn't recognized his own wife on the mortuary slab. He hadn't told anyone.

'Can you identify this lady as your wife?' he'd been asked.

'Yes. That's my wife,' he'd said, because she had after all been found in their garage. Who else could it have been? But he hadn't recognized her, not really. Her face had been a patchy colour, swollen in parts, her mouth contorted. And the person that had been his wife had gone and left in her place a stranger. He'd been so unsure that he spent a long time searching for her. In the house, around the town. Once he'd caught a glimpse of her back view and he'd accosted a complete stranger. It took three months for him to accept the fact that she really was dead.

Fran waited patiently but she could tell O'Neill was thinking about something else. Eventually she said quietly, 'If you look carefully, boss, you'll see the eyebrows are the same. She's wearing make-up here and she's smiling.'

'I remember,' said O'Neill absently. 'I remember.'

Remember what? thought Fran. Surely the wine hadn't affected him. He was after all a seasoned drinker.

O'Neill signalled to the waiter for the bill. He wanted to leave, the atmosphere he had at first enjoyed so much had gone now. That the dead woman wasn't Trudi Miller had been confirmed but he also guessed that if the woman found in Trudi Miller's house was killed by mistake, then Trudi Miller, wherever she was, was still in danger. Their next step had to be to pay a visit to sister Wendy again, because why had she so easily assumed that it was her sister they had come about and not her husband? It was as if she had expected something to happen to her sister.

After lunch they set off for the home of Miss Carol Sykes. The address on the back of the photograph was 24 Sandstone Gardens, Bloomsbury. They toured Bloomsbury street by street, asking local-looking pedestrians for help and receiving only blank stares or 'Sorry, I'm a stranger here myself.' Eventually they found a postman who told them patiently that Sandstone Gardens did not exist.

'Mother of God,' muttered O'Neill. 'Now what?'

'Give the photo to the media,' suggested Fran, 'someone must know her.'

O'Neill shrugged. 'I'll be thinking about that,' he said. Then he added thoughtfully, 'It does seem possible now that perhaps our Carol had something to hide and was the intended victim after all.'

'Battered wife trying to escape from deranged husband?'

'Maybe. That's as good an idea as any. But where exactly is Trudi and why has she run off? Unless she already knew her housekeeper was dead and she panicked and fled. And more to the point, why didn't Mrs Theodolou tell us that her sister had employed someone?'

The train back was crowded and O'Neill found himself sitting next to Fran. Sitting far too close, squashed together in the uncomfortable narrow seats, their legs occasionally touching, they were unable to talk about the case because they were not alone and so their conversation limited itself to a discussion of Fran's future plans for the house. After a while Fran closed her eyes and lulled by the steady rhythm of the train she fell asleep. At first her head lolled forwards but after a while as she eased her position her head found a resting place on O'Neill's shoulder.

Initially he stiffened, reminded of the journeys he and Jenny had taken, journeys where she too had fallen asleep on his shoulder so that he could smell her hair and feel the warmth of her body. Consciously he made the decision to not think about either Jenny or Fran. He closed his eyes and tried to concentrate on cricket but even there a woman sat by his side. It disturbed him that his mind's eye couldn't tell him which woman, but under the brim of a wide straw hat it could have been anyone. . .

'Wake up, boss. Fowchester Station.'

O'Neill felt the light touch on his arm. 'I wasn't sleeping,' he said, 'just resting the eyes.'

The small station had a desolate air that flower beds and hanging baskets couldn't cure. It was growing dark and the faces of the commuters seemed tight and gaunt. Winter has worn them out, thought O'Neill. And then he saw a few men outside waiting for their lift home and he knew he couldn't face going home alone.

As they walked out of the station O'Neill said, 'How about a drink?'

Fran shook her head slowly. 'Sorry, boss, would you mind if I went home? I'm really tired.'

'I'd be minding,' murmured O'Neill. They walked a few more paces before he said, 'All right, no drink, but how about paying another visit to Trudi's sister Wendy?'

'So soon?'

'You've heard the old adage about Greeks bearing gifts.'

'He wasn't bearing any gifts.'

'True, but perhaps we should be wary of Greeks not bearing gifts.'

Fran knew now she had no option. In the CID there were no set off-duty hours, you worked for as long as it took, which was why so many marriages floundered. It wasn't as if she had an excuse, no husband or child or boyfriend. A hungry mouse didn't count for much, did it?

'Fine. Don't suppose my tiredness is terminal.'

O'Neill smiled. He could put off going home. He might, just might, be able to wangle an invitation to Fran's place; or maybe she would come to his.

They walked side by side into the town, O'Neill managing to suppress a sudden desire to take Fran's arm.

At the Theodolou house the lights were on but the BMW had gone. Wendy seemed relaxed, almost pleased to see them.

'Chief Inspector,' she said. 'It's nice of you to call again so soon. I didn't expect that. Do come in.'

They followed her to the second floor and into the sitting room.

This time Fran noticed more about the room, the

plush gold-striped curtains to match the gold-striped wallpaper and on a circular onyx coffee-table a jigsaw three-quarters finished. Fran wondered idly as she sat down why there were no children of the union.

'You'll be wanting to help us with our enquiries,' said O'Neill.

'Of course, anything, Chief Inspector. That poor woman. . .'

'Her name was Carol Sykes, this is a photo of her.'

Wendy took the photo and stared at it for some time.

'That poor woman,' she repeated. 'I did know she had arrived but I'd never met her. Wendy said she planned to have a housekeeper companion but she couldn't seem to find the right person. She was lonely living there on her own. She looks a little like my sister, you know, the same colouring, the same build. . .'

'Why didn't you tell us about Carol Sykes?' interrupted O'Neill. 'Was it deliberately done to mislead us?'

Wendy Theodolou crossed her arms defensively. 'I was upset, she hadn't been there long, I just forgot, that's all.'

'We'll leave it there for the moment,' said O'Neill. 'Let's be talking about your sister's whereabouts. Do you know where she might have gone?'

Wendy smiled briefly, not able to hide her relief that O'Neill hadn't pursued his line of questioning. 'She was planning to go to Provence, to find a small house to buy. She hoped to sell Last Chance Farm, you see. I expect that's why she employed someone to look after everything while she was away.'

'Strange she didn't take her passport, then,' said O'Neill softly.

For a moment Wendy seemed taken aback. 'I only know what I've already told you. She was planning to sell the farm and live in Provence.'

O'Neill shrugged slightly. 'That's a pity. She could be in great danger. If the dead woman was killed by mistake, the killer could still be looking for your sister. Very soon the media will be having a photo of your sister and the murdered woman – Carol Sykes. If you know where she is I would advise you to tell us.'

Wendy looked about to cry but then she put her hand across her mouth and made an obvious effort to control herself.

'It's my fault,' she said, 'I tried phoning a couple of times but there was no answer. I should have got Chris to drive me over there but he's always so busy and he did take some wine to her. He's a very generous man. He would have said if there was anything wrong.'

'When was that?' asked O'Neill sharply.

'Last week some time – I'm not sure when.'

'We'll be finding out from your husband. When will he be in?'

'I don't know. He works in London mostly. He just provides wine locally for businessmen's lunches, that sort of thing.'

'I see. DS Wilson, do you have any questions?'

Fran nodded. 'Only one or two.'

Wendy smiled in a vaguely relieved fashion at Fran

as though her questions wouldn't pose so much of a problem.

'Although you say,' began Fran slowly, 'you don't know where your sister is staying, you must have some idea of the friends your sister might. . . visit. Unless of course you don't know her very well.'

'Of course I know my sister well – we've always been close – very close.'

'Well, then?'

Wendy shrugged resignedly. 'Trudi didn't have many friends really. We have a cousin and an aunt in Scotland but she wouldn't have gone there.'

'Why not?'

'They didn't get on. Trudi is a real home bird anyway, she prefers warm weather and she says that compared to Scotland Lincolnshire has warm weather.'

'I see,' said Fran. 'Just one more question – why did you suspect we had come about your sister and not your husband?'

Looking anxiously towards O'Neill Wendy asked, 'Did I? I wasn't aware I did. I suppose it's because I know Chris can take care of himself, that's all.'

'Perhaps,' said Fran. 'But I think it was because you knew your sister was worried about something. And I mean worried enough to run away. If she knew Carol Sykes was dead wouldn't the more normal thing be to phone the police? After all it makes it look as if she had a hand in the murder or in fact she did indeed kill Carol Sykes—'

'No, no,' interrupted Wendy. 'That's not true. Trudi wouldn't hurt anyone, she wouldn't. She was worried, but only about money.'

'Perhaps Carol Sykes had money with her. Maybe she was desperate enough. . .'

'Never! Trudi was phobic about blood. She could not have done such a dreadful thing.'

Fran smiled then. 'I had to be sure. If in the mean time, Wendy, you think of anything, please be sure to let us know.'

'I will. I will,' answered Wendy. 'I promise.'

As Fran and O'Neill approached the front door, he said, 'One final question. Did your sister always leave a key outside?'

'Yes,' said Wendy. 'Under a flowerpot.'

'You'll be thinking then on who else knew about that hiding place?'

Wendy didn't smile as they left and before they were out of sight she picked up the telephone receiver and began dialling.

As they walked up the drive O'Neill was silent. At the front gate he said, 'We're missing something very basic here and I wish I knew what the hell it was.'

Then he fell silent again until Fran asked, 'All right if I go home now boss?'

O'Neill, ignoring the question for a moment, asked, 'You'll be alone tonight?'

'Yes. Well, apart from the mouse.'

'I'll catch it for you.'

'I don't want it caught. I like it.'

'I'll cook supper for you.'

'I've no food.'

'I'm not going to beg,' muttered O'Neill. And then

he strode off into the darkness leaving Fran staring after him bewildered.

Christopher Theodolou started cruising as soon as darkness fell. The back of King's Cross station loomed out of the darkness, both majestic and gaunt. At first the side streets and back alleyways seemed empty but he knew they were there. Like sewer rats, he thought, scavenging for survival. Tonight his eyes scoured doorways and parked cars for a glimpse of a young one. Really young, fresh. The older ones were addled by drink and drugs. He wanted one tonight that would make him feel young too, would be prepared to be enthusiastic.

In the shadow of a car he saw one. She wasn't alone, there were two of them. The shorter one was definitely young. Her cheeks were round and soft and she wasn't hardened. He slowed his BMW and then stopped by the girls. He wound down the window. The older of the two pushed her head through the window to check the back seat was empty. Theodolou knew the score. The older one checked only one man was in the car and then she gave the would-be punter a look over and asked what he wanted.

'What do you want, mate?' she asked. He wanted to answer, 'Not you, that's for sure.' She was well into her forties, her eyebrows were plucked, and her hand must have been shaking when she replaced the brows with black pencil. Her eyelashes were false, as big as spiders' legs, and close up he could see all the lines in her face.

'Straight sex,' he said, 'condom, with the girl. How old is she?'

'Fifteen. Her name's Sharon. She's not experienced and she's expensive. Cost you thirty quid.'

Theodolou nodded. He was disappointed she wasn't a virgin but then it was unlikely she would be at fifteen and on the streets.

The older prostitute turned to the girl,

'He's all right Sharon,' she said. 'I've clocked his number. Make sure you're back in half an hour.'

Sharon got into the back of the car. Theodolou watched her move. Good legs, a glimpse of knicker as she sat down. Not beautiful, but fresh.

'It's round the corner, mister,' she said as he drove away.

She lived in a basement flat that smelled of mould and air freshener. The one lamp was on, a pink shade giving the room shadowy corners. The bed was stripped to the bottom sheet and one pillow. From a drawer she took a huge roll of white paper, tore off several sheets and covered the bottom sheet.

'I 'ate washing sheets,' said Sharon as she took off her skirt and knickers and lay on the bed.

Theodolou took off his jacket and by now sweating and fumbling struggled with the button and zip of his trousers.

'Take your top off,' he said.

'Nah,' she said. 'Straight sex don't include no extras.'

He didn't argue. He was soon on top of her. At one point he tried to kiss her on the mouth.

'None of that, mister. That'll cost you.'

Again he didn't argue. As he was finishing she said: 'Are you rich?'

'I'm rich,' he said as he got dressed.

'Come again then, mate,' she said. 'I could show you a good time for the right money.'

He handed her the thirty pounds which she carefully counted and then he drove her to where he had picked her up. She joined her minder and they turned their backs towards him as he drove away. And he knew deep down that he was the one who had been exploited.

In the car he tried to justify going to a prostitute, tried to remember the pleasure. There wasn't much. All he could really remember was the crackling sound of the paper undersheet and the fact that her knickers too were made of paper. Next time he wouldn't wear a condom. Pay more, have the works. Next time. . .

Chapter Thirteen

In her room in Higham Merrils College Alison sat on her bed and stared at the calendar. When she missed one period she hadn't panicked, hoping it was somehow a mere blip in her biological clock. Now she'd missed two and she knew it was no blip. Andy didn't know yet. They had been planning to marry – some time – when they had saved enough. At the moment their savings ran to the grand sum of two hundred pounds. Hardly enough for a cot and a few disposable nappies. Was it enough though for a private abortion? There was a rumour that Phillippa knew all about abortions. Alison had wanted to ask her the morning they found the arm but since then she had only seen her once and then she'd been surrounded by people. Perhaps it wasn't true anyway, about Phillippa. *She* seemed the sort who wouldn't get into such a mess. She was the sort who would be on the pill. I should have gone on the pill, thought Alison. Now it was too late.

Alison placed the calendar back on the wall and tidied her bed. She still couldn't face breakfast, even the smell of bacon frying turned her stomach. What was important was that she carried on normally. Tonight she might tell Andy about the baby, or she might not. It depended on his mood. The police going to see him had upset him, though she didn't know why. If his father was dead then Andy would be glad. They had always hated each other, and although Andy never spoke much about his childhood Alison guessed he had been ill-treated.

At just before nine Alison left her bedroom to go to her first class. At least the finding of the arm had got her out of early morning farm duties. Andy didn't need to do a course on farming, he'd had some practical experience. Alison was doing the course so that one day they could run their own farm. Meanwhile Andy worked at the Cottage Hospital and they tried to save.

As Alison approached the classroom she could see Phillippa in the middle of a group of students. Holding court, thought Alison. She almost hoped Phillippa wouldn't see her, but she did. 'Hi, Alison. You feeling better?' she asked in her hearty way. A tone that denied admitting you felt less than perfect.

'I'm fine,' said Alison with a false smile.

'That's good.' Then as Alison passed she whispered, 'I thought you might be preggers.'

Alison felt the colour rush to her face but she walked on, sat down at her desk and opened her file. She looked up, her eyes registering the title on the blackboard: 'The Care of New-Born Animals'.

At the cottage hospital Andy had just finished delivering

samples for the path. lab and was on his way to the porter's lodge for his morning coffee. He'd hardly slept the night before, he really needed his coffee this morning. He didn't know quite what to do. For the last two days he had imagined the police had been watching him. That Irish chief inspector suspected him, he was sure of it. He'd stared at him as if he could read minds. What was he supposed to do now? Should he just wait or contact the others? Why had that other arm turned up anyway? As he entered the porter's lodge the head porter, Bill Southwaite, was mouthing something at him. Andy didn't understand. Then Bill pointed to the phone. There was a message on a pad by the phone, in capitals, as if Andy couldn't read joined-up writing: TOM RANG. SAYS HE WILL SEE YOU IN THE PUB TONIGHT FOR THE DARTS MATCH.

He tore the paper from the pad and put it in his pocket. If he went the police might be there, if he didn't go they might wonder why. He couldn't win. Maybe he and Alison should just run away. He'd find a job somewhere, he was strong, he could dig roads, Alison could do shop work or waitressing. Perhaps Mum would lend him some money. As he drank his coffee he kept thinking about running away. That was definitely the answer. He'd tell Alison his plan tonight. He'd just been paid, they had some savings. Maybe they could go to Scotland, there were some isolated places up there. Perhaps he could even rent a croft and farm the land.

'You all right, Andy?' Bill mouthed at him.

Andy smiled and gave him the thumbs-up sign. It

was a pity Bill hadn't been his dad, he wouldn't be in this mess now if he had.

Andy finished work at four. Alison would be round about five thirty for her tea. Today was Andy's turn to do the cooking and as he only had a quarter share of a fridge he went shopping for perishables most days. Each day he took a certain amount of money and never spent more than that. Today he had three pounds. Spaghetti with meat sauce, he decided. He could buy half a pound of mince, a packet of spaghetti, a tin of tomatoes, two bananas for dessert, and maybe even a carton of single cream to go with them. He made his purchases at the small Co-op in the High Street and then walked back to his boarding house.

He felt a little surge of pleasure that the communal kitchen was empty; he could cook the meat, make the sauce, and then decide what to do with the bananas. Cooking his own meals still gave Andy a source of satisfaction, cooking for two was even better. Alison enjoyed her food, well perhaps not for the last couple of weeks. She'd seemed a bit pernickety but Andy had put that down to her being on a diet. Not that he approved of diets. Perhaps tonight though she'd be hungry. He'd bake the bananas with some brown sugar and a drop of sherry he had left over from Christmas. Alison had told him to buy some sherry in case they had visitors but no one had come so that was why there was still some left. Thinking about cooking stopped Andy thinking about other things, like if he should turn up at the darts match. When the meal was

144

well under way Andy made his decision – he would go to the pub later.

If the police wanted to see him again they knew where to find him anyway.

At five thirty on the dot Alison turned up. Her eyes were red and puffy.

'What's wrong, Ali?' he asked, kissing her, hoping that his kiss could make things better. It didn't.

'I'm all right,' she said wearily.

'Is it college?'

She shook her head. Andy sat her down on the bed. 'Come on Ali, what is it? Is it me?'

In the long pause before Alison spoke it crossed his mind that maybe she wanted to send him packing. It was still a source of wonder that he had a girlfriend like Alison. She was his first and he hoped his last love.

Alison smiled. 'It's not you, Andy. It's. . . I think I'm pregnant.'

At first Andy wasn't sure he'd read her lips properly. He patted her stomach and said the word 'baby'. She nodded miserably, 'What are we going to do, Andy?'

Andy didn't answer at first, he just stared at her. His seed in her belly. Once, when he'd been about six or seven, his mother had shown him how to plant seeds in the garden. In a few weeks she had promised him his seeds would grow into forget-me-nots. Then his father found out and just as the seedlings had begun to surface he had trampled the lot down.

'That's great,' said Andy, 'I'm really pleased.' But

he could feel tears somewhere in his body. 'I love you,' he said, kissing her, and then like legions of young fathers before him he said, 'We'll manage, don't worry.'

Chapter Fourteen

Fran's bewilderment didn't last long because it was replaced by anger. Who the hell did he think he was? Did he think he was so irresistible that any woman would jump into bed with him? Once home she continued to abuse him, only this time aloud to the mouse who didn't of course make an appearance. Feeling a little foolish and hoping the loneliness wasn't sending her over the edge she decided to ring a friend whom she knew had just finished late duty. Lyn had been at training school with Fran, was now married to a detective sergeant, and had a gloomy but sensible attitude towards men.

'Fran! Great to hear your voice. I've missed you. How's it going in the country?'

'So so.'

'Come on, Fran, tell Auntie Lyn all about it. No doubt some male is giving you a hard time? Is that it?'

'Well, sort of. . . he's my boss.' Even as Fran spoke she knew how lame it sounded. She could take care of herself. She'd really only been upset by the fact that he'd walked off and left her in the middle of Fowchester.

'If it's sexual harassment, Fran – forget it. Women in the force never get very far with that. The general consensus is if you work in the force you're among men and if you can't cope with the odd grope or innuendo then you're in the wrong job.'

'I know that, Lyn. I'm not quite adjusted yet to working here or to being a sergeant. And he is my boss so it makes it a little more difficult. He told me to stick to him like a toffee sticks to paper but I didn't know he meant it literally.'

'You quite fancy him, then?' asked Lyn with a laugh in her voice.

'I didn't say that. He's quite attractive but sort of sad. Every so often his eyes mist over and he's not there any more. . .'

'I see,' said Lyn. 'You just be careful, Fran. You know how you fall for lame dogs.'

'That's not true and I didn't say he was a lame dog.'

'You didn't have to.'

Fran was silent for a moment wanting to change the subject but not knowing how. Eventually she said, 'We're on an interesting case. Have you read about the arm in the bag? Well, I'm on that.'

'Lucky old you. I'm on the granny run. I've dealt with six shoplifters in the last month and not one has been under sixty-five. It's soul-destroying. But tell me about your case – go on, make me jealous.'

Fran told the bare details and every so often Lyn muttered 'Wow!' or 'I see.'

148

'The trouble is, Lyn, I suspect everyone I meet. I haven't yet met anyone who has a good word to say for the male victim and as for the female victim we have a name but that's all. Everyone seems to close ranks. Other murders I've heard about, someone, somewhere, seems keen to help the police.'

'Maybe they all have something to hide and when you find out what it is, all will become crystal clear.'

'I hope you're right. My boss is an Irishman and I think half the time he's daydreaming about the Emerald Isle.'

'Don't underestimate him, Fran. I worked once with an Irishman. He'd have charmed confessions from a priest.'

Fran laughed. Suddenly things were back in perspective. O'Neill was slightly odd but he wasn't obnoxious and he did seem to have a way with people – well, some people, some women.

Later that night as Fran lay in bed she heard the mouse scratching but it didn't disturb her, it consoled her. Tomorrow, she thought, I'll talk to O'Neill, explain that I just want a simple, friendly, inspector–sergeant relationship. Perhaps she could invent a long-distance lover, someone who would provide a whole range of excuses.

That same night O'Neill had slept, or tried to sleep, on the sofa. He couldn't face going to bed, any bed. Twice he had picked up the phone to ring Fran, to explain, to apologize, but he'd lost his nerve. Instead he tried to concentrate his thoughts on the case. He'd sifted through all the old newspaper reports about Frank Melksham's disappearance. Not that a farmer's disappearance was all that newsworthy, farmers were always disappearing or committing suicide, but they didn't often reappear three years later in the pub on the night of a darts match. And, more to the point, never to be seen again. His car had been left in the pub car park so someone must have given him a lift, or, as the witnesses said, he had just walked off into the night. Only to reappear after two years in bits? Well, one bit. Why haul him out of the safety of cold storage and parade him like a trophy? Or maybe the arm was the last bit of him. Perhaps he'd died on that night and systematically over the past two years his bodily parts had been disposed of. Usually murderers who tended towards dismemberment left the head till last. Why that should be O'Neill didn't know. If *he* had been a murderer he would have wanted to get rid of the head first.

In the early hours O'Neill had started making a list of all those who might have benefited in some way from Melksham's death, because it now occurred to him that Melksham's reappearance caused someone discomfiture. Murderous discomfiture. But who? Andy Melksham was his first choice but then would he benefit from his father's death, confirmed death? And where could he have kept the body? Melksham's wife? But she was already rid of her husband, what motive could she have for killing him? Steve the boyfriend? He said he hadn't known Melksham, only of him. Was that in fact true? And finally, of course, Trudi Miller.

She had been devious enough to employ a house-keeper who looked somewhat like her, perhaps she had intended Carol Sykes to be the victim. Perhaps Trudi had been ill treated, just like his wife. But, unlike his wife, she had cleverly plotted her way out. On that night she could have driven her own car to the pub at Clopstock, maybe he was a little drunk, taken him home. Killed him perhaps by battering him over the head, chopped him up and frozen him and then set about making herself seem extremely worried by his apparent sudden and mysterious disappearance.

O'Neill began to feel drowsy then, when he woke he felt sure he would crack the case. All he had to do was find Trudi Miller. . .

Daylight, sharp and bright as a scalpel, slipped through a gap in his curtains. O'Neill squinted at his watch. It was eight fifteen, he was fully dressed, stiff, stubbly and his head felt constipated. He picked up the phone. Vaguely he remembered he'd left Fran on bad terms and as he started to dial he also remembered he'd forgotten her number. 'Sod it,' he said aloud as he replaced the receiver.

After two cups of black coffee, a shave and a shower, he found her number in his notebook. He dialled the number and she took so long to answer that he thought she hadn't made it home.

'You'll be wanting to. . . berate me,' he said, relieved that she had at last answered the phone.

She didn't answer at first but he waited and then he heard her mutter what sounded like 'castrate'.

'What was that?'

'Nothing, boss. It can wait.'

'I'll be round to pick you up in half an hour. I thought we'd pay another visit to Mrs Theodolou. Put the pressure on, I'm feeling she knows exactly where her sister is.'

'I'll be ready, boss.'

'Good,' said O'Neill.

As he put down the phone he realized he was actually looking forward to the day. He hummed to himself as he dressed. Maybe his luck was changing, maybe Fran would fall for his Gaelic charm. He splashed on some aftershave, checked he hadn't developed a bald spot on his head overnight, and without his usual backward glance he left the house.

Fran had been in the bath when O'Neill rang. She had been expecting an apology and his rather bantering tone had irritated her. Even his loud knocking on the door jarred her sense of equilibrium.

As she opened the door his brisk, 'We'll be away then,' made her realize she had to say something.

'You'd better come in,' she said.

He smiled somewhat sheepishly before following her into the front room and without being asked sat down and crossed his legs.

'Now then Fran,' he began, 'before you start I want to get one thing straight. I'm sorry about last night. I shouldn't have walked off and I've been feeling guilty about it ever since. Last night was. . . well it was an anniversary of sorts. The day is over now and I promise you my behaviour will be impeccable from now on. We can still be real friends I hope?'

'Of course,' said Fran, her irritation sagging quicker than a fat man's mattress. She had almost relished a row and all he had on offer was the white flag. There seemed to be nothing else to say.

'I'll get my coat,' she said quietly.

Once in the car O'Neill said, 'I'd like you to be responsible for one or two interviews today. I'll be watching you in action. First to Mrs Theodolou, then on to young Andy. Think you can manage that?'

'I'll be managing,' replied Fran. O'Neill raised an eyebrow at her copying his phrasing but said nothing.

A cleaning lady answered the door of the Theodolous' house. Thin and middle aged, with straggly greying hair and pencil eyebrows, she had a surprised look, which after a few moments Fran realized was her normal expression.

'You'd better come in. Madam's in bed,' she said with reluctance and with one hand firmly holding the tubing of a cylinder vacuum cleaner. She made the word *madam* sound like an insult.

'I'll wake her up. You two sit in the library.' Pointing to the right-hand door with the vacuum tubing she added, 'I've done that room.'

'Thank you, Mrs. . . ?' said O'Neill, flashing her a smile.

'Vera Charlesworth.' Mrs Charlesworth didn't smile back but she put down the tubing and said, 'You sit down, sir, and wait. She'll probably be a while.'

They waited in awkward silence each on one end of

a leather sofa. Fran gazed round the room. If this was the library it had been misnamed. There wasn't a book in sight. There was a leather-covered desk with a spotlight lamp, the sort with a green top and a miniature strip light, that when lit highlighted the pen tray beneath. There were also various vases of dried and fresh flowers in the room, a cabinet full of crystal, and a pervading smell of polish and pot-pourri. The desk was empty save for a silver ink well and a blotting pad. Fran walked over to examine the blotting pad but it was a virgin sheet and just as she peered at it the door opened and Wendy Theodolou walked in.

Fran had to admire the fact that in such a short time the woman who appeared looked as if she had spent hours on her appearance. The pony tail was gone and in its place was a neat shoulder-length style. Gone too were the casual clothes: she wore a pastel-green long-jacketed suit with a cream blouse and a double row of pearls; real by the look of them.

Wendy glanced quickly from Fran to O'Neill.

'I didn't expect to see you again quite so soon, Chief Inspector,' she said in an injured tone.

'My colleague wishes to talk to you, Mrs Theodolou.'

She turned reluctantly towards Fran.

'Oh. I see. Well?'

'Please sit down. This won't take long.'

Fran realized she sounded like a dentist but dentists always lied.

Wendy walked over to the sofa and perched on the edge.

'I'm rather busy this morning so I'd be most grateful if you would be quick.'

As she spoke O'Neill, with a brief smile, stood up and walked over to the bay window and stared out.

'Firstly,' said Fran, 'I'd like to know more about the type of person your sister is. Her likes, dislikes, where she went on holiday, that sort of thing.'

Wendy stared at Fran for a moment as if trying to see a hidden catch in the question.

'She likes a quiet life. I'm the opposite. She married young and divorced young. She had quite a few boy-friends but she always preferred . . . well, hard men, real bastards, if you know what I mean. I warned her about Frank Melksham but she wouldn't listen. Mind you I still think he was more interested in the farm than in my sister. She didn't go out much. He went out quite a bit. I must admit I was relieved when he disappeared that night, Trudi was as well, but she did seem convinced something had happened to him.'

'I see,' murmured Fran. 'And what about holidays?'

'Holidays,' echoed Wendy with a trace of irritation. 'She wasn't keen on holidays. She went abroad a couple of times but she said none of the places she saw compared with. . . Bournemouth.'

'Bournemouth?'

'Yes. Bournemouth on the south coast. We went there nearly every year as children.'

'Is it likely your sister has gone to Bournemouth to start a new life?'

Wendy shrugged and looked away uneasily, as if she knew she couldn't get out of this one.

'I wouldn't have thought it likely,' she muttered, 'but I suppose it's possible.'

'What work do you think she'd try?'

'I don't know, Sergeant. She could do a bit of book-keeping, I suppose, and she is a good cook. She's the domesticated sort.'

'Right, Mrs Theodolou. I think that's about it,' said Fran, putting away her notebook.

'I'll get Mrs Charlesworth to show you out,' said Wendy quickly. Too quickly for Fran's liking. It was as if she had been let off lightly.

'Just one more question,' said Fran as she stood up. 'How does your husband get on with Trudi?'

'Fine. Absolutely fine,' she said sharply, and then just as sharply called out: 'Mrs Charlesworth!'

O'Neill thanked Wendy Theodolou for her time and Fran noticed how relieved she seemed now that they were leaving.

Vera Charlesworth appeared and Wendy mumbled, 'Do excuse me,' and left the room. At the front door, Fran said quietly to Mrs Charlesworth, 'While we were waiting at the front door I thought I heard the phone ring. Did you answer it?'

'That's funny,' said Mrs Charlesworth frowning. 'I didn't hear it. Only time the phone's been used was when I came in just after eight. I always start early, *he* leaves at the crack every morning so I can get on because madam always stays in bed. I leave her room till last, see.'

'I do,' said Fran. 'So it was unusual for. . . madam to be on the phone so early in the morning.'

'Well, yes, I suppose so,' said Vera Charlesworth

uncertainly, as if she guessed she had said something important or disloyal, or both.

As they walked down the drive O'Neill said, 'What the hell was all that about? I didn't hear the phone ring.'

'Neither did I. I was just trying it on to see what response I got. I guessed that she either made a phone call or received one while her husband was out of the house. And I think she was lying about Bournemouth. Did you notice, in the kitchen at Last Chance Farm, one of the pictures on the wall?'

He shook his head, wishing he had noticed it and feeling his powers of observation were on the wane.

'I did. It was a pen and ink drawing of a seaside resort.'

'Bournemouth?'

'No, that's just the point. Tenby. Did you notice how Wendy hesitated before saying Bournemouth? I think her sister is in Tenby.'

O'Neill was silent for a moment, then he said, 'Where exactly is Tenby?'

'South Wales. And I think she was warning her sister this morning. Her husband was in last night so the best time to catch her would have been early this morning after he'd left the house. She would have wanted to warn Trudi that we knew she was still alive. I think she's probably working as a waitress or a chambermaid, something in a hotel anyway. Somewhere she can live in.'

'You could be wrong, we could go haring down to Tenby and still not find her.'

Fran smiled. 'I know I could be wrong, boss, but

there were no pictures of Bournemouth in her house, which is strange, if she was that fond of the place.'

At the car O'Neill said, 'We'll go back to the agricultural college now, find out if anything's cropped up, and at lunchtime we'll be going to the pub at Clopstock, to make thorough nuisances of ourselves.'

As O'Neill drove off it occurred to Fran that if she was right in guessing that Trudi Miller was in Tenby, someone else might have made the same connection.

Chapter Fifteen

Norman Crick paused with a razor in his hand. The mirror of his bathroom cabinet had steamed up. The light being soft there it was his favourite mirror, it made him look younger and fresher; somehow the lines disappeared. Then he remembered that in the loft he had a cut-throat razor and a strop and he smiled almost inanely at his own reflection. After all, all he had to do was find it, sharpen it, and if the time came, use it.

Breakfast was eaten in sulky silence. Barbara did speak once; she said, 'Pass the butter, Norman.'

Even that sounded like a criticism coming from her lips, the inference being that he should have seen she needed the butter.

He spoke once too, 'I'll be out tonight. Darts.'

Barbara acted as if she hadn't heard and shortly afterwards Norman left for the agricultural college.

As he drove he felt himself smiling. Fancy remembering about his dad's old razor. If it came to the crunch he might even take Barbara with him. After all she was depressed. Her first, then him, simple really. He was surprised he hadn't thought of it before. But then he hadn't remembered about the razor before, strange that he should have remembered it now.

He arrived at Higham Merrils buoyed up. Sod Malcolm! He wasn't growing any younger either, one day he'd be on the verge of retirement too. And in just a few years Malcolm Kilsby would be jealous – 'Lucky old Norman, he got out,' he'd be saying.

Malcolm was standing just outside the office door. Standing as usual as if someone had put itching powder on his feet or like a robot in overdrive.

'Come on in, Malcolm, sit down.'

Malcolm stopped jigging up and down for a moment.

'You sound cheerful this morning, Norman.'

'Mental health, Malcolm, mental health. That's what matters in the long run.'

'I'm sure you're right,' said Malcolm. 'But I've come to complain about the presence of the police. It's causing total disruption, especially amongst the female students. Surely they have been here long enough now? I've had a word but it didn't make any impression.'

'I've been doing that for years,' muttered Norman.

'What?'

'Nothing, nothing at all.'

Malcolm frowned and continued to pace up and down by Norman's desk. Too near to his desk for Norman's liking.

'I did tell you to sit down.'

The surprise showed on Malcolm's face and he sat down. Norman sat the other side of the desk. There was a long silence in which Norman felt completely in control.

'I'll speak to the police today and ask them how much longer they plan to be here. I expect you, Malcolm, to keep the students under control and minimize any disruption. I'll organize a meeting if you think you can't cope—'

'I didn't say that I couldn't cope,' interrupted Malcolm.

Norman smiled. 'No, you didn't,' he said slowly.

Malcolm got up abruptly and left the room. Norman punched the air in victory, for once he was a winner. And all because of a razor. He felt so good he decided to ring Keith, they could meet for lunch.

Keith's receptionist answered the phone. He had been called out on an emergency farm visit. Norman left a message. 'Tell Keith I'll be in the Plough at one, hope he can make it.'

'Wilco,' said Gladys Thruxton. 'TTFN.'

Norman smiled. Gladys was well past retirement age and stuck somewhere in a time warp between 1939 and 1944, for her the war had never ended. Anyone born north of the border was a 'nasty foreigner', the Germans were still Huns, and the thought of being thought a European appalled her. 'People have such short memories' was her favourite saying, not realizing the shortness of her own.

'TTFN,' Norman had responded. And then he put

down the phone and said aloud: 'Ta ta for now.' And then he smiled again.

Keith, stripped to the waist, found the soap lurking in the bottom of the bucket like some slimy creature. He washed his hands and arms up to the shoulders and then turned to Tom and said, 'You give her a good wash, I'm clean now.'

Tom soaped a piece of old cloth Jessie kept for just such an occasion and with one hand soaped the cow's vulva. With the other he patted her rump, saying softly, 'There there my beauty, soon be done, soon be done.'

The cow stood patiently and Tom guessed that she knew they were trying to help. He'd been worried about the cow for hours; a second timer, she had been in the first stage of calving far too long for his liking and she was off her feed now.

Keith covered one arm with an antiseptic lubricant and entered the cow gently so that he wouldn't rupture the water bladder. Up and up till at last he could feel the calf's two forefeet and head. As he thought, all was well, a normal presentation.

'Could be calcium deficiency causing the delay,' said Keith as he withdrew his arm. 'I'll inject her and then we'll leave her alone. Just make sure you put plenty of grit on the floor, we don't want her slipping and fracturing her pelvis.'

'I know what to do, Keith,' said Tom, aggrieved at being told his job.

Later as they sat in the farm kitchen Keith rang his

surgery and was given the message from Norman.

'You fancy a drink in the Plough, Tom?'

Tom nodded. 'What time?'

'One o'clock.'

'What about the cow?'

'I told you, Tom, leave well alone. She'll be fine.'

Jessie came in then carrying shopping bags. 'Hello, Keith,' she said smiling with pleasure. Then turning to Tom she said, 'You could have put the kettle on.'

He grunted. Jessie made the tea, cut a large slice of fruit cake for Keith, and sat down with them.

'Don't I get offered any cake?' asked Tom.

'You never eat it.'

'Well, I feel a bit peckish today.'

Grudgingly Jessie cut her husband a piece of cake, far smaller than Keith's slice. Tom scowled at it but said nothing.

'I heard a rumour in the town while I was shopping,' Jessie announced.

'What was that?' asked Keith.

'Just a rumour, mind you, but I think it was true.'

'What is, woman?' demanded Tom.

'That body found at Last Chance Farm. . .' She paused to sip her tea. 'It wasn't Trudi Miller. The police think it was her housekeeper.'

Tom lifted his cup and lowered it again noisily into the saucer. His hand trembled slightly but he didn't know why. Keith pushed his plate away, the cake only half eaten.

'I'd better be off now. See you in the pub at one, Tom.'

Jessie watched Keith drive away. Funny that, she thought, he's never left any of my fruit cake before. I must be losing my touch.

Chapter Sixteen

Sandra Melksham, standing on a ladder, dipped her pasting brush into hot soapy water and began to 'slop and strip', as she called it. It was quite satisfying to get the gleaming edge of the scraper underneath the soggy wallpaper and manage to strip it off in one large piece. She couldn't help feeling disappointed that Steve wasn't there to help her. He was busy today, he had 'a few jobs to do'. She didn't know where exactly he was working and between slopping and stripping she paused occasionally to wonder if he actually was working.

Two years they had been together now. Two really happy years that had flown by. More than two years now. They had met at the Hallowe'en party at the Plough. Bill always put on a good do at Hallowe'en and although he charged £3 for the food everyone knew he chipped in himself with prizes and a few bottles of champagne.

She had worn a tight red dress that night to show off her new slim figure. She'd felt good and she knew she looked good, young even, in the subdued pub lighting.

She and Steve had spent the evening together but it wasn't until the New Year party at the pub that he really showed his interest. They had gone home together in a taxi and he'd just stayed on. He'd moved from London to find work, had been staying in lodgings at Mrs Jake's place, and he still hadn't found work, so it made sense for him to move in with her. He'd really improved the farm, fixing fences, digging ditches, but he'd never got used to the animals, in fact Sandra thought he was a bit scared of anything bigger than a chicken. One by one they had sold the animals and now they were going to turn the farm into a hotel. At least that had been the plan, but just lately Steve had seemed preoccupied, worried even. Maybe he was tiring of her, perhaps he'd found someone else, someone younger. Sandra hadn't kidded herself, she knew it couldn't last for ever, knew her looks when they did fade would fade quickly and then he would roam. But not yet, please not yet.

When she'd finished stripping one wall she decided to think about cooking their evening meal. She could make a casserole, she had plenty of meat in the freezer. There was lamb, pork, two or three chickens and plenty of beef. It was while she was washing her hands she decided on a beef in ale pie. Steve liked hearty food. She'd have a bath first though, change out of her old jumpsuit, give herself a manicure, pamper herself a bit. But first she ought to get the beef out to let it defrost.

She lifted the lid from the chest freezer and peered inside. It was full almost to the top. The beef would be underneath. On tiptoe she reached into the freezer. She was concentrating so hard that she didn't hear Steve come in.

'What are you doing?' he demanded. 'Didn't I tell you to let me get things out of that freezer? You're too short. Just tell me what you want and I'll get it.'

Sandra straightened up, turned round and smiled.

'I do love you,' she said. 'I was looking for the beef to make you a pie.'

'I'll be out this evening, darts match. I did tell you. Come on, move out of the way, I'll get that beef for you.'

Easily from the freezer he lifted out a plastic box labelled stewing beef.

Handing it to her with a wide and beautiful smile, he said, 'We could have it tomorrow Sandra, I'll be in tomorrow.'

'Oh good,' she said as if somehow he'd done her some large favour.

They kissed then. Steve was aware how much he still fancied her.

'I've stripped the wall,' she said softly as she nuzzled into his ear.

Steve didn't need a second invitation. They made love on the floor.

When it was all over Steve thought how much he enjoyed older women. They were keen, they were grateful, and there was always that edge of fear. An older woman never took a younger man for granted. They knew it couldn't last which was why they tried so hard. It was such a pity the farm hadn't been more lucrative. Sandra was dead keen on the hotel idea but he knew they were clutching at straws. Hotels didn't make money in a recession. He certainly didn't fancy working for months and months for no return. He was fond of Sandra, in fact if the farm had been a goer he might have stayed, but as it was he couldn't stand it much longer. He wouldn't leave her a note like that bastard Frank. He'd do it gradually, let her know he had found someone else, make it obvious, make it so that she *wanted* him to leave. He smiled.

Sandra raised herself on her elbows and in the fading daylight she saw his happy boyish smile.

'I'm so glad you're happy, Steve. It makes me feel secure,' she said as she nuzzled once more into his strong young neck.

O'Neill and Fran left the pub just after two.

'It's a pity we couldn't talk to Bill's wife,' said Fran as O'Neill opened the driver's door of the Mercedes.

'We'll be having plenty of other opportunities. There's a darts match tonight. Maybe we can jog a memory or two then.'

Fran drove as she always did, quickly and efficiently, far too quickly for O'Neill's liking.

'You're not on a bloody motorway. Just slow down.'

Fran slowed. 'It's a novelty for me to drive such a good car.'

'It's a novelty for me to be a passenger and believe me if I hadn't had a drink I'd be driving.'

They didn't speak again until they neared the college. Fran parked the car with elaborate slowness and care. O'Neill seeming deep in thought sat and stared at a brick wall.

'It's a conspiracy,' he said quietly, 'it's a cover-up job. Everyone we've spoken to has only told the truth about one thing and that was that none of them liked Frank Melksham, even his own son. But why kill the woman? Why? And why the hell get rid of her arm so obviously? And just how easy is it to get in the college at night?'

'Or the morning?'

'Or any time,' said O'Neill slowly. 'We can't be sure, can we, when the arm was put there. Remember what Jessie said, "We don't have dead animals every day." We'd better interview those two girls again and the college farm labourers.'

The incident room was noisy with activity once again and O'Neill decided that he needed a proper interview room, or at least a suitably quiet room to question staff and students. He commandeered a large store cupboard next door to the classroom and asked one of the uniformed constables to clear out some of the old books and get in a table and a couple of chairs. Then he turned to Fran. 'We'll be away now to look at the scene again.'

At the site O'Neill stared thoughtfully at the empty stone round lined with a black plastic bag.

'What's worrying you, boss?' asked Fran, shivering in the chill wind and wondering exactly what staring into an empty plastic bag would achieve.

'Why the hell don't they bury dead animals? Farmers always used to.'

It wasn't really a question because O'Neill knew quite a bit about farming, every time he had a drink in a pub there was a farmer cursing some new piece of government interference.

'Pollution,' answered Fran.

'Of what?' asked O'Neill, knowing perfectly well, but wanting to test Fran's grasp of matters rural.

'Pollution of the rivers and streams. Fear of the spread of BSE.'

'So they'd be letting the hounds eat it?'

'Perhaps it's an EC ruling.'

O'Neill turned away then from the stone round and watched the few people that seemed to be working, pushing wheelbarrows or merely looking intent on getting to some destination or other.

'I wonder,' he said slowly, 'how many people came up here on the day *before* the arm was found. That was a Sunday but of course it might have been left any time from say Thursday or Friday onwards.'

Fran shivered again, hugged her arms around herself, and between teeth that were starting to chatter said, 'We could try to find out, boss, make a graph. We'd need a lot of statements, though, wouldn't we?'

'A graph? That's a grand idea you'd be having, Wilson. You good at graphs?'

Fran smiled weakly. 'I think I could manage it. I've seen it done. It takes a long time, though.'

'You be starting it. I'll find the pig man and have a word with him.'

Fran walked quickly away, glad to be leaving the farm and the north-easterly that seemed to cut through her thin anorak. She could plan the graph and ask Pete, the inspector and manager of operations, to delegate a few constables to get statements from all those who passed near, or by, the stone round. She imagined that at least twenty people, if not more, had done just that. And one of them might have left a grisly deposit. Might have, thought Fran, because surely it was unlikely that anyone would be carrying around an arm in broad daylight. How exactly would you transport it? Cardboard box? Plastic bag? Suitcase? Wheelbarrow? Wheelbarrow! Fran decided her graph would have to include persons carrying . . . virtually anything bigger than an envelope and those delivering via cars or vans. She wished now she'd concentrated more on graph lessons in school. Still, maybe the simpler the better.

By late afternoon Fran had fashioned a graph of sorts. A few sightings were already filtering through. One important fact to emerge was that those who worked in the farm area of the cottage had their meals and breaks in the farmhouse, even at weekends, although the numbers were smaller. This of course increased the toing and froing; especially mid-morning, from twelve till two and again from three-thirty to four.

Deciding on four types of sighting Fran used a different colour for each. Red was for those seen carrying something, green was for students, yellow for those who normally passed by the area, and finally black for those unidentified or those not normally seen in the vicinity.

On the horizontal line the time and the day were

Chapter Seventeen

Fran had a bath, dressed, and lay fully clothed on the bed staring at the ceiling. O'Neill it seemed was intent on solving the murder of Frank Melksham but the murder of Carol Sykes was getting much less attention. Fran knew the Tenby police had been alerted and were in fact looking for Trudi Miller. If Fran had been in charge of the case Trudi Miller would most definitely have been suspect *el primo*. She would have had opportunity and motive for both murders.

Had it occurred to O'Neill, Fran wondered, that there might be *no* connection between the murder of Frank Melksham and the murdered woman? Just because two arms had been disposed of on the same day and in a similar way did not necessarily mean they were murdered by the same person, just that someone as an afterthought had decided to copy a method of disposal. But that of course did imply a knowledge of Frank's death and ultimate destination; no coincidence could be that strong. The assumption that Trudi Miller was the intended victim might have been wrong all along. Maybe Carol Sykes had always been the intended victim. Some sort of smoke screen perhaps.

Surely now was the time to search out Carol's next of kin or friends. There must be someone, somewhere, mourning her. Sure to goodness there was.

Fran closed her eyes and dozed and as she did so somewhere, far off in the house, she heard the mouse scrabbling.

O'Neill rang the door bell three times before Fran answered. He smiled at her. Her right cheek had a definite crease mark and she smelt of soap and bath oil.

'We'll be away,' he said, deciding not to cross her threshold unless invited.

Grabbing her anorak from a peg on the wall she smiled back. 'I'm ready, boss.'

'I'll drive to the pub and I'll be having a drink or two, you can drive back so don't be drinking.'

Fran didn't answer, thinking of all the films on TV where some stalwart detective refuses a drink on the grounds he's on duty. Not so in real life, although of course hours of duty on a murder case were so ill defined that only major surgery qualified for 'off duty'.

O'Neill hadn't driven far before he said, 'Tomorrow or maybe the next day we'll be off to London again. I want to find out where Carol Sykes really lived. I've seen her references and got one of the team to check them out. They were false, nonexistent referees.'

'Have scene of crimes come up with anything yet?' asked Fran.

O'Neill nodded. 'Indeed they have. Fingerprints found at Last Chance Farm match the dead man's and combined with the physical assessment that's fair enough proof that Frank Melksham is the dead man.'

He didn't speak again until they drove into the car park behind the Plough in Clopstock, then he said, 'Think on this, Fran Wilson, tonight *all* our suspects could be under the one roof. And if I'd be having the inclination I could do an Agatha Christie, make a dramatic announcement that I'm going to unmask the killer.'

'But you won't,' said Fran as she stepped from the car.

O'Neill stood for a moment in the muted light cast by the pub and stared at the three parked vehicles. One was Keith Quinton's Land-Rover, the other Norman Crick's elderly Jaguar, the third he didn't recognize. Then he turned, locked his car, and said slowly, 'No, Fran. Miss Marple and Poirot were amateurs, a busybody old lady and a foppish Belgian. They could afford to make fools of themselves. Professionals can't afford to guess. Mind you, I do promise you that at least one person will leave here tonight more worried than when they arrived.'

'You know more than you're telling me, don't you?' queried Fran, suddenly suspicious that O'Neill was keeping some piece of vital information from her.

He shrugged. 'I'd not be calling it information exactly. One thing bothers me, though. . .'

Fran opened her mouth to reply but O'Neill didn't give her a chance to speak. He simply strode off in the direction of the public bar.

Inside the darts match had already begun. As

O'Neill and Fran entered there was no marked hush, just the normal eye-turning as virtual strangers are scrutinized. The publican smiled somewhat half-heartedly but the woman who stood by his side at the bar, middle aged and attractive in a black and white polka-dot dress with huge white plastic beads round her neck, greeted O'Neill enthusiastically enough.

'Connor, nice to see you again. Sorry I missed you last time. What will it be? The usual?'

O'Neill nodded. 'You're looking grand, Liz. This is Fran Wilson, we're on the case together.'

Fran smiled and knew by Liz's expression that she was trying to work out if 'on the case together' included the night shift.

'I'd like to talk to you privately, Liz, when you've got a chance,' said O'Neill as he accepted a whisky and ordered an orange juice for Fran. A sudden shout of 'Well done, Norman!' went up, and those at the bar turned to watch the darts players.

Norman Crick had obviously been concentrating heavily on his darts because as he turned to pick up his pint of beer he noticed the police presence and Fran saw in his face not only surprise but fear. Interesting, she thought, but then facial expressions could be misleading. Maybe he was just irritated.

O'Neill smiled at Liz. 'Just let me know when you have a minute to spare.'

Liz nodded and O'Neill walked over to an empty two-seater table with a good view of the dartboard. Fran stood by the bar for a moment and looked at the clientele. Apart from the publican's wife she was the only female. As she turned back to pick up her orange juice she noticed the publican looking at her with his good eye. He winked, smiled, and then took another swig of his drink. It looked like a tumbler of water but Fran guessed it was vodka. It was only then she noticed his one eye was slightly bloodshot and that underneath his artificial eye was a neat scar running its length like a dark circle.

Sitting opposite O'Neill Fran asked, 'Did you know mine host was hitting the vodka?'

'Sure I did. He used to run a pub in north London. The punters were a bit rough and one night he tried to eject the ringleader. Got a faceful of jagged glass for his pains. Liz says he's never been the same since. He drinks to forget, or to dull the fear, or to cheer him up, or just to survive. It does work, temporarily anyway.'

They fell silent then, watching as Steve threw his darts, a treble 20 and two 20s.

'One hundred!' exclaimed an excited home team customer.

O'Neill stared thoughtfully into his whisky. After a while he looked up, smiled at Fran, and said: 'I want you to be imagining Frank Melksham walking in here now after a three-year absence. Who would be most upset by his reappearance?'

Fran glanced towards the door, seeing in her mind's eye the door slowly opening and Frank moving in. Tall, arrogant, the bad man of Fowchester. Maybe there was a lull, eyes turned towards him, maybe shock, surprise on their faces, and then a strained resumption of normality. But not quite normality. Someone might have been frightened or disappointed to see him.

'I think,' replied Fran slowly, 'on what we know, that two people would have been quite put out to see him. First, young Andy. And then – Steve.'

'Why Steve?'

'I think he was vague about when they met. Maybe he had already set his sights on the attractive deserted wife, with farm.'

O'Neill laughed. 'There's more to you than meets the eye.'

'And talking of eyes,' said Fran, 'I had a one-eyed cat once. He was always under my feet, because he was blind on one side.'

Puzzled, O'Neill frowned. 'There's a touch of the Irish in you, Fran. You'll be explaining.'

'The landlord is blind in his right eye, his blind spot if you like is to the right of him. He said that he thought Frank got up to leave just before the others. Someone else though could have left the group earlier to go to the gents, then as he opened the door to the public bar saw that Frank was no longer there and followed him out. Our landlord's one eye may have missed quite a lot of the action.'

'He's got two ears,' muttered O'Neill. 'And then what?'

Fran shrugged. 'Maybe the person who followed him out gave him a lift and killed him *en route*.'

'*En route* to where?'

'I don't know.'

O'Neill smiled. 'Sure you know, Fran. Think about it. A man like Frank didn't come back after three years for the darts. He didn't play darts. So why did he come on that particular night?'

'We've come full circle, boss. He must have come to see someone.'

'Sure he did. My bet is he came to see that person and waited outside for him to leave.'

'But if he'd come to see Andy and Andy was scared of him wouldn't Andy have waited for the others?'

'Yes. The others. . . Andy grew up in the area. Keith and Norman wouldn't have wanted anything to happen to Andy. He's a star player. And he's popular.'

'So you think—' Fran broke off as Liz approached.

'Come into the back room, Connor, I've a few minutes, the glasses are all topped up.'

Fran stood up to follow but Liz said quietly, 'Just him please.'

In the back room behind the bar Liz said, 'Make yourself at home, Connor.'

If he hadn't known her better he'd have thought she was trying to be funny. The back room was merely a store for boxes and crates and although there were two armchairs both were laden with cardboard boxes. O'Neill lifted them carefully and stacked them into the one empty corner of the room.

'Sorry about all this mess. I would have taken you upstairs but well. . .'

'Here is fine, Liz. Sit down and stop your worrying.'

Liz didn't sit, she lifted boxes and lids as though Aladdin's lamp was missing.

'Oh, sod it!' she exclaimed. 'I've left them in the bar.'

O'Neill guessed she meant cigarettes and matches.

She returned triumphant with a lit slim brown-papered cigarette in her mouth and an ashtray in her hand.

'Now then, Liz,' said O'Neill. 'Tell me about the last time you saw Frank Melksham.'

Liz kicked aside a box and perched on the arm of the chair. She balanced the ashtray in her hand like the scales of justice and said, 'You've got to promise me, Connor, that you won't tell a soul. If I don't get that promise I'm not saying a word.'

'I don't have to make that promise, Liz, because I've just guessed. You don't have to say anything but what you do say may be taken down in evidence and used against you.'

Liz inhaled deeply and watched O'Neill's face. It was grim. Oh, God. He really meant it. Once a copper always a copper, she thought. The bastard was going to charge her.

Chapter Eighteen

O'Neill sat watching as Liz drew sharply on her cigarette. His caution had really been a joke and he'd been surprised that Liz had taken it seriously. Now he waited for her to talk.

'I'm sorry, Mr O'Neill. I'll tell you all I know but for God's sake don't let my husband know I've told you. He'd kill me, he can be evil when he's drunk – really evil.'

'Just be telling me,' said O'Neill softly. Her reversion to 'Mr' seemed to reflect a change in the status of their erstwhile friendly matiness and Liz had indeed been a very good friend when he needed one.

'Come on Liz, tell Uncle Connor all about it.'

Liz smiled, lit another cigarette from the stub of the last one, and said, 'The night Frank came and went. . . well, you see, it wasn't just a chance visit. He'd rung up, wanted to know when exactly the darts match was on. I didn't think there would be any trouble. And. . . I wanted to see him.'

O'Neill raised an eyebrow and smiled. 'Lizzie, you should be ashamed of yourself.'

'I know I should, Connor, but he wasn't all bad, you know. When he was sober he was OK. And he was sober most of the time. Not like Bill. He's drunk now during the day as well as at nights. Somehow though he manages to wait till closing time before he collapses. Occasionally Frank used to give me a hand putting Bill to bed. And then. . .'

She broke off and gave a little shrug as if to say she couldn't help herself.

'Did he come that night to see you or did he have another reason?' asked O'Neill.

'He came to see Andy. That's what he said. I think he may have had plans to go back to his wife. He said he'd seen her from a distance.'

'What do you think he meant by that?'

Liz shook her head. 'I don't know, but I got the impression he'd seen her with a man.'

O'Neill fixed Liz with a gaze that made her uncomfortable.

'What is it, Connor? I've told you everything, I have!'

'I'm just wondering why,' he said slowly, 'you couldn't have told me this two years ago.'

'Two years ago I didn't know he was dead, did I? I thought maybe his wife had told him to clear off again and he'd done another runner.'

'Don't be lying to me, Liz. You'll be wanting to tell me the truth after all this time. I did think we were friends.'

'We are Connor, we are. There is something else. The night he left here, I saw him in the car park. Andy was with him and there was a bit of shouting going on. I couldn't stay and watch because it was near closing time and I knew Bill had had a skinful so I went back into the bar and that was the last time I saw Frank.'

'You heard nothing more.'

'Bill went upstairs and slumped in front of a video. I ran a bath. I didn't hear or see any more. I just went to bed.'

'And Bill?'

'Bill?'

'Yes, Bill. What did he do?'

Liz frowned. 'Bill was just sitting there, the worse for drink. He came to bed later. When I woke up he was in bed fully dressed. You won't tell the brewery about his drinking, will you? We'll lose the pub and it would finish Bill off. Please, Connor.'

O'Neill patted her shoulder. 'Stop your fretting, Lizzie. All I need to be sure of is that Bill didn't guess about you and Frank.'

Liz stared at O'Neill for several seconds as the full meaning of his casual comment hit her.

'Oh, God, you can't think Bill could have anything to do with Frank's death! He didn't know about Frank. I was exaggerating when he said he'd kill me. Really, Mr O'Neill, I swear on the Bible he didn't have an inkling about me and Frank. I swear he didn't know I swear he didn't. . .'

'Calm down, Liz. I'll be speaking to Andy next. There may be no need to speak to Bill at all. Just one more question. Did you see Frank's car in the car park?'

Liz shook her head. 'I noticed the car but I didn't

know it belonged to Frank. It was really clapped out, bald tyres, the lot. We often get cars left in the car park these days, sometimes they stay for as long as a week, sometimes they're just abandoned. To be honest I thought it was abandoned. We reported it about a week later.'

O'Neill smiled. 'Now, Liz, you be away back to the bar. Tell Bill I was after asking about the times of people leaving.'

'Thanks, Connor,' said Liz, smiling with relief and then kissing him on the cheek. 'I owe you one.'

O'Neill sat for a few moments in air more than tinged with tobacco fumes. He had hoped that Andy had not been involved but it seemed he was one of the last people to see Frank alive. Father and son. Father and abused son. What could be more natural than wanting revenge? But Andy? O'Neill doubted the boy really had the killer instinct. Self-preservation, though, tended to sharpen the wits, and Andy was young and strong.

O'Neill returned to the public bar and a disgruntled-looking Fran.

'I felt a real prat sitting here on my own,' she said, 'and I hate darts.'

'We have to stick it out till closing time,' said O'Neill, 'so I suggest you tell me your most intimate secrets and I'll listen.'

'You tell me yours,' said Fran. 'I haven't got any secrets, intimate or otherwise.'

'I was hearing a different story – about Birmingham, and a certain young sergeant. You'd be wanting to tell me the right version, wouldn't you?'

'Right version!' replied Fran swiftly. 'There's the truth and the truth and you can't have a version of it.'

O'Neill smiled with great charm and Fran's irritation vanished as quickly as it had flared.

'Boss, you shouldn't smile at women like that, it puts them at a disadvantage.'

'Come on now, Fran, don't you be trying to distract *me*. I think it's time you told me why you were transferred.'

Fran supporting her chin on cupped hands said calmly, 'I know you've got written reports on me and if you're not satisfied with my work I'm sure the Super would find you a another bagman.'

'Jasus, woman! I'm only trying to make conversation. I'll get you a drink and I'll tell you the story of *my* life. That'll make you wish you'd done the talking.'

Even as O'Neill talked, and talk he did, he watched the darts team. He was sure that Andy had become aware that he was under particular scrutiny and his uneasiness soon seemed to filter through to the rest of the team. Some very poor darts were thrown and then the match was over. Last orders were called and the darts players, both winners and losers, milled around in desultory groups, knowing that the night out they had looked forward to was now over.

O'Neill knew that soon the pub would empty and they could lose track of Andy.

'Fran,' he said, 'you go outside into the car park at the back. Stop anyone you like for any reason but don't let Andy Melksham leave the area. I'll follow you out.'

Quite why she had to be the one lurking in the car park Fran wasn't sure, but she was quite sure that detective sergeants did exactly as they were told.

Light from the pub's upstairs rooms played on to the tarmac in a patch that left the rest of the car park in darkness and shadow. Fran stood back against a wall and waited.

A surge of people seemed to leave at once. 'Andy,' she called softly and amongst the noisy group there was a sudden hush broken only by the sound of Andy's voice because he had failed to hear or see her. Fran stepped out of the shadows and said. 'Andrew Melksham. Could I have a word, please?'

His young face seemed to register emotions like the clicking of a camera: surprise then fear then reaction – for with sudden flailing arms and legs he pushed past Fran and ran and ran. Fran, unsteadied by the thrust of his arms, fell to the ground. She could hear the sound of his running feet thumping away and then abruptly she was being helped upright by O'Neill.

'Did he hit you?' asked O'Neill.

Fran shook her head. 'Just charged off like the proverbial bull.'

'Are you sure you're not hurt?' asked O'Neill as he brushed dust from her back.

'I'm fine, I sort of lost my balance. I don't think he meant to push me, I was just slightly in the way.'

The small crowd had dispersed now, car engines were being revved. Together they watched the car park empty until O'Neill's Mercedes was the only car left.

'Any ideas, Sergeant Wilson?'

'About arresting Andy?'

'That too. Shall we do it now, bring him in for questioning tonight, or shall we go home to bed?'

Fran didn't answer immediately, she wasn't quite sure what he meant.

Be a keen detective, she thought. 'I think we should find him tonight, boss. He probably hasn't gone far.'

'My guess is he's going home to mum,' said O'Neill with no trace of disappointment in his voice.

Relieved that O'Neill had decided to take immediate action, Fran drove towards the farm half expecting to catch Andy in the car headlights running along the road. But the roads were empty.

'He'll be taking a short cut across the fields,' said O'Neill, 'and there's no need to be breaking any speed limits.'

Fran reluctantly slowed. She'd taken the police advanced driving course and she was a good driver and a safe one. Just because she drove a little over the speed limit occasionally didn't mean she was some sort of speed freak.

Nearing the farmhouse Fran could see the downstairs lights were on: the curtains were not fully closed and the cracks of light showed up the barns alongside in black relief like giant silhouettes.

'This place gives me the creeps,' murmured Fran.

'You'll be telling me next you think Frank was murdered here.'

'I do think that, boss, I always have.'

That wasn't quite true, Fran knew, but as she spoke the words she felt it was. Frank's deserted wife and her young lover. Who else? Andy? Either he knew they had done it and that's why he had run away or all three had a hand in Frank's death.

It was Steve that answered the door and he was obviously surprised to see them.

'Saw you in the pub, didn't I?' he said. 'Something up?'

'We're looking for Andy,' answered O'Neill. 'He ran off, he seemed to be scared of us.'

At that moment Sandra appeared by Steve's side and there was no disguising her anxiety at her son's name being mentioned.

'What's happened? What's going on? Where's Andy?'

'We'd be hoping you'd tell us that, Sandra,' said O'Neill gently.

'You'd better come in,' she said. 'I don't know where he is.'

The kitchen was still in a state of half decoration and O'Neill refused the offer of a sheet-covered chair.

'Andy was playing darts tonight, my sergeant just wanted to ask him a few questions and he ran off. Now why would he do that, Sandra?'

Sandra shrugged and looked genuinely mystified. Steve put a protective arm around her.

'Now look,' he said, 'she hasn't seen him. He was in the pub and then he wasn't. I knew he'd run off but he hasn't come here, he's probably gone back to his place.'

O'Neill was about to go when Sandra suddenly stiffened. 'What was that outside? I heard a noise.'

There was silence in the room then. Fran strained to hear something but couldn't. O'Neill stood and listened. Had he heard anything? He wasn't sure.

'Maybe it was the wind, a barn door slamming.'

'There was a noise,' said Sandra, 'the barn doors are closed. He's out there, that poor boy, he's out there!'

'Calm down, Sandra,' said O'Neill. 'We only want to talk to him. We'll have a look round. I think Steve's right, though, he's probably gone back to his lodgings.'

'I heard something. I did,' she repeated fiercely.

O'Neill nodded at Fran to leave and outside he said, 'We'll be checking the barns just in case. You take the left, I'll take the right.'

Fran wished she had a torch, more than likely all she'd find in the barns would be rats. Mice she could cope with, even grow quite fond of, but rats were different and of course there could be spiders and webs that would touch her face. . . she kicked open the first door. It budged only slightly for there was a bale of straw in the doorway. She used her foot to kick the bale away and then the door was free and swinging. And there in the darkness was a black shape and that too was free and swinging.

Chapter Nineteen

Fran screamed out, 'Help in here!' and then began to haul bales of straw under the dangling feet, for Andy was not yet dead but slowly choking to death. His face seemed blackish in the murky light but gurgling noises still rose from his throat. Take the weight, take the weight! Fran told herself as she tried to lift his feet. It was then that O'Neill rushed in and together they managed to raise more bales to support his legs and release the strain on the rope.

'Get Steve, get a ladder, and ring for an ambulance,' ordered O'Neill.

Steve, having heard the commotion, was already running towards the barn.

'Ladder, fetch a ladder quick!' Fran's voice resounded in her head like a scream.

Steve responded immediately and began to run for a ladder. Fran followed him with the breath catching in her throat and her head pounding. Dragging a wooden ladder from a barn wall Steve grabbed one end and Fran picked up the other and together they ran back to the barn where Andy still hung, his legs supported now by more bales and O'Neill's arms. Steve and Fran must have paused for a second at most.

'Get the ladder up!' shouted O'Neill hoarsely.

Steve grabbed the ladder from Fran and propped it by the wall next to the beam from which Andy had tied the rope.

'I'll go up,' said O'Neill, and whilst Steve held the ladder O'Neill climbed up the few rungs necessary to get to Andy. For a while O'Neill struggled to loosen the loop of rope from around Andy's neck. He's not going to manage it, thought Fran, but then O'Neill shouted, 'It's off, get ready to hold him.'

As the body slumped down Fran couldn't stop him, the bales collapsed and he toppled on to her. Pushing his body away, Fran knelt down and looked at his chest. It wasn't moving. His face was blue and his tongue protruded.

'I think we're too late.'

'Start mouth to mouth – *now*!' shouted O'Neill.

Fran didn't hesitate. It was something she had done once before on a child. The child hadn't survived. Conscious of her own heavy breathing she pulled back his head and began breathing into his mouth. Seconds later O'Neill began cardiac massage.

The sounds of their breaths and O'Neill's disciplined 'One and two and one and two' began a period of immeasurable time that seemed not part of the real world. Only Sandra's scream as she entered the barn broke their concentration. Steve bundled her out and then suddenly the ambulance crew had arrived and O'Neill and Fran sat back on their heels as though they were bit-part actors in a play and suddenly the main characters had come on stage.

The ambulance crew worked for a while and then one of them said, 'There's definitely still a pulse.' And then an exultant, 'He's breathing on his own.'

Moments later Andy was stretchered out.

'We'll follow,' said O'Neill.

'Well done, mate,' called out one of the ambulance men as they left the barn.

'I notice you get all the credit,' said Fran rising stiffly to her feet.

It was only then Fran noticed how much she ached and she started to shiver. O'Neill looked pale and exhausted but he took her arm and they walked back to the farmhouse slowly, like wounded soldiers coming back from a battlefield.

Sandra was by now sobbing quietly and Steve stood over her patting her back and looking ineffectual. At the sound of their entry Sandra looked up, her eyes red and wild-looking with anxiety.

'He'll be making it, Sandra,' said O'Neill. 'He's a strong lad but he couldn't tie a decent noose. That's what saved him.'

'Thank God,' breathed Sandra. 'I must get to the hospital now.'

'I'll be taking you,' said O'Neill.

The hospital was five miles away and on the journey Fran was conscious of a pain low down in her back and a sense of anticlimax. Just the body's adrenalin on the wane, she thought, but even so she felt slightly guilty that all she longed for now was a cup of hot sweet tea and a disgustingly long filter tip.

The Accident and Emergency department was empty save for an elderly lady with a face set in pained resignation and a mother with a screaming baby. A young nurse soon came to tell them that Andy was in a stable condition and semi-conscious.

'If you'll just sit and wait the doctor will see you shortly,' she said, adding cheerfully: 'If you'd like tea there is a vending machine in the hall.'

The baby continued to scream. The elderly lady sighed. Fran eased her back on to a chair and hoped O'Neill wouldn't send her for the tea. He didn't, he made two trips to the vending machine. It was as he handed Fran her plastic cup she noticed his hand trembled and she looked up into his eyes and was surprised by the anguish she saw there. She looked away quickly and sipped: it had no real taste but was still comforting.

An hour later a doctor appeared, took Sandra aside, and spoke quietly to her. For a moment Fran suspected the worst but when she saw Sandra smile weakly and respond to the doctor's questions she knew all was well. The doctor left abruptly and thankfully took the mother and screaming baby with him.

Sandra clutching Steve's hand couldn't hide her happiness and relief. 'He says Andy's out of danger now and trying to talk but no one is able to understand what's he's saying and he couldn't seem to understand their questions. The doctor thought he might be brain damaged but when I told him Andy's deaf he said that could explain it and I wasn't to worry too much. He says I can see him now but they'll want to keep him in for a couple of days and maybe he'll have to see a psychiatrist. . .'

As she said the word her euphoria vanished. In the drama of Andy's near death she had forgotten what had led him to hospital. She began to sob quietly. 'Why did he do it? Why did he do it?'

Steve put an arm around her tightly. 'Now come on, love, pull yourself together, Andy won't want to see you looking upset.'

Sniffing, Sandra looked up fondly at Steve. 'What would I do without you, darling?' she said wonderingly.

Fran and O'Neill watched as they walked off still arm in arm in the direction a passing nurse pointed them.

'Ain't love grand,' said Fran.

'You're jealous.'

'Maybe,' answered Fran thoughtfully, 'but once bitten I don't think it's twice shy, I think it's. . . immunized.'

'Tell me about it.'

'Here?'

'Some other time then.'

'Maybe.'

Ten minutes later the couple reappeared. Steve said tersely, 'He'll live. I'm taking Sandra home now.'

Sandra looked up as if about to speak but then changed her mind and looked down.

As they hurried out O'Neill said quietly. 'We've cocked up. We should have gone in to see him first.

Did you see the expression on Sandra's face? There was no relief there. Andy's said something and they've probably sworn him to secrecy.'

'Not necessarily. Perhaps relief has changed to anger. It sometimes does.'

O'Neill nodded. He knew all about that. The shock. Then the anger. Then the despair.

'Come on,' he said sharply. 'Let's see what Andy's got to say.'

Andy lay propped upright on a hospital trolley. His neck showed the livid marks of the rope. His face was no longer blue but ashen, his eyes were closed. O'Neill touched his arm and Andy's eyes flickered open.

'I did it,' he said in a gravelly voice. 'I killed my dad.'

Chapter Twenty

O'Neill mouthed, 'Tell me all about it. From the beginning.'

'I killed my father,' repeated Andy and then he closed his eyes and seemed to fall instantly asleep.

O'Neill sighed loudly in exasperation and tried to wake Andy up by shaking his shoulder but to no avail.

'There's no point, boss,' said Fran. 'He won't be saying any more tonight.'

'No, I suppose not,' said O'Neill, 'but we'll be having to arrange for a uniformed man to sit here overnight just in case he does decide to talk.'

'Shall I do that?'

'No, Wilson. I'll do it and then I'll drive you home.'

'There's no need. I could get a minicab.'

'I'll be taking you home, so don't argue.'

Fran saw in his face the strain of the last few hours and in his eyes the blurring effect of the Irish whisky she had seen him pour into his tea from a silver hip flask.

Told to wait in the car she did just that and after about half an hour O'Neill returned.

O'Neill was just conscious of the fact that dark roads
sped by, that the sky was pocketed by bright stars,
that every so often a little light from a house or farm
window cast a glow that was as comforting as earth-
based stars. As he drove he stayed silent, trying to
dredge from his memory a past life with his wife;
happier times, hopeful times. But still the one overrid-
ing memory came flooding back – her face in death.
Now that death and near death had become so much
part of his job he thought maybe he should get out.
He was still young enough, he could find a new career.

He wasn't going home on his own that was for sure.
If Fran wouldn't let him stay with her. . . well, he
wasn't prepared for arguments. They could talk about
the case all night. He wouldn't lay a hand on her but
there was no way he was going back to an empty
house.

'Fran,' he began tentatively.

'Yes.'

'I'm wide awake. I want to discuss the case tonight.'

'Fine,' she answered, smiling.

'At your place.'

'Ulterior motive?'

'None. I promise you'll be as safe as Mother
Superior at matins.'

'Fair enough,' said Fran, relieved that she too
wouldn't have to be alone. Andy's close brush with
death had upset her. Death itself could be in a strange
way an anticlimax – the end – finito – extinguished.
But near death with a hope of survival *if* you did the
right things was edged with fear and panic. And it was

from that she was feeling the effects.

Once back in Fowchester and nearing the house O'Neill cheered up.

'I do a great line in scrambled eggs, Fran.'

'You'll need one,' she said, 'I haven't got any.'

Fran noticed as she opened her front door the strong smell of damp but it had begun to have a familiar homely connotation like her Granny's lavender bags.

'That smell could be bottled and sold,' she said.

O'Neill smiled. 'I wouldn't buy it. Are you sure it's not the drains?'

Fran smiled back. 'You don't have to stay. But if you are planning to, you'd better light the gas fire first, I'm frozen.'

After much swearing and calling on the only two saints he could remember, the gas fire's ignition mechanism finally succumbed. After a few minutes the fire's glow transformed the room. And Fran's appearance with bowls of tomato soup and toast made it seem as if those two unforgotten saints had indeed been persuaded to work on his behalf.

After the soup they began to talk about the case.

'How's the graph coming on, Fran?'

She shrugged. 'More time consuming than I thought. Most people have, I think, now been accounted for. We've only got a couple of stray reds.'

'Reds?'

'My colour coding. The reds are real possibles, seen in the area and carrying something. It gets difficult of course when you only have one witness and they may have caught a sighting from some distance away.'

'What about reasons for being in the area?' asked O'Neill as he stretched out his legs towards the gas fire so that the heat could travel comfortingly up his legs.

'Very varied. From working there, to meals at the farmhouse, to delivering things—'

'Collecting things as well,' interrupted O'Neill.

'Well, yes.'

'Right, let's be making a list then.'

'It's three a.m., boss. I don't think I'm going to be much help.'

'I'll do the thinking, you write them down, and do call me Connor in your own home. It makes me feel. . . less awkward.'

O'Neill began making his imaginary list as if it were gospel and in a loud voice. Fran supposed that this was in case she dare fall asleep. The gas fire roared on and after a few minutes of listening to his list, which included one or two discrepancies, she excused herself and went upstairs to fetch pillows and a duvet. He looked up in surprise as she handed him his share of the bedding.

'Double duvet!' he said. 'A scarlet woman after all.'

'Just because I sleep alone doesn't mean I shouldn't have some comfort.'

He laughed and Fran grew hot with embarrassment. Lying under duvets to discuss CID matters was not how she had envisaged the job. Although he'd probably noticed her embarrassment he didn't pursue it. He stared at the list for some time.

'Let me have a look,' said Fran.

O'Neill handed over his notebook in which he had drawn up his two lists; deliveries on the right, collections on the left. The left-hand margin was empty save for one word – rubbish.

The right-hand margin listed: bread, milk, groceries, animal food, newspapers, hay, compost, and seeds.

'That's wrong,' said Fran reading through the list, 'the only deliveries to pass the area in question are for the farmhouse so items like hay, compost, and seed don't have to pass that way.'

'Have the people who delivered them been checked out?'

'Of course, and eliminated. So far the graph has been a waste of time.'

'Keep at it, Fran. Someone delivered more than they should. What puzzles me,' he said, 'is why the limbs were not wrapped up properly. Who would have noticed the odd arm covered in brown paper? It's as though our murderer wanted to be caught.'

'Or maybe they thought the wrappings would be good fodder for forensic.'

O'Neill laughed. 'I see you're into farming vocabulary already, but that's a very good point. Who would want to touch dead flesh?'

'No one in their right mind, but of course Andy would have rubber gloves.'

'So too would Keith Quinton.'

Fran nodded. Then she said, 'Don't you believe Andy killed his father?'

'He may have,' agreed O'Neill, 'but he had help. Two years ago he was nineteen, no car, and he wasn't as muscular as he is now. If he did kill his father he'd have needed help disposing of the body. So who helped him? And why kill a housekeeper? No, it doesn't ring true. There's more to Carol Sykes than meets the eye. She's the key to everything. Frank Melksham's death was perhaps inevitable if you believe in natural justice but Carol's is much more of a mystery.'

'You could be right,' said Fran as her eyes began to close and her head lolled sideways on to the pillow.

O'Neill watched her sleep for some time, listened to her quiet rhythmic breathing, and fought the desire to put his head between her firm young breasts and inhale the fragrance of her skin.

Finally as dawn was breaking he fell asleep. And for the first time in weeks he didn't dream of his wife.

The telephone woke Fran. She was awake instantly, surprised by the noise and the stiffness of her neck. She eased her shoulders, shrugged off the duvet, and stepped over O'Neill's feet to get to the phone.

'Is DCI O'Neill there?' asked the voice.

'I think he's just pulled up outside. Just hold on, I'll let him in.'

Covering the receiver she kicked O'Neill's out-stretched legs.

'I've said you've just arrived, it's the incident room, I think.'

With eyes struggling to open O'Neill took the receiver and listened for some time before he said, 'Yes, fine. We'll be straight down. Get a statement from Andy Melksham. Be making sure it's a good one. As he put down the phone he said, 'That was the incident room.' The Met. have come up with an address for Carol Sykes. Someone has reported her missing. So we're off to London. And forensic have come up with something too. We'll be going to the college first, then London.'

'Any chance of breakfast before that?'

'Not a hope,' said O'Neill. 'But I'll treat you to rolls and coffee at the college.'

In the incident room Pete, the inspector manager, greeted O'Neill and Fran with a faxed forensic report. O'Neill read it in silence.

'What does it say, boss?' asked Fran, eager to read it herself, and disappointed when O'Neill gave it back to Pete with instructions for it to be filed.

'It says, DS Wilson, that traces of a fine white powder were found on the arm of Frank Melksham. A minuscule amount, but enough, and a single hair.'

'Yes? And?'

O'Neill smiled. 'I'll be telling you on our way to London.'

Fran couldn't contain her curiosity once they were on the train. At least the compartment was empty and they could sit opposite each other and talk about the case without the risk of being overheard.

'What did that fax say, boss?' she asked, trying to appear nonchalant.

O'Neill smiled. 'I've kept you waiting long enough, Fran. The white powder, it seems, is flea powder of a type used and sold only in veterinary practices. And the hair, not human, belongs to a shaggy dog.'

'So that means either Tom Harrington or Keith Quinton.'

'Looks like it,' agreed O'Neill. 'Although my bet is on Keith Quinton. He, it seems, was having or at least was suspected of having an affair with Sandra Melksham even before Frank came on the scene. I knew they were friendly but then Keith is a friendly soul and women do seem to have a soft spot for him. Jessie Harrington, for instance, always brightens up when he's around.'

'What do you think happened that night?'

O'Neill stared out of the train window at the countryside fast flashing by and said, 'My guess is that Andy accidentally killed his father. It certainly wasn't premeditated – well, not for that moment anyway. He didn't know his father would be turning up but once confronted by him and with the threat of his father returning there was his chance to prevent that and get his own back. And he did.'

'What about the others?'

'The others,' echoed O'Neill. 'Steve and Keith I can understand. They, after all, had an interest in Sandra. Norman and Tom – that I don't understand. But of course they did know Andy, they've known about him from a young lad. Someone years ago had reported Frank to the NSPCC but nothing much happened. It seems they couldn't prove that his deafness had been caused by blows to the head and most of the time Andy managed to keep out of his father's way. Maybe on that night they were simply sucked in by the drama of it all. Tom and Norman conspired to get rid of the body simply to help a friend.'

'That doesn't solve Carol Sykes's death, though, does it?'

'It surely doesn't. Did someone in Fowchester know her from London? Not likely, I would have thought. It reeks too much of coincidence. Perhaps she came with a purpose. . .'

O'Neill tailed off as the train stopped and their solitary status was disrupted by four excited children and two already harassed adults.

Fran liked stations and Euston was particularly busy. She would have loved just to stay and watch the toing and froing but O'Neill was obviously grimly determined today and they were climbing into a taxi bound for Camden town within minutes.

As the cab stopped in a back street the driver turned his head. 'You sure you want this place, mate? It's a bit rough round here. Used to be where the nobs lived but not any more. Bloody disgrace it is, some of these houses ought to be condemned.'

Fran stepped out of the taxi while O'Neill paid the driver and reassured him that they did indeed want Park Mansions. She stood for a moment staring up at the tall Georgian house which no one had bothered to gentrify or even slap on a bit of paint. Park Mansions could only have been described as a multiple-occupancy slum. Crumbling walls and paintwork, a front door thick with dust and windows with fist-sized holes in the woodwork. And the whole house the colour of dirt grey.

The intercom system had five sections, all abbreviated

– M, S, C, T, and finally MM. O'Neill rang the bell marked MM. It was some time before anyone answered. A pretty girl of about sixteen opened the door. She wore a blue towelling bathrobe and her long dark hair hung in wet strands to her shoulders.

'Police,' said O'Neill.

'Oh, yeah, about Carol. I reported her missing. Come on in.'

The hall was a complete contrast to the outside. Fresh white paint and green plants in every corner gave the hall a summery feel. A huge yellow paper lampshade hanging less than true and walls decorated with a collection of straw hats added to the summer atmosphere.

'I'm Mandy, mad Mandy. M.M. Have you found her yet?'

'We may have,' answered O'Neill gravely.

Mandy looked at him sharply, 'Are you an inspector?'

'Detective Chief Inspector Connor O'Neill and Detective Sergeant Fran Wilson at your service, madam.' He bowed slightly and Mandy giggled.

'You'd better come up to my room,' she said. 'Follow me, it's right at the top.'

Mandy's room was painted on all four walls in shades of darkest lavender; on a bedside table a stick of incense poked into a black candle smoked its sickly fumes.

'You'll have to sit on the bed,' said Mandy as she sat down on a bean bag that she pulled from beneath it.

O'Neill sat next to Fran and for a few moments there was an awkward silence.

'Tell me about Carol, was she a friend of yours?'

Mandy smiled. 'You could say that,' she said, 'she's my best friend.'

O'Neill hurriedly tried to think what to say next but during the pause Fran asked, 'Where did Carol say she was going?'

Mandy shifted her position on the bean bag. 'She didn't say exactly. She just told me she had got a month's work in the country. She gets so fed up with London especially in the spring.'

'So she didn't plan for it to be a permanent position?'

Mandy threw back her head and laughed. 'Of course not, my mother doesn't go in for permanent positions.'

'Your mother!' O'Neill tried to keep the surprise from his voice.

'Yep. My mum. Where did you say you found her?'

'I didn't,' mumbled O'Neill awkwardly and glancing at Fran as if she should now take over.

Fran knew that if she gave Mandy the bad news now the interview would be over and although it seemed cruel not to tell her immediately, it had to be delayed.

'Tell me about your mum,' said Fran.

Mandy shrugged. 'Not much to tell, really. She had me very young, never married, and she wants me to get a nice safe office job.'

'And what do you want?' asked Fran.

Again Mandy shrugged. 'I don't really know. I'd

like to move out of this dump and I'd like me and Carol to live somewhere in the country. That's her dream – a cottage in the country, a horse, a few sheep, and some money in the bank. That's one of the reasons she works for a few weeks in the country every year. She looks at places to buy and tries to imagine us living there. She never tells me where she's going but she writes or rings once she's there. I hope she isn't ill, one year she had to have some sort of operation. She didn't even tell me until she got home.'

'Who looks after you when your mum's away?'

'I am eighteen,' said Mandy indignantly.

'When you were younger?'

'One of the girls. They've always looked after me.' She laughed. 'Carol always said I'd had more mothers than most people have hot dinners.'

'Girls?'

Mandy stared at Fran for a moment with a look of incredulity.

'I bet you haven't been in the police force long,' she said. 'Fancy not knowing this was a brothel.'

Fran didn't know how to respond to that and O'Neill spoke then. 'Are any of the girls in now?'

Mandy nodded. 'They're all asleep, though.'

'No matter,' said O'Neill. 'Would you wake one of them up? I'd like to have a word with them about Carol.'

'Why? There's nothing wrong, is there? You're not going to do us, are you? Carol keeps a good house, you know, there's never any trouble. . .'

'It's nothing like that,' said O'Neill gently. 'Away

with you and wake up one of the girls.'

Mandy looked at him suspiciously but then very slowly got up from the bean bag. As she got to the door she turned and gave O'Neill a searching look. He found it hard to return her gaze: she had seen the bad news in his eyes. They both listened as Mandy walked upstairs and knocked on a door.

'I can't believe it,' said Fran, remembering how Carol looked in death. 'She was wearing a pinny.'

O'Neill didn't respond but instead stared at the thin spiral of incense that drifted upwards. He tried to keep his thoughts on Carol's killer and not on Carol's death. If her daughter didn't know where she was it was unlikely her friends did. The one person that knew had disappeared. Who else knew where she was and did Trudi Miller know what her housekeeper did for a living – and if she did, who did she tell?

Mandy walked in then with a young woman in a just long enough T-shirt, hair flattened by sleep and with the crumpled look of the just woken.

'This is Sue,' said Mandy.

Sue, smiling laconically and looking directly at O'Neill, said, 'I'm Sassy Sue or Sexy Susie at work. I don't think I've had the pleasure of you ever taking me in.'

'We're from the Midlands, Sue,' said O'Neill. 'We'd like to ask you a few questions about Carol.'

'Yeah, OK, but what's happened? She usually gets in touch, you know. She's a minder, we prefer to work with a minder.'

'Minder?'

'Times have changed, Mr Plod. Carol went out with us but she did the minding.'

'You'll be explaining,' said O'Neill, 'for the benefit of my colleague.' He smiled then at Fran as if saying she was a simpleton.

'Carol comes with us to check out the punters,' explained Sue. 'We give her a percentage of the take. She checks the back of cars, clocks the number of the car, and gets a good look at the punter's face. Then if we're not back she comes for us. For years a lot of women on the game had a pimp – times have changed. We've changed – once we were beaten up by pimps and punters – now we look after ourselves.'

'Was Carol good at that?'

'Good! I'll say she was good. Saved me from a few nutters. She could take care of herself, could Carol. Sweet Caroline's her nickname and she is sweet as long as a man doesn't cross her.'

O'Neill sighed. 'I'm sorry to have to tell you both this, especially you, Mandy, but Carol must have been taken unawares. I'm afraid. . . she has been found dead. Murdered.'

There was a ghastly pause as they both tried to take in what he'd said. Then Mandy let out a howl of anguish. Fran stepped forward to comfort her.

'Leave her,' said Sue sharply. 'I'll look after her.'

Mandy's howl changed to choking sobs whilst Sue held her tight.

'Who the fuck did it?' demanded Sue.

'We don't know yet,' said O'Neill.

'Well, get your finger out and find out. You won't

find the bastard here, will you?'

'Is there anyone you can think of who knew where she'd gone?'

'She never told anyone where she was going, ever. . .' She trailed off as her eyes filled with tears.

'No men friends?'

'She didn't like bloody men. She hated them. Now leave us alone – go on, piss off.'

O'Neill and Fran were at the door when Mandy cried out, 'How did my mum die?'

'She was strangled,' said O'Neill softly. 'She was found in a farmhouse in Lincolnshire.'

'Was it a burglary?' she asked in a whisper.

'It doesn't appear so—'

'I'll tell you something,' interrupted Sue. 'She might have spent her life on the game fucking strangers but she'd never open the door to one. She was too careful for that. She could tell a nutter a mile off. I'm telling you she wouldn't have let a strange man into the house. She bloody wouldn't.'

Chapter Twenty-One

The news of Andy Melksham's suicide attempt had spread through Fowchester as rapidly as smoke from a large bonfire. Keith Quinton had called a pub meeting (not at the Plough) and it was suggested that the Red Lion, being in the centre of town, would be the most suitable.

They met at one. Tom Harrington, Keith, Steve, and Norman. At a round table well away from other customers they spoke in the hushed tones of conspirators.

'This has been a real cock-up,' began Keith. 'I never wanted young Andy to be involved in the first place. I knew he was the weak link.'

'He *was* involved from the start, Keith,' said Norman. 'He had to do his share. We all did.'

The others nodded and for a while everyone stared morosely into their drinks.

Norman, though, whilst trying to appear as worried as everyone else, was glad everything was coming to a head. He half smiled at that thought. Keith had been responsible for the disposal of the head. Of course they should have come clean when it first happened, but for two years everything had worked according to plan. Why had Andy tried to kill himself now? Perhaps his girlfriend had asked too many questions, perhaps he was plagued by conscience? More to the point why hadn't Andy got rid of his. . . responsibility. . . in the first year? The others had. They had been home free and then. . . this. And of course Trudi Miller's death. . . unless of course Andy had killed *her*. But why? Andy wasn't a killer. No, someone from outside the group must have killed her. . . surely.

He began to watch the others. And for the first time in ages he experienced a quickening of his senses. He didn't want to die or go to prison. He wanted to live, free of the college, free of Barbara, and free of Kilsby.

'I spoke to Andy,' said Steve suddenly, 'at the hospital.' The others looked up sharply. 'I told him to plead guilty to manslaughter on the grounds of provocation.'

'What about the body, old man?' asked Keith.

'I said to say he'd disposed of most of the body over the two years. The arm was the last bit to go – well, that is the truth.'

They sat in silence for a while all thinking about the implications of that.

'They won't wear that,' said Keith. 'He's not a good liar and he's got little imagination.'

Tom spoke then. 'We're in the shit.'

'Not necessarily,' answered Keith. 'What exactly could the police charge us with even if they find out? I'll tell you – not allowing a body to have a Christian burial. That's all.'

'Are you sure?' asked Steve.

'I'm sure,' answered Keith, but he didn't sound entirely convinced.

'Perhaps we should just go to the police and tell them about our part in all this,' suggested Norman.

No one answered, all were busy trying to work out the drawbacks of this idea.

Then Steve announced aggressively, 'We'll cop it for the woman, you know. Bound to. The police will think we've done it once and got away with it and so we'd do it again.'

'That's what worries me,' said Tom. 'After all, whoever killed that housekeeper must have known we chopped up Frank's body.'

Keith looked round the table at his darts companions.

'Did anyone here tell?' he said slowly. 'We swore to secrecy but it would be better if it was admitted now. Come on, own up lads if you did tell anyone.'

There was a long and embarrassed silence. Then Tom spoke. 'I can only speak for myself but I'd swear on the Bible I haven't told a soul. Not the wife, nobody.'

'Nor me,' said Steve.

'Nor me,' said Norman.

Keith smiled bleakly. 'That just leaves Andy. Poor little bugger. He must have told someone. If he's not careful he'll be charged with both murders.'

'What are we going to do?' asked Norman.

'Get him the best lawyer we can afford and make sure we all stick together. What else can we do?'

No one answered him so Keith said, 'It's agreed, then.'

A murmured consensus passed around the table and then Keith spoke again. 'For Christ's sake,' he said, 'let's have another drink.'

Andy didn't mind the policeman sitting in his room watching him. In a strange way he felt safe. Mostly he pretended to be sleeping but when he did open his eyes, there sat the policeman. He wasn't much older than himself. When Ali had turned up he'd introduced himself and apologized for not being able to leave the room. It didn't matter anyway. Ali whispered and Andy read her lips. Mostly though she sat crying and sniffing and saying she couldn't live without him. Andy felt strange, as if he were an onlooker, as if somehow he had died and he was just an unfeeling shell in the bed. It wasn't unpleasant, not feeling, it was as reassuring as the policeman who guarded him. And suddenly his deafness became an added bonus, giving him the ability to cut off when he wanted to. One thing was certain. He wasn't going to grass. He would remain silent. He smiled to himself. He would become deaf *and* dumb. He'd admitted killing his dad. That would be enough. He still didn't regret killing him.

His only regret was telling Mrs Miller. And Steve.

Chapter Twenty-Two

Norman Crick had planned to tell Barbara not only about his part in Frank Melksham's death but also that he was leaving the college and her. But she was asleep when he left and her face in repose had looked soft, warm with sleep and untroubled. He just didn't have the heart to wake her with bad news.

Malcolm Kilsby came into his office about eleven, looking healthy and cheerfully optimistic.

'Morning, Norman, wonderful morning. I've started swimming down at the sports club, six thirty start but it sets you up for the day. No sport is as good as swimming at giving one that feeling of wellbeing.'

Norman, looking up from his desk, studied Kilsby from top to toe, until Kilsby said, 'Is there something wrong with the way I look?'

Norman smiled. 'You look the same little prat as you've always looked – now piss off!'

Malcolm flushed and without argument turned round and left.

One down, thought Norman, one to go. He didn't think he could use quite the same tack with Barbara but it would probably have the same effect. He would go home and tell her this very minute whilst his courage lasted.

Barbara was sitting in her favourite chair staring at the garden when he walked in.

'What's the matter, are you ill?' she asked, turning at the sound of his footsteps and injecting into her voice a rare note of consideration.

'No. I've come home to talk to you – specially.'

'You want to leave me, don't you?'

'No, I. . .' What did he want? 'It's something else. A very serious matter.'

'We're not a serious matter, then,' she said caustically.

'Just shut up, Barbara, and listen.'

She listened then, neither interrupting him nor prompting him when he faltered. At last he finished.

'Why didn't you tell me all this before?' said Barbara. 'I've been so depressed because I thought you had another woman. I could have shared the worry.'

She came then to sit by him on the sofa. Tentatively she rested her hand on his knee.

'You should have told me, you silly boy.'

Norman cried then for the first time in years. Barbara let him cry, cuddled him, kissed him like a child, then said, 'We'll find the very best lawyer. I'll take a job if necessary to pay for it.'

Norman managed a wry smile. 'I'm taking early retirement. I can't take any more of that creep Kilsby.'

'We'll make the best of it, won't we?' said Barbara. 'We had some good times in the old days didn't we?'

Norman remembered then the good times when they were younger, more optimistic, more loving. He kissed her full on the lips and she didn't turn away. In fact she seemed to enjoy it.

'It's been a long time, Norman,' she said.

Keith Quinton's only oral confession was to his dog.

'I've cocked up my life, old son,' he said to the black and white collie who sprawled on his lap. 'I should have married when I had the chance. Now look at me, just a bit of booze every now and again and you – you mangy old thing.'

The dog licked Keith's face in appreciation of his master's reference.

'Women have always been a problem to me, Tozer. Once it was better-looking men who took my women, now they're just younger.'

Tozer wagged his tail.

'Agree with me, do you? Well, you would. It was down to her you were rescued. That bastard deserved to die. Well, what would you have done? Torn him limb from limb I expect.' The dog yawned. 'Boring you, am I? How about a walk?'

Tozer immediately sprang into action and ran to the door barking excitedly.

The walk did Keith good. He wasn't a criminal, neither were the others. He thought back to that night in the pub car park. Frank attacking Andy. They had come across the fight unexpectedly and for a moment they had stood, shocked, not quite knowing what to do. Then Andy had fallen and Frank had kicked him in the head and then amazingly before they could do anything Andy was once again on his feet landing his attacker one almighty punch on the jaw. Frank had blinked in surprise, staggered, and then fell. Someone cheered. They all stood waiting for Frank to get up again, but he didn't.

Keith had felt his pulse then, it was weak and thready but he was still alive.

'He's dead,' he heard himself saying. 'Come on, quick, let's get him in the back of the Land-Rover.'

They had dragged him into the back of the Land-Rover and Andy, still groggy from the blows, had sunk to his knees as though that kick to the head had suddenly taken effect. He'd been helped up and taken home by Tom.

It was the next day they met and discussed disposal of the body. And for two years they had been safe. Andy had insisted that as it was his blow that killed his father (or so he thought), he should help to get rid of the evidence. Two years on, it seems, he had still not done so. Why? Why had he decided to ruin everything, just as they seemed to be safe? Perhaps his girlfriend had something to do with it. Women often caused complications. And then of course there had been the other death. And now Andy's suicide attempt.

Keith smiled to himself. Perhaps Andy had just wanted to be free. And if a man had a son maybe that was all a father could want for him. Andy was *his* son, he was sure of that. There had been some doubt in Sandra's mind but not in his. A man knows his own son even if that son can't recognize his father. He'd had to kill Frank Melksham to protect both Andy and Sandra. It was such a pity that the good-looking Steve had come along, all youth and solid biceps, but one day he would go and Sandra too would be free.

Until then he would maintain his story that Frank was already dead when he was lifted into the Land-Rover. Who was going to find out? The only bit of the body left had been that arm. Cause of death couldn't be established from that.

'Come on, Tozer,' he called. As the dog ran up to him, tail wagging, Keith thought how lucky it was that dogs have such undiscriminating devotion and such undiscriminating tastebuds.

Tom Harrington looked up from his *Pig Breeders' News* to watch Jessie unobserved as she took out scones and an apple pie from the oven. Apple pie was his favourite pudding. Sometimes with a wedge of cheese, sometimes with thick clotted cream.

He'd have to tell her, of course. She'd probably shout and swear at him but she'd calm down after a while. Really he hadn't known why he'd agreed to Keith's plan. But Keith was a vet and as a farmer he couldn't afford to lose a vet, a darts player, and a drinking partner. And of course there was young Andy, poor little bugger, deafened by his thug of a dad as a kid. Not forgetting those cows that Melksham had sold him – infected with BSE. At least though he'd managed to put the boot in a couple of times that night, even if he had been dead at the time. One wallop from Andy and he was down, felled like a tree. His skull must have been smashed on the concrete. Tom had been given the torso to get rid of. Well, he'd done his duty and the pigs had done theirs. Now all he had to do was to explain everything to Jessie.

Jessie listened to Tom's recounting of events in silence. Every so often she caught him looking at her – worried and nervous. And yet he insisted it hadn't really been a crime, not a proper crime. Well, she hoped it was a proper crime and that he'd get at least two years inside. Two years would be just perfect. Time enough to make a new life for herself, have some fun before it was too late. Perhaps go dancing again, dye her hair, buy some new clothes, get a job, make some friends. And never cook a sausage again.

Chapter Twenty-Three

Andy had time to think in hospital.

A psychiatrist had been to visit him but he seemed to speak between clenched teeth and Andy had trouble understanding him. He'd also been seen by an ear, nose, and throat surgeon who suggested that they again examine his ears under general anaesthetic with a view to improving his hearing. Andy said he'd think about it. But he knew he wouldn't. His mind was made up; he dreaded the idea of losing consciousness, or at least the coming round after anaesthetic – he might say something he regretted.

Alison had also been to see him, bringing him grapes and a few puzzle books. They helped to pass the time. She didn't ask too many questions, she talked mostly about the baby and if she should have an abortion. He didn't say much. What could he say? He'd probably be in prison when the baby was born and that would grieve him more than her getting rid of it. Somehow lying in a hospital bed their relationship didn't seem real any more. He was glad to see her because she broke the monotony of his day but other than that it seemed he had no real future and he still felt remote as if he were acting a minor role of a patient in a play and the drama was going on elsewhere.

He'd given a statement to the police, of course. He admitted to killing his father accidentally, he admitted not being sorry he was dead, but when pressed about how he got rid of the body he refused to say more, other than that he was responsible for leaving the arm in with Tom Harrington's dead animals.

After he'd given his statement he feigned incomprehension at their questions. The police offered to get someone in to sign for him but since he'd never learnt sign language that wouldn't have helped much. Besides, he did have some hearing, he wasn't completely deaf, nor was he stupid. The onus was on them now. He'd confessed, what more could they want?

Steve read the morning paper, or at least tried to appear as if he were reading the paper. Sandra sat opposite wanting to talk. He knew she was going to ask him to get on with the decorating. All he wanted to do now was get out.

Sandra had known about Frank's death the night it happened. Tom had brought Andy home dazed and shocked and later Steve had spent time making out he had fought Frank to save Andy's life. Ever since then he'd been a real hero in Sandra's eyes and she hadn't questioned Andy too much on what happened that night.

'Oh, Steve, I'll always be grateful,' she'd said. And

she'd shown plenty of gratitude ever since.

What she hadn't known then was that the body had been chopped up and stored in freezers. Two bits of him stored at the bottom of her freezer for a very long time. Anything at the bottom was too deep for her to get easily and she was always well stocked on top. Keith Quinton had dealt with the chopping up, he had the facilities at his vet's surgery. He'd kept a cool head in more ways than one. But now Andy had been struck by conscience and they were all in danger.

Leaving the arm to be found had been Steve's idea. He'd been up in the loft laying new insulation when he'd found a box of Frank's old papers. In there he'd found a life insurance policy. A hefty amount. Sandra didn't seem to know anything about it but there it was in black and white – £80,000. Not payable on suicide, or of course just being missing; but missing believed dead, well, they paid out on that, didn't they? It could have worked out very nicely for the three of them – if Andy hadn't met Mrs Miller.

Andy had been walking through outpatients' when he'd heard her name being called and saw her stand up and walk to the consulting room. Outside he'd waited for her, told her that Frank Melksham was his dad. Of course she questioned him and he let it slip that Frank was dead.

It was then that Steve had decided to pay Mrs Miller a visit at Last Chance Farm. Now that he thought back on it she had been nervous that night. Perhaps he'd come on too strong. He'd told her she could have a quarter share – if she kept her mouth shut about

Andy's little slip of the tongue.

It took her a while to make up her mind. She offered him a glass of wine and by the end of the bottle they had shaken hands. Not that the wine had convinced her, he'd been sure of that. That had been down to his personal charm and the fact she had fancied him. He'd wanted to see her again so he said he'd come again in a couple of weeks to discuss the final arrangements. These posh birds, he'd said to himself, needed a bit of time.

The next time had been a disappointment though. She'd employed a woman about her own age as a companion housekeeper and of course he couldn't talk freely and this time he wasn't offered any wine. After that there was no point in shilly-shallying.

Now that a woman's body had been found at Last Chance Farm the money when it came would only have to be shared three ways. But even that wasn't consolation enough for the police sniffing around and now that Andy had tried to top himself they wouldn't be handing out insurance on a plate.

'It was your son that struck the fatal blow, not me,' he'd told Sandra, wanting to distance himself from anyone named Melksham and from Fowchester itself. The town was too small for a man like him, a man with real ambition. He smiled to himself. He wanted a woman to be ambitious for him so that he could sit back and reap the benefits. So far all the town had brought him was aggro and grief. Would Andy really keep his mouth shut? Would he be better off doing a runner now?

'Don't go out tonight, Steve,' begged Sandra in the whiny voice she reserved when she wanted something – usually when she wanted him to stay in. Steve looked up from his newspaper. He was past caring. He just wanted out – permanently. He put down the newspaper and walked over to her.

'Now look, Sandra, love,' he began, holding her close and whispering into her ear. 'All this has blown up and no doubt the police will be round soon. It's not looking good for me, is it? You wouldn't want to see me in prison, would you?'

'No,' Sandra whispered back, frightened and uncertain.

'Well, then. I've got to do the sensible thing and think of us both, haven't I?'

'I suppose so. Does that mean we've got to leave? I don't mind, not if we can be together.'

'It's not as easy as that, love. You'll need to be around for Andy's sake. Being in court – that sort of thing. It's me that will have to go. You'll need money for his defence. I could make quite a lot on the oil rigs – they're always looking for good men.'

Sandra began to sniffle. 'Please, Steve, don't leave me now. I need you more than I need money.'

'Come on now, Sandra, be a brave girl. I could be back here in a few weeks.'

Sandra continued to sniffle. Steve began to get irritated.

'If you carry on like this I shall have to stay. How will you feel when they come to arrest me? You'll blame yourself.'

Sandra thought about that for a while. She could see she was being selfish. She didn't want Steve to go to prison because of her so what choice did she have?

'I'm sorry, Steve. Of course you must go. I couldn't bear to think of you in prison because of me.'

'That's my girl!' he said kissing her.

He made love to her then, quickly. Promising afterwards he'd soon be back, so soon she'd hardly notice he'd gone. And no he didn't want her to drive him to the station it would upset him too much. He'd prefer it if she went out for the afternoon. He'd be gone by the time she got back. Reluctantly, Sandra agreed.

Later that afternoon he packed all his belongings into two suitcases, pocketed the two hundred pounds she had insisted he take with him, and left by minicab. He whistled cheerfully as the car drove away from Fowchester.

Sandra returned to an empty house, no note, and not a sign left that a man called Steve had ever lived with her. He'd even taken his plastic clothes hangers with him.

She sat down amongst the paint pots and white sheets and wept.

In an empty store room near the college incident room O'Neill sat alone with Fran and examined her graph. He felt ashamed of his drinking. He was definitely going on the wagon. Drinking was stopping him thinking properly. He'd seen the clues but he'd failed to see their significance. The night the arm had been left on the Harrington farm the dog hadn't barked, because he'd recognized friend not foe – Andy: simple

as that. And more to the point, the finding of the
second arm had been a deliberate ploy to ensure the
police thought there was a connection between the
two murders. But still he wasn't sure. A hunch wasn't
enough. They needed proof, cast-iron proof, and a
sighting was a beginning at least.

'Right, Fran,' he said, 'who have you identified and
who's left?'

'It's been difficult, boss, getting accurate sightings.
The farmhouse cook is well past retirement age and
she's a bit absent-minded. One of the statement readers is going over her questionnaire and I've got a list
of all the regular deliveries and occasionals like the
electricity man and the gas man. That leaves two reds
left – unidentified but thought to be carrying something. And just one unidentified white van – no mark-
ings seen.'

'Right,' said O'Neill, 'let's have lunch at the farmhouse and see what we can find out from the cook.'

The farmhouse kitchen boasted two large scrubbed
pine tables and a chalk-board menu of four items:
roast beef, steak and kidney pie, Irish stew, and roast
pork. The tables were already full and the heads of
the customers lifted occasionally as a voice boomed
from the Aga – one beef, large Yorkshire coming up!
A girl with dark straggly hair and a demented
expression rushed to take the plate from the cook
whose most notable features were her extremely thin
body, feet encased in red trainers, and bifocal glasses
through which brown dots peered like the eyes of a
dead fish.

'The cook is Miss Hilda Hawkins, known to the

regulars as Hawkie,' whispered Fran.

'And the assistant?'

'That's Tracey, ex-YTS, hopes to take over the cooking when Hawkie retires.'

They stood near the doorway for some minutes watching the action and hoping that soon they would be able to sit down. No one took any notice of them, least of all Tracey who glanced at them angrily, resentful that they were proposing to increase her workload.

Eventually two men left and O'Neill and Fran sat down opposite each other. Fran faced the window.

'What exactly can you see?' asked O'Neill.

'Not much, a few sheep in the field. None of the customers can see much, all the deliveries come to the side of the farmhouse.'

O'Neill nodded. 'Does Tracey work here all the time?'

'Five days a week – eight to four. Has one weekend off in three. Days off in the week in lieu. She doesn't sign for deliveries though, Hawkie always does that. And Hawkie seems to work seven days a week, although if she wants a break they get a relief cook over from the main kitchen.'

Ten minutes later Tracey stood waiting sullenly for their order. At least she was sullen at first, until O'Neill turned on the charm. The smile first, then the chat.

'It's Tracey, isn't it?'

She nodded listlessly.

'I hear you're a very good cook.'

Surprise animated her face for a moment then vanished. 'Pretty good,' she said. 'Why?'

'I just thought that a young keen girl like you would keep an eye on supplies. So that when you're in charge you know what's what.'

'I know that already,' said Tracey. 'There's not much I don't know about ordering and supplies.'

'That's just what I was thinking. Take a seat, Tracey, DS Wilson will explain to your boss you'll be out of action for a few minutes.'

Fran, somewhat reluctant to miss the rest of the interview, stood up and walked to the kitchen area. Hawkie wasn't pleased.

'I can't be doing the cooking and the serving,' she said as she thrust a bowl of apple pie and custard into Fran's hand.

'Who's it for?'

'I don't know,' said Hawkie irritably. 'I just do the cooking.'

Fran didn't waste any time, she simply shouted: 'One apple pie and custard coming up!' and a hand shot in the air in quick response.

When Fran returned Tracey was just beginning her list of suppliers.

'And on Saturday – well that was just the milkman. No one else. It was dead quiet all day. Friday was the busy day, fish and chips at lunch time, that's always popular, and then at night there was a small cheese and wine party. A private do, for the deputy. He was celebrating something. I got well paid for that.'

Fran, puzzled, said, 'Hawkie didn't tell me about that.'

'I did it all,' said Tracey, 'Mr Kilsby said it didn't need two people. It was just a few vol-au-vents, French bread, and cheese, and he supplied all that. I just laid the tables and put the glasses ready.'

'And the wine?' asked O'Neill.

'Oh, yeah. I forgot about that. Mr Theodolou delivered that Saturday about six.'

'In a white van?' asked Fran hoping that time spent on her graph was being justified.

'I didn't see no van. He just sort of appeared.'

O'Neill was just about to ask another question when Hawkie yelled: 'Tracey!'

Tracey made a move to stand up but O'Neill put a hand on her shoulder.

'Just one more question, Tracey. Did you see Mr Theodolou leave?'

Shrugging, she said, 'Don't think so, can't remember really.'

'Well, thank you, Tracey, you've been a great help.' O'Neill flashed her another smile. 'You'd better get on now.'

Tracey stood up. 'I've just thought,' she said. 'He came back the next day to collect the unused bottles. I remember now seeing that big black car of his. A bit tight of him I thought, there was only two unopened bottles. Two bottles of red – Bulgarian – just cheap plonk but he came and collected them. Hawkie wasn't here then, said she was in church. I think she thought I'd nicked them but I didn't get a chance, did I?'

Chapter Twenty-Four

Wendy Theodolou watched her husband undress in the dark. Soon he would be beside her in the bed. She breathed deeply, hoping that steady breathing would convince him she was asleep. In the first years of their marriage sex hadn't been a joy but it had been tolerable until she had suffered the miscarriages. After that she could no longer bear him to touch her.

She heard the gentle thump of his feet on the thick carpeting and as he got in beside her she smelt his hair oil, heady and strong and foreign. He had it sent over specially from Greece. Grease from Greece. She smiled sadly into the darkness. Perhaps if they had lived in Greece their marriage would have worked. . . perhaps. Maybe if he was at home more she would have felt more. . . affectionate. As it was he was like a tom cat, out a lot but attached to his own territory. In the first years of their marriage she had wanted to work but gradually she had changed. Chris couldn't bear the idea of her working, he wanted her in the home, waiting for the hunter's return.

His breathing now became more regular and Wendy

edged towards the side of the bed and lay still hoping that soon she too would sleep. She had misjudged his breathing though for his hand groped for her breast. She kept very still. Please God, she thought, not tonight.

At breakfast Chris reported to her his latest wine coup. She tried to show an interest.

'So the Bulgarian plonk is doing well?' she asked.

'Don't call it plonk,' said Chris, 'it's a palatable wine at a reasonable price.'

'You sound like an advertising man,' said Wendy as she passed him a refilled coffee cup.

'I have to do a bit of everything in my job, as you well know.'

'Did Trudi like the Bulgarian wine?'

'No idea,' replied Chris.

'Why didn't you take her any, you usually do when you have a fresh consignment?'

'Are you trying to upset me?' said Chris. 'Couldn't I just have my breakfast without these continual questions?'

'It was only one question, Chris. Why are you so tetchy this morning?'

'Why are you being so bloody irritating? Ever since that woman got herself murdered at your sister's place you've been nagging and prying like an old woman. Now just leave me alone!'

Chris stood up then and without a backward glance left the room. A few minutes later the front door slammed and then she heard the car start and he drove away.

Not long after Mrs Charlesworth arrived. She had been with Wendy for years and although they didn't really need a cleaner, somehow she brought Wendy a sense of comfort. They sat down at the kitchen table and drank tea. Mrs Charlesworth had all sorts of problems; money problems, a son who was mentally ill, a feckless husband. She managed by having several cleaning jobs but Wendy knew her favourite job was with her. After all, the house was never dirty or untidy and dusting and hoovering and polishing taps at the Theodolou house was easy money compared with some of the houses she had to clean. Mrs C. talked in spasms, little bursts of woe, and then she listened. Occasionally if she was in a good mood Wendy would hear little bits of town gossip but today she did most of the talking.

Later that morning the telephone rang. It was Trudi.

'I can't talk long,' she said, 'I'm on my coffee break.'

'Where are you? Have you heard what's happened? I've been so worried. You must come home.'

'I can't come home, Wendy. I can't explain. I'll stay here for a while and then I'm going abroad.'

'The police are looking for you – they'll find you. They'll think it's suspicious you haven't come forward.'

'I must go, this phone isn't very private.'

'Where are you, Trudi? You must tell me that.'

'I'm in Tenby now, at the Marigold Guest House. I'll ring you again soon but don't tell anyone where I am – not Chris – not anyone – promise me.'

'Come home, Wendy – please.'

'Must go. Don't forget.'

Wendy put down the phone and stared straight ahead. Why was her sister so scared? Did she know who had killed Carol Sykes? Was she frightened he would come after her? Perhaps Chris would know what to do. The best thing to do would be to drive down to Wales and bring her back with them. Trudi would be a lot safer then, especially if she had seen the killer. Protection, that was what she needed.

Chris was in a better mood when he came home that evening, a little merry even. He said he'd had one or two gins and he was sorry he snapped at her that morning.

'I've cooked your favourite spring lamb,' she said. 'And I've got some news.'

'Drink?' he asked at the drinks cabinet as he poured himself another large gin.

Wendy shook her head. 'Do you want to hear my news, Chris?'

'Of course I do, darling. What news?'

'I've heard from Trudi. She's in Tenby and she seems scared.'

'Where in Tenby?'

'Oh – the Marigold Guest House—'

'What's she scared of?' Chris interrupted.

Wendy glanced at him swiftly, his mood was not so merry now. He smiled at her placatingly.

'What's she scared of, dear?' he asked again.

'I don't know, but I think she may know who killed that Carol Sykes.'

236

'How?'

'I don't know how, maybe she saw him, I think we should go to Wales and collect her. She could stay with us, couldn't she? She'd be safe here.'

'If she saw the man why didn't she tell the police?'

'I don't know, Chris. Can she stay here?'

'Of course she can. Does she want to?'

'Oh, thank you, darling,' said Wendy kissing her husband's cheek. 'I didn't tell her we'd come for her, she didn't want me to tell anyone where she was but I expect she'll be delighted when we turn up.'

'Yes, I expect she'll be delighted,' said Chris, 'we'll drive down in a couple of days.'

'Couldn't we go tomorrow?'

'I'm far too busy.'

'A couple of days,' repeated Wendy thoughtfully. 'Well at least the murderer doesn't know where she is, does he?'

'No, of course not. She'll be fine for a couple of days. Just fine. And she'll be so pleased to see us.'

Chris drank another large gin before dinner but it didn't harm his appetite. The spring lamb and cous-cous tasted wonderful.

At the Marigold Guest House Trudi's day's work was over and she sat on the bed and began writing a letter. She regretted telling her sister that she was in Tenby. How long could Wendy keep the secret? Even as a child she had found it hard to keep secrets. Now that she knew, it was only a question of how long before she told someone.

She finished the letter, put it in an envelope, and licked a stamp into place. If she could find the energy she would post it tonight. She closed the writing pad with a sigh. Would Wendy ever forgive her? she wondered. Her marriage wasn't the happiest, but then Wendy valued status and security above physical closeness. Wendy chose the soft options, Trudi wanted change and excitement – or she did until she met Carol. Carol had made her see things differently, had made her see she could manage without a man. She would have to now anyway.

One thing Trudi was sure about though was that it was time to move on. Tomorrow morning she was off duty, she could pack in the morning and be on the way to. . . wherever.

For a while she listened to the radio until she began to feel drowsy. She would post the letter in the morning. No doubt the landlady of the Marigold would be happy to see her go. For the past few days she had been giving her some very odd looks and had asked her strange rather pointed questions. It had been stupid of her to use Carol's name but surely there must be hundreds of Carol Sykes in Britain. Poor Carol, they had got on so well together.

In a strange way she had admired her. Carol had managed to bring up a child on her own; she was independent and her own boss. The fact that she had to have sex with strangers seemed not to matter much. She didn't have to pretend to enjoy it, or flatter the male ego, or feel guilty that she hadn't reached orgasm. Merely perform a business transaction. Carol had also done more 'minding' than soliciting in the last few years so she could rely on others to do the bulk of the work.

Why on earth Trudi had let Frank Melksham into her life she didn't know; and then after that she'd made another ghastly mistake with *him*. She'd been drunk, of course, and he'd got maudlin and told her all about his London activities. The strain of the last few months had been partially relieved by Carol's arrival. Carol told her most people make mistakes through loneliness or stupidity or both. True of course. She had been both stupid and lonely but she could change her life if she wanted to. Tomorrow is the beginning of the rest of my life, she thought just before she fell asleep.

Her sleep was troubled, *he* invaded her brain. She couldn't see him but she could smell him. In the house, in the cellar. Poor Carol. She woke at four, anxious but alert and wide awake, and she decided that if she bathed and packed she could slip out at six and catch an early train to London. London was an anonymous place, she could easily stay hidden there.

First she opened the letter, read it again, and decided that she couldn't possibly send it. Her sister's happiness and peace of mind meant more to her than truth or revenge. She tore the letter into tiny pieces and walked downstairs with her wastepaper basket and threw the contents into the dustbin. Far better, she reasoned, to just disappear. There would be less hurt all round.

As Trudi was running her bath she heard the milkman

arrive. The lobby was always left open for him. The clink of the bottles reassured her. She lifted the sash window of the bathroom a few inches to release the steam that had begun to fill the small room and dull the wall mirror. Pouring bubblebath into the running water she watched the bubbles grow satisfyingly large and frothy. She stepped into the bath and gasped a little as the hot water flowed over her body. Then as she became accustomed to the heat she sighed, appreciating the soothing warmth, and lay back and closed her eyes.

It was a few moments later that her eyes sprang open at the slight metallic sound outside, a noise on the fire escape. A footfall. She sat up in the bath, all senses quickened. Then came a scraping noise as the window was lifted higher. At first she only saw a shadow. And then the hands. She tried to scream, opening her mouth wide. But the scream was trapped deep within her brain and all that emerged in her terror was a sharp rush of air and the knowledge that she could no longer close her mouth.

Chapter Twenty-Five

O'Neill insisted that they spend the next day at Fowchester police station. He had become convinced that as well as being implicated in Frank Melksham's death Keith Quinton was also a firm suspect for the killing of Carol Sykes.

'I'll have them all in. Formally interview the whole lot of them – together.'

Fran smiled. 'I can just see the headlines, boss: "Five men are being held for questioning at Fowchester police station." There's only two cells and two interview rooms, we wouldn't be able to cope.'

'We'd be managing,' said O'Neill, 'it would be good practice for you. How is your formal interview technique?'

'I've not done much and never for anything serious.'

'That's a big failing in the police,' murmured O'Neill. 'We spend so much of our time interviewing people and yet we're not taught how to do it properly so, when all else fails, up comes a concocted confession. Rule one, Fran, of O'Neill's interviewing practice, never raise your voice. Rule two, never lose your cool. Rule three, help them relax, and rule four, keep them talking.'

'You make it sound easy,' said Fran.

O'Neill laughed. 'I've still got a few more rules up my sleeve but if you add them all together it comes to the same thing.'

'Which is?'

'Make them feel safe.'

Fran couldn't help frowning. 'Surely suspects should feel nervous not safe.'

'That's what a lot of policemen think. Detectives should develop the gentler, subtler arts of getting people to talk. Tell me a few places where people actually give away little secrets.'

Fran thought for a moment, 'At their GP's, with their shrink. . .' She paused. 'I can't think of anywhere else.'

'Now if you were a good Catholic girl you'd be thinking of the confessional. . .'

'The hairdresser's,' interrupted Fran.

'Sure, and why do they do that?'

'Because they feel safe.'

'Correct. Badgering and hectoring makes people feel unsafe, insecure, secretive, frightened. No one would be divulging even the simplest information when they feel threatened. Make them feel safe and you're there, if you're patient. Put the innocuous questions first and make all the real questions seem innocuous.'

'So you want to start with Keith? What about Steve?'

'He's an opportunist, I think, which no doubt was why Sandra had made enquiries about Frank's life insurance – that was after his death but before the finding of the arm so premeditation on that score can be ruled out.'

'What about the Sykes murder? Don't you think Steve is a strong contender for that one?'

'No,' replied O'Neill. 'Call it an Irish hunch if you like but a man who can charm most women into bed rarely ends up strangling his source of satisfaction.'

Fran remained sceptical but looked forward to her first formal interview. The phone rang then. It was for O'Neill. Fran left the office to get coffee from the machine and when she returned he said, 'Interview's off. How do you fancy a trip to the seaside instead?'

'Sounds fine to me,' said Fran. Fran's first sight of the sea had been as an eight-year-old. A day trip with the school. Just a few hours on the beach at Skegness but glorious sunshine and the only thing marring the trip was vomiting in the coach on the way home. The sea had been wonderful, vast and blue and exciting.

'I notice you haven't asked where we're going.'

'I guessed. Tenby. To find Trudi Miller.'

'You're half right. But not to find her. She's been found. And guess how? You were right, she was silly enough to use the name Carol Sykes.'

O'Neill felt cheerful as he began the drive to Tenby. At lunchtime they stopped for lunch in a pub that had an extensive menu of bar meals but no customers. Even so their meal took forty minutes to arrive. Fran had deliberated for some time choosing her meal. She

243

of course declined steak saying she had visions of the poor cow staggering around in a field as if it was execution day and no one had noticed it staggering who would know if it had BSE or not. O'Neill said he'd take his chances on BSE. Fran eventually chose vegetable lasagne.

O'Neill watched her eat. 'Many more meals like that you'll plump up nicely,' he said.

'Like a chicken, I suppose, all breast and skinny legs.'

'There's no need to be so prickly. I'm a good-natured soul really, in the right company.'

'And you think I'm the right company?'

'Sure I do, Fran, sure I do.'

His hand rested on hers briefly and although Fran had expected something to happen as she moved her arm slightly her sleeve caught on the edge of the plate and it went crashing to the ground.

'Sure to goodness that was their best Spode,' he said, trying to lighten the awkwardness of the moment.

Flustered Fran began to pick up the broken pieces but soon the barman came with a dustpan and brush and O'Neill insisted on paying far more than the plate was worth.

As he drove away from the pub O'Neill cursed his clumsiness but vowed to do better next time. That was all he needed – time.

'That phone call from HQ told me something else, Fran,' he said as they drove west towards the Welsh border.

'What was that?'

'The reason the Welsh police cottoned on to Trudi

244

so quickly was because they checked CRO and found Carol Sykes had a record. The usual, soliciting, but once for causing a breach of the peace – chased a naked punter down the street. It created quite a stir. It was the middle of the rush hour and he had to weave in and out of the traffic.'

'Serves him right,' said Fran.

The sun shone weakly in Tenby. Slivers of sunlight managed to slip between bulky grey clouds. Fran was delighted with the town. It had an old-fashioned quaintness; wide, empty beaches and an angry sea. She closed her eyes and imagined the town on a warm summer's day when the sea lapped the beach in ripples, the sand felt soft under bare feet, and gulls flew in contented silence. She would come back, she decided, in the summer.

O'Neill watched Fran's obvious happiness. There was no disguising her pleasure at seeing the sea and the beach. He wished they had more time to enjoy it. He would come back in the summer, he promised himself – with Fran.

The CID at Tenby police station directed them to a small hotel near the sea front. Their door to door enquiries had proved quite difficult. Casual labour in seaside towns was indeed casual. Many employers were reluctant to tell the police anything about their employees, especially if they were good workers. Engaging staff, for the most part, consisted of asking few questions and taking those willing to work for the lowest possible wage.

Mrs Alice Fairbrother had long ago given up being

too fussy about whom she employed. Workers had been known to stay only a few days and she always insisted they work a week in hand. A week in which she had a chance to sum them up. Cleanliness and neatness of appearance came first, honesty she didn't necessarily expect, and she did watch new employees with a suspicious intensity born of years of being let down by 'foreigners'.

'We'll not be saying we're police to the landlady,' said O'Neill as they approached the narrow lane that led to the Marigold, 'we'll say we're Carol's friends just down for a short holiday.'

'Right, Chief Inspector,' said Fran. 'Roger – over and out.'

'You're very cheerful,' said O'Neill.

'I regress to childhood when I'm near the sea. It's the smell of the place. Goes to my head like. . .'

'Irish whisky?'

'Not that much.'

'Good,' said O'Neill with a smile. 'I could do with a drink. You won't be needing one.'

It was Mrs Fairbrother who opened the door. Fran could see past her wide bulk to the fussiness inside: all lace placemats and bunches of artificial flowers. Fran guessed that the toilet rolls would be disguised in fluffy holders with rabbit tops or as crinoline ladies.

'Mrs Sykes is not on duty,' said Mrs Fairbrother in a pseudo-posh voice that made her sound like a RADA actress of thirty years ago. She was square in shape, with a comparatively small head that sported a tight perm with a hint of lavender in its silky whiteness.

Her matronliness was accentuated by a navy-blue crimplene dress with a white collar. She was quite probably seventy years old.

'Is she in her room?' asked O'Neill. 'It's a grand day, if she's off duty perhaps she could come out to tea with us.'

'Well,' replied Mrs Fairbrother, 'I don't know. She has a day off, she may have gone out.'

Fran smiled and copied the accent. 'How lovely, Connor. Carol has a day orff. Could you please direct us to her room?'

'Oh, very well,' said Mrs Fairbrother reluctantly. 'I'll go up and see if she's in.'

'We could save you the trouble and go up ourselves,' suggested Fran.

'It keeps me young and fit,' answered Mrs Fairbrother, walking stoically towards the stairs and pausing there as an elderly lady fought her way down the staircase with the aid of a walking stick.

'The lift will be working again soon, Mrs Wells,' she said.

Mrs Wells paused. 'I'll be buggered if I'll use it anyway,' she muttered as she got to the last stair.

O'Neill and Fran stood and waited in the hall. By the time Mrs Fairbrother returned she was out of breath and pink.

'She's not in. I knocked very hard and she's not in. The lift broke down last night. It makes such a racket I would have heard her go out if she'd used it.'

'We'll come back later,' said O'Neill. 'You've no idea where she's gone?'

'Hardly. She hasn't worked here long. I expect she's gorn shopping.'

'We'll be back if we don't find her, Mrs Fairbrother.'

'How do you know my name?' she asked dropping her accent for the first time.

'She wrote to us. We're her best friends,' answered O'Neill with his most winning smile. It was lost on Mrs F.

'That's funny,' she said sharply. 'Mrs Sykes gave me the impression she hadn't told any of her friends where she was because she was worried her ex-husband would find her.'

'Ah!' said O'Neill, stretching out the word to give him time to think. Fran came to his rescue.

'Mrs Fairbrother,' she said, using her best conciliatory tone, 'we come from Carol's home town and we know her ex-husband is on his way to look for her. I'm sure you wouldn't want any trouble at your splendid establishment. He is a rather violent man.'

'No, of course not. I certainly don't want any trouble here. In fact I shall have to let Mrs Sykes go if there is any danger of that.'

'Perhaps,' said Fran pressing home her advantage, 'we could wait for her in her room – just to be sure we don't miss her.'

'Oh, I suppose so, there's no harm in that. But shouldn't you be out on the streets looking for her? I don't want him coming in the mean time.'

'I can assure you if we are here there will be no trouble at all.'

'Very well,' said Mrs Fairbrother. 'I'll get you the

key. I do vet my workers extremely thoroughly, you know. If I'd been aware that her husband was violent I'd never have employed her.'

'Quite,' murmured Fran trying hard to keep a straight face.

'Yes, quite!' said Mrs Fairbrother, noticing.

Moments later she reappeared with a key.

'Third floor, second on the right. You'll have to walk up.'

O'Neill and Fran were aware that she watched them till they were out of sight.

'You were grand,' said O'Neill when they reached the second floor. 'But I was hoping we could have a saunter round the town before we confronted her.'

'Hedonist!' said Fran laughing and feeling that for the first time in this case she had scored a Brownie point.

The third floor was in fact a large attic area but with low mock-Tudor beams. O'Neill had to stoop slightly. There was one small sash window with a swath of white net curtains leaving a gap and a glorious view of the sea. Fran stood mesmerized for a moment watching the waves rise up and the clouds move across her line of vision. . .

'Fran – the door!'

Reluctantly Fran moved to the second door on the right and inserted the key. The lock was stiff and it took two or three tries before the key turned and even then the door was hard to open.

The room was quite small and dark because the heavy blue curtains were still drawn. The duvet on the pine bed had been thrown back. An open paperback book was on the bedside table next to a writing pad and a half-drunk mug of cocoa.

O'Neill opened the curtains and as he did so the light illuminated underwear and clothes neatly arranged on a chair. The cupboard door was slightly ajar. It was the only door apart from the one they had just walked through.

'Bathroom,' said Fran.

The door next to the bedroom wasn't locked. Fran could smell soap and bath oil as she slowly opened the door.

'Mrs Miller,' she called softly. 'Mrs Mill. . .'

The word trailed off, caught deep within her. She tried to speak but she was mesmerized by the sight. The bath water was red with bubbles of blood, the body in the bath was a deeper red, the face untouched apart from the blood that had trickled from the pulpy mass of her head. The eyes were half open and the air remained perfumed with the smell of soap and bubble bath. Fran, without turning her eyes, put out her hand to O'Neill. She was afraid to stop viewing the scene in case somehow the body should rise up. O'Neill took her hand and pulled her towards him. Fran saw he had become ashen.

'Mother of God,' he murmured. 'Let's get out of here.'

Fran took a deep breath and disengaged her hand.

'Just one thing,' she said moving to the bottom of the bath and dipping her hand in the water. It was icy cold and yet it looked warm, hot even. She stared for a moment at her wet hand expecting it to be bloody but the residue of bubbles hardly seemed pink. She looked then at the sink. Bloody smears showed the murderer had paused to wash his hands.

'I said *out*, Fran, come on. Forensic can do the rest.'

Back in Trudi Miller's room Fran watched as O'Neill took a swig from his hip flask.

'Don't look so po-faced at me Fran. I have trouble with dead bodies.'

Fran watched him anxiously. Her heart was thumping but at least *she* could cope without swigs of whisky.

O'Neill went downstairs to ring the local CID and Fran sat on the bed for a few moments until her heart stopped being in overdrive. How the hell did he get in? When did he get in? Early morning? Or did he spend the night? As that thought struck her she jumped up from the bed. Forensic would come up with something if he'd spent the night. Even a single hair would nail him. But how long would that take? He could have disappeared by then.

O'Neill returned still looking somewhat pale.

'Tenby CID and scene of crimes are on their way. Found anything?'

'I haven't looked. I was wondering if he stayed the night.'

'No way of knowing that yet, is there?'

He stared around the room and then picked up the writing pad. It was blank but there were faint indentations.

'Let's hope she pressed hard enough for forensic to be able to make something of this.'

'It's a new pad,' observed Fran, 'but she's used a few sheets. Maybe she wrote a letter last night.'

'The murderer could have taken it, or maybe she posted it. Or perhaps. . .'

O'Neill picked up her wastepaper bin. At the very bottom he found a tiny scrap of paper – blank paper.

He sighed. 'We'll check the dustbins then the bathroom. Find out exactly how the bastard got in. There's no sign of a break-in downstairs. I've had a word with Mrs Fairbrother, it seems there is an arrangement with the milkman that the milk is left in the inner lobby so that it can't be seen from the road. The outer door remains open all day but only the inner door is locked and bolted after midnight. That's superfluous information really because she also told me that a fire escape leads from the top-floor bathroom. We'll just be needing to check the window.'

'Why did she lock her door?' asked Fran. 'Who was she afraid of here? I mean if she was just going for a bath—' She broke off, realizing that it might not have been her who locked the door but the murderer. Indeed he may have forced her to lock the door. . . that was unlikely though, in view of the bubbles.

'Did she have something to hide in the room,' murmured O'Neill, 'something that would suggest she knew who had murdered Carol Sykes? Maybe she was afraid Mrs Fairbrother would nose around in her room and she'd lose her safe haven—'

'But it wasn't safe, was it?' interrupted Fran. 'Someone knew she was here. The murderer knew she was here.'

O'Neill nodded. 'Indeed he did. He's killed once too often now. I'll get the bastard. So help me. And quickly.'

The room didn't take long to search. The drawers contained only underwear, no address book or diary, and the cupboard contained clothes, mostly classic styles of good quality, all well worn. The only item of real interest remained the stationery, there was only one envelope missing from a pack of twenty and one stamp from a book of stamps.

'Who would you write to if you were scared and away from home?' asked O'Neill.

'An old boyfriend, a trusted girl friend, a relative. I hope I'd be able to trust quite a few people in those circumstances?'

'Who would you trust the most?'

Fran shrugged. 'A relative.'

'Precisely. Trudi Miller wrote to her sister.'

Before Fran could answer, the police surgeon arrived then, short and brisk and Welsh. It took him only a short time to come to his conclusion.

'Death by bludgeoning with a blunt instrument. Judging by the bruises and the amount of water on the floor she struggled quite a bit. Death occurred some hours ago but difficult to say when exactly because rigor mortis would have been delayed by the warmth of the bath water.'

'But you'd be betting on a time?'

Davies managed a tight smile. 'Early hours, between four thirty and six thirty.'

He'd packed his bag and was just about to leave

when he handed O'Neill a plastic envelope.

'She did you a favour. Forensic should have a field day.'

O'Neill held the evidence to the light. Several strands of black hair lay curled under the plastic.

'All the saints be praised,' he murmured. Then turning to Fran he said: 'We'll be away back to Fowchester as soon as the SOC boys arrive. By tonight we could have him in custody.'

'Don't forget the rubbish bin, boss, we were going to check that.'

'Are you wanting to get your hands dirty? Have you seen the size of the bins? We'll let SOC do that, they actually enjoy that sort of thing.'

On the drive back to Fowchester O'Neill insisted they stop frequently and at each stop he managed to have a drink. Fran got the impression he was celebrating in advance. She drove as fast as she dared to compensate for time lost. O'Neill became increasingly morose as the drink took effect and Frán knew that with each drink and the hours that passed their murderer had more than enough time to either make his escape or plan his lies. And if he escaped she would blame O'Neill. Oh yes, she would definitely blame him. But would she shop him?

Chapter Twenty-Six

Their return to the incident room the next day was greeted with the news that the hair found on Frank Melksham's arm had come from a collie dog and that Andy was sticking to his story that he and only he had been involved in Frank's death. He had admitted to borrowing a car and said he cut up the body in the hospital morgue, he had access to the key and complete privacy. He remained unwilling to go into any more detail.

'It's a pack of lies,' said O'Neill tersely.

Fran noticed that Pete recoiled a little from the still present whisky fumes on O'Neill's breath. She might have thought of shopping him but she certainly wasn't going to let anyone else do it.

'There's been another murder,' she said swiftly, to turn Pete's sense of smell to more abstract thoughts, 'but the chief inspector has the perpetrator clearly in his sights.'

O'Neill looked at her sharply. 'Yes, that's right,' he said. 'I want Wendy Theodolou and her husband brought to the station for questioning but I don't want them to know why.'

Pete, obviously puzzled, nodded. 'Right away, Chief.'

At the station O'Neill and Fran waited in the interview room.

'I don't want Wendy to know her sister is dead yet, and no doubt Theodolou will have an alibi, but we do have this—' From his trouser pocket he brought out the strands of hair neatly encased in see-through plastic.

'Boss! Forensic should have that. That's vital evidence you've stolen.'

'Don't be taking the high moral tone with me, Fran, I only filched a few strands so that if my interviewing techniques fail I have that to fall back on. We'll be having him in custody by tonight.'

Fran shrugged. 'You seem sure he's done it, but why? What possible motive could he have?'

'We'll soon be finding out, you and I.' O'Neill turned away from her then to take another swig from his hip flask.

'Please, Connor – don't,' said Fran gently. 'Alcohol won't help.'

'You'd know that, would you?'

'You'll ruin your career.'

'Sometimes that seems like a grand idea.'

'You don't mean that.'

'I bloody do.'

Minutes later Wendy was led into the interview room by a police constable – she was alone.

'Mrs Theodolou, good of you to come,' said O'Neill, shaking her by the hand as if he were at a school parents' evening. 'It was really your husband I wanted to see. Do sit down.'

Wendy eyed the straight-backed chair and the table warily as if by sitting down she might not be allowed to leave. She seemed slightly breathless as if she had been running and for a moment she paused and breathed deeply, then, tugging her cream linen skirt beneath her so that it didn't crease, she sat down and said, 'What's all this about, Chief Inspector? Have you found my sister?'

'We'll talk about that presently, Mrs Theodolou. As I said, it was really your husband I wanted to see.'

'He's gone to London. He won't be back till this evening.'

'I see. What train did he catch?'

'He went by car.'

'What time did he leave?'

'Nineish. What is this all about?'

'What about yesterday? What time did he leave yesterday morning?'

Wendy frowned slightly as if trying to remember. 'I was half asleep when he left. We'd gone to bed very late that night, I was rather tired.'

'So you went to bed when?'

'About two, we'd watched a video. Does it matter?'

'Your husband was in bed all night?'

'Or course he was. This is ridiculous. Where else would he be?'

'We're just making routine enquiries, Mrs Theodolou. So you were not aware that your husband left the bedroom the night before last?'

Wendy frowned in puzzlement. 'Why would he go out?'

'Did you sleep soundly?'

'Yes. . . I. . . I take sleeping pills. So I did sleep soundly.'

'You wouldn't perhaps have been aware then that he had left your bed. It is a double bed?'

'A double bed!' repeated Wendy. 'Yes! What difference does that make? We went to bed that night, in our double bed. There really isn't anything more I can tell you. What on earth is he supposed to have done?'

O'Neill smiled soothingly. 'I knew you'd be a grand help.'

Wendy relaxed back into her chair, smiled, and obviously thought the interview was over. 'It's all right if I go now, then?'

'In just a few minutes. Only one or two more questions.'

'About that poor woman?'

'That's it,' said O'Neill. 'What can you tell me about her?'

'Nothing. . . I never met her. I didn't know her at all.'

'I see,' said O'Neill slowly. 'Tell me what your sister said about her.'

Wendy paused and rested her hand on her face.

'I suppose there's no harm in you knowing. Trudi told me that after she'd been there a couple of days they had a chat late into the night and Carol Sykes told her the story of her life, of how she became a prostitute and how she had a young daughter and had brought her up on her own. They got on really well.'

'Were you jealous?'

'What of?'

'Of their friendship?'

Wendy tried to smile as if she thought the question ridiculous.

'No, of course not.'

'Really?' said O'Neill, raising one eyebrow in disbelief. He continued to stare at her.

'Oh, if you must know, I was a bit jealous and annoyed. Trudi was full of her, how much fun she was, how interesting, how resourceful. . .'

'And now she's dead?'

'I didn't do it, if that's what you're implying.'

'But you're not sorry she's dead?'

Wendy hung her head as if in shame and then looked O'Neill straight in the face. 'I wasn't heartbroken – but then I didn't know her, did I? I was shocked, though. Murder isn't something you expect in a place like this, is it?'

'Did you tell Chris how you felt?'

'No, why should I?'

'But you told him that Carol Sykes was a prostitute?'

'Well, there was no harm in that was there? I mean, we don't really have that much to talk about, do we? He has his wine and I only have the house.'

'Ah yes,' said O'Neill, 'the wine. We found two bottles of Bulgarian red at Last Chance Farm. Was that a present from your husband?'

Wendy shrugged. 'I'm not sure. He did take her his

new varieties but she did buy wine as well. After all, Bulgarian red is sold in supermarkets and shops all over the place.'

'With a black swan motif?'

There was no reply.

'What motif does your husband's Bulgarian red sport?'

'I don't know, Chief Inspector. I really don't know.'

'He doesn't bring any home, then?'

'We drink a good quality white. I never drink red.'

'But your sister drank red?'

'Yes. . . what do you mean? Drank? Why are you using the past tense? Why?'

O'Neill realized he had made a mistake. There was no avoiding telling her now.

'I'm sorry to have to tell you this, Mrs Theodolou, but in the early hours of yesterday morning your sister was found dead. . . murdered.'

There was an agonizing silence whilst she tried to take in the news. The colour had drained from her face but eventually she said in a hoarse whisper, 'No, that can't be right, it can't be. I spoke to her on the telephone. We were going to collect her. . . she would have been safe with us. . . she—'

Wendy broke off in a choking sob and O'Neill stood up and put his arms around her.

'Fran – get a WPC in here and inform her GP she'll need a home visit.'

Wendy Theodolou continued to sob but occasionally she looked up and said, 'It can't be true. . . it can't be true.'

As the WPC arrived O'Neill said, 'Just one more question, but I have to ask.'

Wendy looked up at him with tears flowing unchecked down her face.

'Who did you tell, Mrs Theodolou? Who did you tell your sister was staying at the Marigold?'

She didn't have to answer. The doubt was there in her eyes.

O'Neill disappeared then until nearly lunchtime and much to Fran's relief he didn't appear to have had any more to drink. Fran's other worry she had to voice. 'She could tell him, boss, ring him up and warn him not to come home.'

'Would you if it had been your sister?'

Fran shook her head. 'I wouldn't but some would. I've got a sister but she's in Canada, I haven't seen her for years.'

'Any other family?'

'My dad, he lives in Devon. I see him once or twice a year. My mum died and Dad remarried. He's very happy.'

'Don't you like his new wife?' asked O'Neill noticing Fran's expression.

'It's not that I don't like her exactly, it's just that. . . she's the image of my mother. I just can't bear to see them together. Sometimes I catch the back view of her and I think it's Mum, then she turns and I feel so disappointed. Even her voice is similar but it's not her and I resent her for it.'

O'Neill didn't quite know what to say. There was

nothing to say. Instead he changed the subject.

'Before we see Theodolou let's go and see Keith Quinton. Don't forget we've still got Frank's murder to sort out.'

'It wasn't murder, though, was it?'

'I'm not sure and I've got a gut feeling we never will be sure. We can try, though.'

It was four when they arrived at the Quinton veterinary practice. The waiting room was already half full: a fearful dog salivated and cowered in one corner, a small boy sat clutching his rabbit next to two owners carefully guarding their cats in cardboard boxes. The receptionist with a badge that said Tracy showed them through to the surgery. Keith had just finished giving a mongrel dog an injection. He turned in surprise as they entered.

'I won't keep you,' he said.

The dog slunk away from the table, tail between his legs as if expecting another attack from the rear, and its owner, a middle-aged man, breathed an obvious sigh of relief. 'Whew, I'm glad that's over.'

Keith showed dog and owner out and then returned saying, 'Male dog owners are the worst, show them a needle, the dog hardly minds a bit but their owners sometimes pass out. Women never do. Strange that. It's the same when you have to put dogs down, it's nearly always the women who bring the animal and stay with them until the end.'

'This is just a routine visit, Mr Quinton,' said O'Neill. 'A few simple questions about. . . recent events.'

'Call me Keith, everyone does.'

'Keith, it is,' said O'Neill. 'I've been wondering about how well you knew Mrs Miller?'

A look of surprise crossed Keith's good-natured face.

'Mrs Miller?'

'Mrs Trudi Miller,' repeated O'Neill.

'I didn't know her well at all. I did meet her because of her sister. Last Christmas the Theodolous invited me for Christmas dinner, she was there. Nice woman.'

'So you know the Theodolous?'

'I've known them for some time. Chris supplies my wine.'

'Red Bulgarian?'

'That was the last batch, it wasn't bad at the price.'

'Did you ever take Mrs Miller any wine?'

'No,' replied Keith. 'Why should I?'

'What about Sandra Melksham? Now you were friendly with her.'

'I was before Steve came along.'

'I'm surprised you could bring yourself to play darts with him. After all he stole your woman.'

Keith didn't blink. 'I don't hold grudges. Anyway Steve is a good bloke, likes a drink, throws a mean dart. Sandra made her choice and who can blame her? A young buck instead of a jaded old vet – no contest, was there?'

'What about Andy?' he asked Keith sharply. So sharply that he said softly, 'Did I step on a raw spot there, Keith?'

'I'm fond of Andy. . . I think he's had a rough deal in life.'

'You want to protect him?'

Keith smiled as if seeing the trap ahead.

'I've always liked him. He's a good lad.'

'Not the sort to manage any post-mortem surgery though, is he?'

Keith didn't answer.

'He'll cop for it, you know. He said he killed his dad. With no witnesses and his confession he could well go down for murder in the first degree.'

'That's nonsense,' Keith blustered. 'It wasn't murder, it was self-defence.'

'And how could you be sure of that?'

'It's what I've heard,' said Keith, 'it's only what I've heard.'

'Ah, to be sure. We'll be going now, Keith, but perhaps you'll be interested to hear the forensic report.'

'Of course,' said Keith.

'Frank Melksham's arm showed traces of flea powder – Nuvan Top to be exact, the same stuff you sell here, and more to the point a single dog hair. I'm surprised there weren't more dog hairs considering this place must be full of them. Still, a single hair from your dog on a two-year-old arm must be pretty conclusive forensic evidence. Where did you chop him up, Keith? In the surgery? And more to point why?'

Keith's face suffused with colour like an adolescent girl but he stayed silent.

'Think about it, Keith. Come into the station tomorrow and make a statement. After all, you did want to protect Andy then, and I hope you'll get him off the hook now. Think about it. He's in line for other kill-ings as well.'

'What are you talking about?'

'The two women. Carol Sykes and Trudi Miller. Both dead now. Andy may have got a taste for murder. Think about it, Keith. Carefully.'

Chapter Twenty-Seven

Later that afternoon Superintendent Ringstead phoned from his sick bed. He shouted rather than spoke and Fran could hear every word of their conversation.

'Come on, O'Neill, I want some results. . . not next week or next month but bloody soon. It can't be that difficult! A town this size, how many murderers can we have here? The one in Wales has really put us in shit. What must they think of us? Is it too much to hope that you have a suspect?'

'That's not too much at all, sir. We do have a surplus of suspects, but I hope to have someone in custody very soon.'

'Who, exactly?'

'Christopher Theodolou for the murder of Carol Sykes and Trudi Miller. . .'

'Oh, Christ!'

'What's the problem, sir?'

'O'Neill, the man is a Mason. He also supplies wine to all police functions and to the chief constable personally.'

'I don't care if he's the Ancient Mariner, sir. He's guilty and forensic will prove it.'

'I hope you're right, O'Neill. If you're wrong they'll get rid of you. You must have your reasons, but just make sure the evidence is cast-iron.'

'Absolutely, sir. Sure to goodness I will.'

'Are you being funny, O'Neill?'

'No, sir, perish the thought.'

'How's that DS of yours getting on?'

'She's a real treasure, sir, a real treasure.'

'I hope you're not laying her.'

'Not yet, sir.'

'Watch yourself, O'Neill, she'll report you.'

O'Neill put the phone down and glanced at Fran who smiled back, mischievously, he thought.

'You heard all that?' he asked.

'Probably the whole of Fowchester heard it. You couldn't be wrong about Theodolou, could you? I mean he hasn't got a record or anything and I can't see that he had motive, whereas Steve, he's a real opportunist.'

'I'm right. He did it and it's true I don't know why, but he did it.'

O'Neill paused for a moment to rearrange papers on his desk when there was a knock at the door. A uniformed police constable opened it and said: 'There's a Keith Quinton to see you, sir, says it's important.'

'Send him up, Constable.'

O'Neill couldn't help a faint smile of victory.

Quinton came straight to the point. 'I want to make

a statement,' he said, 'for Andy's sake.'

'Take a seat, Keith. Tea? Coffee?'

Keith shook his head.

'DS Wilson will take down your statement. Start when you're ready.'

It was brief and to the point.

'On the night of November the twenty-third I left the Plough pub at Clopstock a few minutes before closing time. At the back of the pub in the car park I found Frank Melksham attacking Andy Melksham. Andy was on the ground. I pulled Frank away but he struggled free and then Andy was on his feet again and managed to punch Frank quite hard on the jaw. One blow felled Frank. He didn't get up again. Andy was breathless and a bit dazed. I still expected Frank to come round. I felt his pulse, listened to his heartbeat – there was nothing. There was no sign of a head injury. Someone took Andy home, I can't remember who, and then someone else (I can't remember who) helped me lift Frank's body into the back of the Land-Rover. I dismembered the body at my surgery. I did that to protect Andy and Sandra from a court case. It had been an accident. I was wrong to have disposed of the body that way but it seemed my best option at the time.'

'Well, thank you, Keith,' said O'Neill. 'I think that's the biggest load of crap I've heard in a long time.'

Keith was definitely taken aback.

'I didn't have to come here,' he said. 'It was an accident. Andy acted in self-defence. There's no reason he should carry the can for everything.'

'I agree,' said O'Neill. 'And your story might have been accepted but for the fact that another severed limb had been deposited in the area.'

'That was nothing to do with us,' protested Keith. 'That was a coincidence.'

'High odds for a coincidence. I'd call it a copy-cat killing.'

'That was murder. I'm telling you this was an accident, manslaughter at worst.'

'You're trying to tell me, Keith, that no one put the boot in while he was lying unconscious on the ground?'

'He was dead. He was clinically dead. His pupils were dilated, there was no respiration, no pulse. He was a goner.'

'Right,' said O'Neill. 'We'll be accepting that for now. You say he was dead. Did anyone else feel his pulse?'

'There wasn't anyone else there. I am a vet, I do know a stiff when I see one.'

'So how did you lift him into the back of the Land-Rover?'

'I dragged his body, it was a struggle but I managed.'

'And you took it out again at your surgery?'

'Yes.'

'Were you breathless?'

'A bit.'

'I ask that,' said O'Neill, 'because of your girth. To get to this office you walked up only one flight of stairs and yet I could hear your breathing becoming more laboured than normal. Dealing with a corpse is no easy matter but of course if you had help – witnesses – they could verify Andy's story and yours.'

Keith shrugged but stayed silent.

'I'd be grateful if you would stay in the station for a while to think on things. The more witnesses the better for both of you. You'll be doing that, will you?'

Keith nodded miserably. He knew he had no choice. He also knew that eventually they would all be dragged in. Just the two of them made it sound – planned. And if anyone found out that Andy could possibly have been his son it was all the more reason to believe that Frank's murder was deliberate. All the more reason to believe the hand that chopped up Frank might have also chopped off the woman's arm.

'I'll think about it,' he said.

'You be doing that, Mr Quinton,' said O'Neill, 'and get the others to think about it too.'

After Quinton had gone Fran asked, 'What do we do now, boss?'

O'Neill gestured at the window with his thumb.

'Jump?' asked Fran in mock surprise.

'Very funny, Wilson. I meant that we should spend time staring out of the window.'

O'Neill pulled his office chair to the window. 'Be fetching yours then, Fran.'

Fran dragged her chair closer to the window and for a while they both stared at the traffic going by and the pedestrians with shopping bags and determined expressions. It was O'Neill who broke the silence.

'Imagine the scenario,' he said. 'Carol Sykes is in the house alone, tidying up. Let's be saying it's daytime.

Someone knocks on the door. What does she do?'

'If Sue was right she wouldn't have answered the door.'

'True, but what if Trudi were there and she said, "That's my brother-in-law, you answer the door and I'll slip out the back"?'

'Why would she do that?'

O'Neill shrugged and continued to stare at the High Street.

'Maybe she just didn't like him.'

'That's possible,' agreed Fran, 'but what if Carol was alone in the house?'

'In that case she would have told Carol that he might call.'

'Why would he call?'

'To deliver the wine. You see, Wilson, I think he called, probably in the afternoon. Carol let him in, after all quite a few people would open the door to a chubby Greek brother-in-law bearing gifts, even some-one as wary as Carol. She thanked him and put the wine in the fridge.'

'Yes? But I don't understand the point you're making, boss.'

'The point I'm making is that red wine isn't usually refrigerated. Somewhere in that house there will be a wine rack, maybe in the cellar. We'll check the photos.'

Fran stared at O'Neill in amazement. 'You can't mean you think his motive for killing her was simply because she put his red plonk in the fridge?'

O'Neill smiled. 'No, but I've known some very

weird causes for murder. Detectives are taught to look for *motives*. The word itself suggests something logical, a justification, a rationale. As though murderers had a choice.'

'But they do, surely?'

'I'm not sure they do have a choice. Choice implies freedom. I view murderers in two ways – I call them impulsive or compulsive. The impulsive have no choice, they react instinctively to stress or jealousy or fear. The man who batters his wife is practising for murder. He's looking not only for silence from the spoken word but even from the reproving glance. Death is the ultimate domination.'

'What about the. . . compulsive?'

'They include serial killers, child molesters, shotgun bank robbers, insurance murderers, that sort of thing. They don't have a choice either, their compulsion is so strong, for money, or power or sex, or simply the need to answer the voices in their heads. Forced into a corner, the only answer they have, the only resource at their disposal, is murder.'

'You think Theodolou then was one of the. . . impulsive?'

'A bit of both, probably. But I don't think the wine triggered him.'

A little later Fran collected coffee and sandwiches from the canteen. O'Neill still sat by the window.

'I thought of something, boss, while I was standing in the queue for these.'

O'Neill turned, glanced at the steaming coffee, and smiled. 'Come on, make my day twice over.'

'It's Trudi Miller. Where was she while Carol was being murdered? We haven't established that, have we? If she was going away then she either went to buy clothes or to the bank, or maybe she had an appointment somewhere.'

'By all the saints, Fran Wilson, you may not only have made my day you may have also saved my career. Because I think I know where she went that afternoon. Eat up and we'll be away, and later we go to the Theodolous'.'

Chapter Twenty-Eight

The town of Ilet in Lincolnshire seemed to Fran to be a relic of her childhood, the sort of place her mother had talked about, where women still shopped with baskets at the market and where the highlight of the day was discussing how well your tomato plants were doing.

The shops surrounded the market place itself. There was a baker's, a butcher's, a greengrocer's, one or two general stores, a shoe shop, and a couple of boutiques that were obviously expensive because no nasty common price tags were in evidence. There was also a travel agent's and a bank.

At the travel agent's O'Neill stopped. 'This is it,' he said. 'Let's hope I'm right.'

A young woman in a red suit, white blouse, and blue neckerchief sat in front of a desk-top computer. Her name badge read Tina Nelson and she worked busily on the keyboard with no other customers in sight but surrounded by posters of happy holidaymakers.

'Good afternoon,' she said cheerfully. 'Welcome to

Paradise Travel Agents, where only the best is good enough.'

'Good afternoon,' said O'Neill with a smile. 'Police. Fowchester. Where our best is never good enough.'

She smiled uncertainly. 'What can I do for you?'

'I'd be appreciating your help. Recently, I believe, you may have had enquiries about a holiday in Provence from a woman named Trudi Miller. I wonder if you'd be good enough to give me any information you can.'

Tina Nelson looked mystified for a moment.

'Do you have an address, Inspector?'

'I do indeed. Last Chance Farm.'

'Of course.' Tina smiled. 'I remember. You don't forget somewhere called Last Chance, do you? She came in a few weeks back, booked a flight to France and a two-week holiday in Brittany. . .'

'Not Provence?'

'I'll check on the computer but I'm sure it was Brittany.'

It took a short time and after staring at the screen Tina reported, 'Yes, I was right. Brittany.'

'When was she due to go?'

'End of May. She said she wanted some good weather because she was house hunting.'

O'Neill raised his eyebrows at Fran as if to say – what next?

Tina looked thoughtful. 'Bit strange really that I should have forgotten her name but I know why I did now, she came in with a chap and I expected her to have a different name – '

'Could you be explaining that?' interrupted O'Neill.

Tina smiled. 'Well, you see, she came in with this little fat Greek man and I assumed at first he was her husband and that she'd have a Greek name.'

'You mean they were going together?' asked Fran, unable to keep quiet any longer.

'Yes. It seemed like that – the booking was for two. Mind you, they didn't make it, did they?'

'What do you mean?' asked O'Neill.

Tina frowned. 'She cancelled three weeks ago. Lost her deposit, said she'd changed her mind and she'd been impetuous.'

'You're sure it was her?' asked O'Neill.

'Positive. She came in person. It was during the afternoon, she said she was going to have a holiday in this country instead. I asked if she minded losing the deposit money. She laughed and said she'd decided, on the spur of the moment, to go on holiday with a girlfriend. She seemed a bit nervous – she's not in any trouble, is she?'

'None at all now,' said O'Neill. 'Thanks a million for your help.'

'Any time,' said Tina smiling flirtatiously at O'Neill, 'I'm always happy to help the police.'

O'Neill was jubilant as they drove away.

'We've got him, Fran, we've got him, the two-timing bastard.'

'Unless he's done a runner.'

'No, he'll turn up. He thinks he's got an alibi for Trudi and he thinks he doesn't need one for Carol.'

'Why did he kill them both, Connor?'

'We'll be finding out soon enough, Fran, and afterwards I'll take you for a slap-up meal to celebrate.'

Fran smiled wanly. If she had been Theodolou she'd have been on the first plane out of the country.

It was dark as they approached the Theodolous' house. The BMW was parked at the front and O'Neill couldn't help feeling a sense of satisfaction that he had been right.

Christopher himself answered the door.

'Chief Inspector,' he said, 'this isn't, I'm afraid, a very good time. My wife is extremely upset, as you can imagine.'

Again, Fran noticed the sexiness of his voice but now it seemed to have creepy overtones. Especially now that she guessed what he'd been up to.

'It's you we've come to see, Mr Theodolou.'

'Fine. Do come in.'

As they followed Theodolou into the hall he turned and said in a hushed voice that was almost a whisper, 'My wife's lying down, she's had some awful shocks, hasn't she? It's just terrible, there really isn't anywhere safe, is there?'

'I don't know,' said O'Neill. 'Brittany's got a low crime rate.'

Theodolou didn't respond, he merely said: 'Do you mind if we talk in the conservatory? I really don't want my wife disturbed.'

'That's fine,' said O'Neill. 'We'll not be keeping you long.'

The conservatory was warm, lit by lamps that looked

like plants and surrounded by plants that looked as exotic and expensive as the lamps. They sat at a wicker table and Theodolou sat on a wicker chair that had a high domed back, the highest back – thronelike. Fran wondered if he thought that gave him an advantage.

'How can I help you?' asked Theodolou calmly.

'Just a few routine questions for our paperwork,' replied O'Neill, reassuringly soft-voiced. 'Mostly to do with your sister-in-law Trudi.'

'Fire away,' said Theodolou.

Fran marvelled at O'Neill's restraint. There was no doubt his suspect felt as safe as a wine merchant in a wine cellar, maybe even safer.

'How often did you see your sister-in-law, Mr Theodolou?'

He looked thoughtful for a moment. 'About twice a month on average, sometimes more. She comes – *came* every fortnight for Sunday lunch, we invited her every Sunday but she often preferred to be on her own.'

'And did you meet Carol Sykes?'

'No, I didn't. My wife told me about her, though, she told me she was. . .'

'A prostitute.'

'Yes. And I have to admit I didn't approve. In fact I told my wife I'd rather she didn't meet her.'

O'Neill stared at him thoughtfully for a moment and then said casually, 'I'm surprised you didn't see her on the day you delivered the wine.'

Again there was no awkwardness or hesitation in his answer.

'I knocked very loudly but they were both out. That was a Wednesday. I left the wine on the doorstep.'

'Yes,' said O'Neill, 'that was the day Trudi cancelled her holiday with you in Brittany.'

'With me?' asked Theodolou in seemingly genuine surprise. Then he laughed. 'You've been to the travel agent's to see Miss Nelson. The trip to Brittany was to have been with Wendy. We were keeping it a surprise. I was going to change the name on the ticket at the last minute – but it was really only a vague hope that she would go: you see Wendy doesn't leave the house. That's not quite true, sometimes she can be persuaded to go out in the BMW if I pull the blinds down. She has panic attacks, you see, has done since she had her miscarriages. One thing she doesn't like is for people to know about her fear of the outside. She tries to act as if the problem doesn't exist.'

'It exists for you, Mr Theodolou. It must affect your life.'

He shrugged then. 'It does, if I'm honest. But I cope.'

'Tell me how you cope.'

Just for a moment there was doubt and hesitation on Theodolou's face but just as quickly it vanished. 'I have my career, which is very successful, I'm a Freemason, and I do work for charity. I keep very busy.'

'And your wife?'

'She has her hobbies, needlework, patchwork, jigsaws. She's a very good cook.'

O'Neill paused. Something was wrong here, very

wrong. Theodolou seemed too composed, too at ease. And yet he was guilty, of that O'Neill had no doubt. He would have to try a different tack.

'On Wednesday, two weeks ago, when you delivered the wine, why didn't you take it into the kitchen via the back door? I'm sure that in the house there is a wine rack.'

'There is,' he said, 'in the cellar. I do know where Trudi kept her spare key but it didn't seem worth the bother, not for two bottles of Bulgarian red, though I can assure you it's a wine that is worth more than it costs.'

'Did you take any wine to the Marigold Guest House?'

Theodolou smiled and Fran felt her heart go out to O'Neill, because she knew that evil little smile was completely fearless.

'Chief Inspector, what possible motive could I have for killing my sister-in-law?'

'Let's forget the motive angle, Mr Theodolou, and concentrate on what you actually did.'

Fran noticed now that O'Neill's voice had a crisper edge now as if he were approaching some sort of conclusion.

'That night,' said Theodolou, just as crisply, 'I was at home in bed with my wife. She has already verified that.'

'Indeed she has, sir, indeed she has. However, a trip to Wales would take an hour and a half to two hours, that's all. How long did she take to die – two minutes, five minutes – longer?'

Again the bastard smiled. O'Neill felt his hand forming a fist. Dear God he wanted to hit him.

'I repeat. I did not leave my bed all night.'

At last O'Neill felt he could play his trump card. Before he lost his temper.

'How was it then, sir,' he said, 'that a handful of your hair was found tightly clenched in your victim's hand?'

Theodolou didn't even blink, he stared for a moment at O'Neill.

'I'm surprised at you, Chief Inspector, really surprised. I thought you were an honourable man, not the sort to plant evidence. There is absolutely no way my hair could have been in Trudi's hand. I wasn't there, you see – and I wear a wig. A synthetic wig, not human hair at all.'

Chapter Twenty-Nine

'A bloody wig,' O'Neill said, and then repeated: 'A bloody wig! Why didn't you notice that, Wilson?'

'It's the best wig I've ever seen. No give-away hair line and somehow that oily sheen made it look more natural.'

'Now what? That bewigged self-satisfied smug bastard isn't going to get the better of me.'

'Of course not, boss. Shall I ring forensic to see if they have anything yet?'

'You be doing that. I'm going to the pub for a drink.'

O'Neill walked out of the station and strode purposefully in the direction of the Red Lion. There he sat in a corner, lined up a draught Guinness and a double Irish and promised himself that at the end of his pint and before his chaser he would know exactly what to do next.

He drank slowly, his speed of thought even slower. What, he asked himself, was the difference between the death of Carol Sykes and Trudi Miller? One was strangled, one was bludgeoned. Carol lost an arm.

Why the hell did he do that? OK then, what was the difference between the death of Frank Melksham and the two women? Answer – two years. Two years and ice-crystal artefacts. Ice-crystal artefacts! Of course. Christopher Theodolou would have assumed, as they had, that Frank's arm was fresh and that no one would find out it had been frozen – except that he couldn't have known about the ice crystals. He'd found out about the disposal of Frank's arm and decided to muddy the waters. And how did he find out? His wife told him. She couldn't keep a secret. And that being so, she was the weak link. His Achilles' heel. A Greek name for a Greek's weak spot. Theodolou was a dangerous man, not only an impulse killer but a compulsive one. He may not have planned to kill Carol Sykes but he sure as hell planned to kill Trudi. *Why*, would have to wait.

He drank the chaser quickly, appreciating the fire in his belly and the fact that alcohol could so quickly turn dejection into resolve.

Back at the station Fran greeted him with a happy smile.

'Forensic have come up with something boss. The hair—'

'Yes?' interrupted O'Neill eagerly.

Fran's smile faded. 'Well, it's not so much good news as odd news.'

'Be telling me, Wilson.'

'Forensic have done tests on the hair and they say the hair wasn't from the attacker, it was the victim's own hair. . .'

'You mean she pulled it out in her death throes?'

'No, she didn't pull it out at all. It was cut hair. The murderer cut her hair and put it in her hand.'

'Jasus! It gets worse. I don't know what you can find to smile about.'

'It's gone now, boss.'

'Good.'

'There's more news.'

'I hope it's better than the last lot.'

'A bit. They think she was killed with a blunt instrument – a cricket bat, baseball bat, or something similar.'

O'Neill shrugged, wishing he'd had two resolve-hardening chasers instead of one.

'This is it, Fran. I'm going to get them both in tomorrow and after that I'm going to get a warrant to search that house.'

'Is it wise to bring Wendy in, especially now we know she's agoraphobic?'

'She came in before, didn't she? Her degree of the condition must be fairly mild. He's probably encouraged it.'

'Well, she won't feel very safe, will she, if she's had to come here in a police car?'

O'Neill put an arm round Fran's shoulder. 'I'm getting to the point, Fran, when I don't care if they are scared shitless as long as I get a result. You interview Wendy, I'll interview him. Do it by the book. Tape it and half-way through I'll send for you to bring her in.'

'Good luck, Connor,' said Fran, experiencing a sudden and rather unnerving feeling of tenderness for him.

'Good luck yourself.'

O'Neill sensed the interview was going badly from the start. And he knew why. His antagonism towards Theodolou kept getting in the way. But there was no shaking his suspect. It was as if Theodolou really believed he was innocent. Each time he asked a question Theodolou answered with the same implacable calm.

At one point Theodolou began to get the upper hand. *He* began to ask the questions.

'Why me, Chief Inspector? My sister-in-law was an attractive woman, she must have had men friends that neither you or I know about – yet. I can only assume you have taken a dislike to me and therefore, with no evidence, other than I knew where she kept her spare key, you think I killed her. Several people could have known that.'

'Would you be implying your sister-in-law was promiscuous?'

'Not at all. I'm just saying you are wasting your time with me.'

'Fair enough, sir. Let's be talking about something else. Your baldness for instance.'

Theodolou's face showed the first sign of surprise and discomfiture.

'Since when has having a wig been a crime?'

'Your wig is anything but a crime, sir, it's a work

of art. It must have been very expensive.'

Between tight lips Theodolou said, 'It was, very. I had it made in the States – it cost the equivalent of three thousand pounds.'

'What about replacements?'

Theodolou frowned angrily. 'It should last me a lifetime at that price. You just have to take care of it. I use a good quality hair oil that I have specially flown over from Greece.'

'Do you indeed?' O'Neill couldn't keep the satisfaction from his voice and Theodolou noticed and began to bluster.

'This is ridiculous, Chief Inspector. I came here today to give you as much help as I could but you seem to be going round in circles and talking so much crap. If you want to keep me here any longer asking me rubbish questions then I think I should ring my solicitor.'

'That's a good idea. I'll have the portable phone brought to you.'

O'Neill glanced at his watch. 'Interview with Mr Christopher Theodolou interrupted at three p.m. to enable him to phone his solicitor.' Abruptly O'Neill stood up. 'Do excuse me. I'll be fetching the phone.'

From his office O'Neill phoned Superintendent Ringstead asking for a search warrant.

'You're sure it's him?' shouted Ringstead down the phone.

'Sure I'm sure.'

'Pity,' said Ringstead. 'He sold some bloody good wine.'

Further along the corridor in the second interview room Fran had settled Wendy in quite nicely, or so she thought. Mrs Theodolou had arrived wan and breathless but now she was composed and seemed ready to talk, especially about her 'problem'.

'It's walking I have a problem with, you see. Everything seems so dangerous on the outside. Chris says I shouldn't watch the news or crime stories but it's all true, isn't it? Everything I dreaded has happened. My babies died, my parents are dead, now my sister. I was lying in bed yesterday and I even thought we might have been burgled. I mean you hear about people being burgled while they're watching television, don't you?'

'Was something missing?' asked Fran.

'Well, I thought there was, but then Chris told me this morning he had put it in the loft for safe keeping. Very sensible of him really.'

'And what was it?'

'Oh, it was a sort of trophy, a prize from some wine organization. A lovely silver-embossed bottle.'

'Made of glass?'

'No, something solid, it was very heavy.'

'It's in the loft now?'

'Yes, that's right.'

Fran smiled reassuringly. 'Would you mind talking about your sister now?'

'Not at all,' said Wendy. 'I'd like to talk about her.'

'How well did the three of you get on together?'

'Very well. Trudi used to come over every other Sunday and after lunch Chris would disappear somewhere and we'd have a good gossip and a chat. It was the highlight of my week and of course we'd talk on the phone nearly every day.'

'But you didn't know of her plans for Brittany?'

'Oh yes, I knew about that, but only after she booked it. Anyway, we had a terrible row. Chris wanted me to go, thought it would do me good. I just couldn't face it. I was glad in a way that Carol Sykes had agreed to have a holiday with my sister. Carol didn't want to go abroad so I knew they were planning to go away but I didn't know when.'

Fran said gently, 'This is something else you didn't tell us. Is there a reason you didn't?'

Wendy shrugged. 'I don't want people to know how weak and stupid I can be. Anyway it wasn't important – was it? Chris was angry with me for wasting his money but holidays abroad aren't something you plan as a surprise for a person with my sort of. . . problem.'

'Were you jealous that Trudi planned to go away with Carol?'

Wendy looked away for a moment, stared at the bare far wall and then said reluctantly, 'I *was* jealous, I suppose. When you're afraid to go out people are sympathetic at first but they get tired of it and then they get irritated.'

'Did your sister get irritated with you?'

'Oh no, she was very kind, very understanding—' Wendy's voice broke off in a sob. 'I'm sorry. I still can't believe she's dead.'

'We can have a break if you'd like.'

'No. I'd rather get it over and done with.'

Fran waited a few moments while Wendy composed herself before starting again. After the pause Fran asked, 'How did Chris and Trudi get on?'

'Fine,' said Wendy quietly.

'You don't sound convinced.'

'Of late they argued a bit. My sister didn't really like Chris. I don't know what he did to upset her, but he did. She always felt he encouraged me to stay indoors. I suppose he did in a way and then I just became used to it.'

'There's still something you haven't told me, Wendy. The reason you were worried about your sister. Do you know who killed her? Is that what you really want to tell me?'

There was a long pause before Wendy finally said, 'I do think I might know who killed her. I just wish I had told you before. It might have saved my sister's life but I couldn't see any reason for him to have killed her and I didn't connect it at first with the murder of Carol—' She broke off. 'I told you I was stupid and I am.'

'Tell me now,' said Fran. 'Take your time.'

'His name's Steve. Trudi knew Frank was dead, she found out from his son. She didn't know how he died but I think she was relieved to know he wasn't coming back. Anyway, this man called Steve came to see her at the farm and said there was a way they could prove Frank was dead and maybe they could claim on his life insurance. She didn't tell me any more, just that she was thinking about it. But I know she had a joint bank account and she must have checked that out because then she told me there was no point in Steve doing anything. The policy was null and void – Frank hadn't kept up the payments. And then Frank's arm was found, so that was the proof, wasn't it? Steve must have been upset at the thought of losing all that money so he killed her.'

'Maybe,' murmured Fran as she glanced at her watch. 'Would you like some tea, Wendy?'

'I'd love some.'

'I'll go and fetch it. The police constable will stay with you.'

Fran terminated the taped interview and signalled to the young policeman in the corner of the room behind Wendy, who had sat still as a garden gnome during the interview, to sit in the vacated chair.

'Don't look so worried, love,' he said as he sat down. 'I don't bite, in fact I'm almost comatose. I do my silent witness routine so often I could get work as an artist's model.'

Wendy smiled bleakly. 'I didn't even know you were there,' she said.

As Fran walked along the corridor one of the civilian staff came hurrying out from an office, 'There's a message for your boss, Sergeant Wilson. Urgent from Wales. Forensic.'

Chapter Thirty

O'Neill felt relieved to be out of the interview room. It was hot and stuffy in there and Theodolou's arrogant nonchalance continued to rile him. Fran's appearance came just at the right moment.

He took the call in an empty office. Fran stood near by waiting expectantly for the call to finish. It was a long call and she became impatient. O'Neill put the phone down and at first his face was grim. Then he placed both hands on her waist and lifted her high into the air and laughed at the surprise on her face. As he put her back on the ground he said, 'Those Welsh wizards have done it. We've got a case. We have got a case!'

'How? What's happened?' asked Fran, beginning to catch his mood of elation.

'They pieced together the letter, and missing bits they managed to get from impressions on the pad.'

Fran laughed. 'Come on, Connor – what did it say?'

'It says everything – well almost. It most definitely puts our Greek into the arena. But I'm not going to tell you. He can tell the both of us. I'll just give you a clue. Sex!'

'Ah,' said the still confident Theodolou as Fran entered the interview room behind O'Neill, 'the cavalry has arrived.'

'Let's be cutting the attempts at humour, Theodolou. We have the letter.'

'What letter? I don't know anything about a letter.'

'The letter Trudi Miller wrote just before she was murdered. In it you get more than a mention.'

Theodolou's face reddened. 'There wasn't a letter, I. . .'

'You looked, did you? In her room?'

'I meant that no letter was delivered.'

'Very well. Let's talk, shall we, about your sex life? Trudi seems to have some experience of that, albeit somewhat drunkenly and by all accounts somewhat reluctantly. Is that when your relationship soured? Is that why you had to shut her up?'

'That's not true. You must by now have realized what sort of person my sister-in-law was, she may not have been promiscuous but she did have a penchant for violent men – Frank Melksham for instance. She was desperate and she's lying. I deny it all totally.'

O'Neill turned to Fran. 'Bring in his wife. Mr Theodolou would undoubtedly like to explain his. . . night-time activities. . . to her.'

Theodolou's shoulders crumpled and his lips tightened into a thin line, O'Neill hoped in defeat.

'There really is no need to bring her into this. She's upset as it is. I'll tell you about – London. She'll blame herself, you see, it's not her fault she could no longer be a proper wife to me and it's true – God forgive me

294

– that I do occasionally visit prostitutes in London. But that's not against the law, is it? What else is a man supposed to do when he can't find. . . affection. . . at home? You of all people should understand that.'

O'Neill clenched his hands tightly. He would have enjoyed knocking his rotund body through the window. The bastard knew about his wife and was suggesting that they shared some sort of bond! Before he spoke again he stared at the wall for a few moments imagining how it would sound at confession. Then he said calmly, 'Cut the euphemisms, please. You were simply looking for sex, nothing more, nothing less.'

Theodolou looked across at O'Neill with bleak watery eyes. 'Who knows what I was looking for? I was never sure. But I didn't kill anyone. I'm not a violent man.'

O'Neill leaned towards his suspect, and putting his face close said softly and with no trace of anger, 'Neither am I, Mr Theodolou, but sometimes I can be understanding about the use of rubber truncheons and forced confessions. But I'm a calm man, most of the time. I'm also extremely patient.' Looking up slowly from Theodolou's pudgy face he turned to Fran. 'Be fetching his wife.'

Theodolou and O'Neill waited in silence for Wendy to arrive. Christopher Theodolou's shoulders were not the only part of him to sag now. His bulky body seemed to shrink into his chair.

By the time Wendy arrived even she could see he was in a state.

'What's the matter? You look awful. What's happening, Chris?'

Theodolou gazed mournfully at his wife. 'I'm not saying anything more until my solicitor arrives.'

'But why, Chris?' she asked anxiously. 'What have you got to hide?'

There was silence then, broken by Fran saying, 'Hiding things is a speciality of yours, Mr Theodolou. I've been told that you have just recently hidden away a rather solid blunt instrument in your loft. A silver-plated presentation bottle, to be exact. And I expect that's where we shall find the keys belonging to Trudi Miller's room at the Marigold.'

'Oh, Chris – what's she saying? I don't understand. You couldn't do anything like that – you couldn't!'

'Sit down, Mrs Theodolou,' said O'Neill. 'And be keeping calm. I'm sure your husband can explain.'

Slowly Wendy sat down, her eyes at first on her husband then lowered so that she stared at the table in front.

Theodolou half rose from the chair, and then, changing his mind, sat forward. 'Wendy, there's no need to upset yourself. It's all a mistake, someone must be trying to implicate me. Trudi was just being vindictive. . . she must have been jealous of us. You know how lonely she was.'

Wendy looked up and O'Neill and Fran both recognized the change in her expression. If she ever had any doubts about her husband they were now being confirmed. Theodolou too saw the expression on his wife's face.

'There's no need to look at me like that,' he said. His anxiety became obvious now in the way his voice had become higher and little beads of sweat appeared on his forehead. 'Come on, Wendy, you know I'm not a violent man. Tell them I wouldn't have done it. Tell them!'

Wendy continued to stare at him as though going through a checklist of all that had happened. She remained silent. Eventually she said with utmost calm, 'I think you had better tell the truth now, Chris. It's time.'

'I didn't—' he began. Then, lowering his head on to his hands, he said, 'I didn't kill her. But. . . I did spend the night with her some time ago. We were both drunk – I didn't plan it or anything, it just happened. Afterwards we . . . weren't friends any more. I did want to tell you but what good would it do you to know?'

'Look at me, Chris. Look at me.'

His sharp brown eyes flicked up to her face.

'Do you really think I'm that stupid? I knew all along. Trudi didn't tell me, I just guessed. I didn't even mind. I used to fantasize about what might happen. I used to dream that she would get pregnant and give me the baby. Silly, wasn't it. Then when I began finding condoms I thought you might be having an affair with someone else—'

'I wasn't,' interrupted Chris. 'I. . . I was going to prostitutes. I couldn't help myself. . . I couldn't help myself, Wendy. I do love you.'

His head sagged again but this time Wendy moved

across to him and put an arm round her husband. For a moment all was silent in the room then Theodolou began to sob. Not loudly, a dry, choking, masculine sob.

O'Neill watched Theodolou carefully. And he knew then he was watching an innocent man. A lonely man who had betrayed his wife but nothing more.

'We'll leave you alone for a few minutes,' said O'Neill. 'There are still questions to be asked.'

Outside in the corridor O'Neill braced his back against the wall and turned to Fran.

'What a cock-up! We're back to square one.'

'No, we're not,' said Fran. 'We're another step forward. Theodolou has just been eliminated from our enquiries. The Super will be delighted.'

'That's one way of looking at it, I suppose. What next, though?'

Fran shrugged. 'More statements?'

O'Neill shook his head. 'No. We're going back to Last Chance Farm. After I've asked Wendy one or two more questions.'

On their return to the interview room Christopher appeared much calmer and Wendy managed a wry but nervous smile.

'Mrs Theodolou,' said O'Neill as he sat down opposite her. 'I have one important question to ask you and I want you to think very carefully about it. Take your time in answering but I'll be trusting you now to be completely truthful with us.'

'I have been, Chief Inspector. I have been.'

'Sure you have. But as it seems your husband did not murder the two women, then someone else did.

And unwittingly you let it be known where your sister was staying. You must have told someone.'

Wendy began to shake her head miserably. 'I didn't. . .' She paused. 'Only. . .'

'Only who?'

'Only Mrs Charlesworth, but she doesn't. . .'

'Doesn't matter?' asked O'Neill.

'No, I didn't mean that, I just meant that she wouldn't have told anyone.'

'How can you be sure of that?'

'I can't. I trusted her. I mean. . . I've known her for years. She wouldn't.'

'Does she clean for anyone else?'

'Yes. She's got several jobs.'

'And does she ever tell you about her other – clients?'

'Well, yes. But she's not malicious. She doesn't gossip. . . much.'

Wendy's voice trailed off in a whisper as the full implication hit her of what she told Mrs Charlesworth in an unguarded moment. A moment that she knew she would always live to regret.

'Who were your cleaner's other clients?' asked O'Neill.

'I don't know,' Wendy answered miserably, 'she's always referred to them as "one of my ladies" or "one of my gents".'

'Not to worry,' said O'Neill, 'she'll be giving us a list.'

'Can we go now, Chief Inspector?' asked Christopher.

'You can indeed, sir.'

'I've just got one question,' said Fran. 'Was there a reason you put your wine trophy in the loft?'

He gave a half smile in reply. 'Yes, Sergeant. It didn't live up to its promise. It was supposed to be silver plated and it began to peel and tarnish. I prefer to have objects around me that are beautiful rather than flawed.'

O'Neill couldn't conceal from Fran the final disparaging glance he gave Christopher as he left the room.

Before O'Neill and Fran left the station O'Neill sent a constable to the home of Mrs Charlesworth for a list of her clients. 'Ring me at Last Chance Farm,' he instructed, and as the young constable sauntered off O'Neill shouted at his retreating back, 'Today, Constable, not tomorrow!'

Once in the car Fran asked O'Neill the question she had been longing to ask him.

'Tell me, boss, why exactly did you dislike Theodolou so much?'

O'Neill stared straight ahead for a moment and then said, 'Jealousy, would you believe.'

'I wouldn't. He's ugly and bald and apart from a sexy voice he's got nothing going for him.'

'He's got a wife though, hasn't he?' said O'Neill. 'And believe me, being a widower isn't all it's cracked up to be. Women of my age are usually married or in relationships. If you've never been married it must be easier. . .' He paused. 'Or. . .'

'Or what?'

'Just more galling to see younger men not only have the pick of young girls but of older women too.'

O'Neill switched on the ignition and began driving in silence. They had only gone a short distance before Fran said, 'This isn't the way to Last Chance Farm, boss.'

'We're not going there, we're going to the Harrington place first.'

His tone of voice didn't suggest to Fran that asking more questions would be wise. Once again she felt those uncomfortable twinges of concern for Connor. As a detective he was, thought Fran, not detached enough. Her erstwhile boyfriend had been like that, only he had manifested his involvement by beating hell out of a criminal who had triggered his wrath. O'Neill seemed to be trying to project some of his own insecurities on to imagined suspects. Steve and Sandra were Fran's favourite suspects but O'Neill had obviously dismissed them. Was that because he liked Sandra, or did he assume Steve simply didn't have the bottle? If not them. . . who?

At the Harrington farm O'Neill said, 'Be waiting in the car, Fran. I'll only be a few minutes.'

Fran sat for a while staring at the watery sky and the sides of barns and remembering that when she was a smoker this was just the moment she would have idly smoked to pass the time. And that of course was the joy of smoking – being idle but not being truly idle.

When O'Neill did eventually return he wasn't alone. He had Jethro with him. An excited Jethro who bounded into the car with much barking and wagging of the tail.

'Lie down,' said O'Neill with the low, authoritative voice dogs seem to understand. The dog laid down immediately on the back seat but once the car moved away he crept to the window to look out with more tail-wagging excitement.

'Why the passenger, boss? He's not a poor man's bloodhound, is he?'

'No, Fran, he's our excuse to call out the vet. We're going to try and reconstruct the crime.'

'Using the dog?' asked Fran in surprise.

'That dog is pretty talented, I'll have you know, Fran.'

'We could do with some talent.'

'Is that meant to be a dig at me?'

'I was just trying to be light-hearted, boss.'

'I was light-hearted once,' said O'Neill. 'Before I joined the police.'

Last Chance Farm stood desolate and sinister in its emptiness. At least it seemed sinister to Fran now. The front door was boarded up and cordoned off by a circle of yellow police tape. The back door was boarded up too; O'Neill produced a crowbar and energetically wrenched them off. They were just entering the kitchen, followed by the dog, when a voice spoke from O'Neill's radio.

'The list you wanted, boss, of the cleaner's clients,' said the voice.

'Fire away,' said O'Neill.

There were four names. The third was Keith Quinton. O'Neill rang the surgery.

'Mr Quinton, it's Detective Chief Inspector O'Neill here. We're at Last Chance Farm and we've found a very sick stray dog here. I don't think he'll last if we move him. I think he must have got himself trapped inside the house.' He paused. 'Give him some water. . . oh, yes, we've done that. You'll be over – good – about half an hour. Thanks a million.'

'Very convincing, boss,' said Fran.

'Glad you liked my performance. And it achieved something.'

Fran frowned. 'That he's coming?' she asked.

'No,' replied O'Neill, 'it established that he knew where to come.'

For a few moments they both stared at the neat kitchen, both reliving the moment they first stepped into the house. First impressions thought O'Neill – count. He shouldn't have ignored his first gut reaction. The house had been too tidy. Even the body had been neatly arranged, the tea towel over the face as if a woman's influence had been at work. A murderer with plenty of time, a murderer with an assistant.

As O'Neill stood silently surveying the scene Fran's glance lingered on the dried flowers and then she remembered. . . those tiny scraps she had picked up and placed in her anorak pocket. Her hand went automatically to the pocket. They had gone! Her fingers searched the pocket lining more carefully. There was a small hole and she felt the edge of her anorak. They were wedged in the lining. Whatever had possessed her to pick them up? Still, it couldn't matter now – could it?

'Are you good at acting, Fran?' asked O'Neill abruptly.

'Brilliant,' answered Fran.

'Modest too. Well, you'll have to prove it now. All along we assumed that, because Trudi escaped with her life when Carol was killed, that Trudi wasn't here when the murderer came. Time of death was only established to within a few hours. I think now we were wrong. Trudi and Carol were here when *he* came. They were happily preparing for their holiday but some of that packing was done after Carol's murder and some of the tidying up. It was all too tidy. No one dies that easily, something gets kicked or knocked over and usually because the murderer leaves in a panic. But the one thing we did underestimate was the deliberate severing of the arm – the organization involved.'

'Yes, boss, but only one arm was cut off.'

'Sure, Fran, that was only the beginning. The intention must have been to dismember the whole body, but that takes time. Either someone disturbed them or one of them lost their nerve.'

'Them?'

'Yes. This was definitely a two-person job.'

'I don't suppose you're going to tell me who?'

'Not yet. First I'm going outside and knocking on the kitchen door. Delay letting me in. Pretend you're tough Carol. You're alone in the kitchen, Trudi is upstairs packing.'

'I don't think I'll win any Oscars for this,' said Fran.

'I'll buy you a damn good meal though,' said O'Neill as he walked out of the kitchen door and closed it behind him.

Fran waited for his knock and when it came she jumped slightly in surprise at its loudness.

'Trudi, it's me. Let me in. I just want to talk.'

Fran didn't know what to say so she didn't answer.

'Come on, Trudi, there's a good girl. Let's discuss it. Open the door.'

Fran realized at this point that she hadn't really got a scenario in mind. 'Connor, for goodness' sake what am I supposed to do?' she shouted at the door.

'Jasus woman – improvise!'

'In that case: Sod off, Trudi doesn't want to see you.'

Silence for a moment, footsteps moving a short distance away. Then the door opening.

'You bastard,' said Fran, getting into her character part and standing square in front of O'Neill. 'I told you to sod off. She doesn't want to see you.'

'Get out of my way. Trudi, get in here!' he shouted. 'I want to talk to you.'

Fran raised her hand to push him back but O'Neill pushed her aside. Fran had expected the dog to come to her rescue – instead she saw him skulking fearfully under the kitchen table. Again Fran resumed her part, pulling at O'Neill's arm. This time though he responded by putting both hands on her throat and tightening.

'Connor – you bastard!' she gasped, all pretence at

acting lost as she genuinely pushed him away.

'Sorry, Fran. . . sorry. I got carried away.'

The knock at the door when it came was at the front door.

'Let him knock for a while,' said O'Neill. 'We'll be ignoring him.'

The knocking continued then the calling, 'Chief Inspector – it's Keith Quinton.'

At this point Fran wanted to answer the door but O'Neill shook his head.

'Let him come round the back. I'll take the dog down to the cellar.'

There was silence, then footsteps and this time banging on the back door. O'Neill and Fran stood in the kitchen and watched as Quinton, obviously frustrated, began opening the door. Seeing O'Neill and Fran waiting there he looked pink faced and angry. 'What the hell's going on? Why didn't you let me in?'

O'Neill ignored the questions. 'I'm glad you could make it, Keith. You obviously knew the back door would be open, you didn't look for the key.'

'What key?' asked Keith irritably. 'And what's all this about a sick dog?'

'He's in the cellar,' said O'Neill.

A puzzled look crossed Quinton's face. 'I'm a busy man. A bloody busy man. I'm not prepared to play silly buggers for people who have time on their hands.'

'You'll have to make time for this,' said O'Neill. 'Sit down.'

Quinton hesitated.

'Sit down!' repeated O'Neill coldly. Quinton slowly

perched his bulky frame on the edge of an upright chair.

'My DS and I have been practising our amateur dramatics,' explained O'Neill. 'We've prepared a little play and we want you to fill us in with the ending. Are you sitting comfortably? Then I'll begin.'

Fran stared at O'Neill and tried to mouth a protest but O'Neill put an arm round her and whispered in her ear: 'I'll put in a good word for you with the Fowchester amateur dramatic society.'

'Don't bother,' she whispered back.

Keith's face by now had turned an ugly red colour and his hands were clenched into fists.

'Settle back, sir. Imagine this is Thursday afternoon, not dark yet. Not time to lock the kitchen door. Carol Sykes is in the kitchen, probably at the sink.'

O'Neill went outside then and began his door-knocking routine. Fran stood at the sink but she couldn't stop herself from looking at Keith and recognizing the sheer fury in his eyes. O'Neill was calling now.

'It's Keith,' he was saying. He even sounded like him. Fran was impressed.

They stretched out their little scenario but it wasn't until O'Neill had his hands at her throat that Quinton stood up – shaking.

'You bastards. It wasn't like that. . . it—' He stopped, realizing he had given himself away.

'What was it like, sir? You can tell us now or we can adjourn to the cellar.'

Quinton sank back on to the chair, his mouth white

around the lips. He said nothing.

'Right, that's it, Mr Quinton. The cellar. We'll follow you.'

Their suspect had two doors to choose from; one was merely a broom cupboard. He chose the cellar door.

The sound of their feet ended at the stone-floor vestibule. Quinton turned round abruptly just before O'Neill held open the inner-door for him. Fran thought for a moment he was going to make a run for it but he turned back towards the door hesitating for a second as if summoning his courage. Like a condemned man entering his cell, thought Fran.

The dog lay on the floor quite still, its face covered by a bright floral tea towel. Fran heard O'Neill say quietly, 'Play dead, Jethro.'

Jethro did just that but only for a few seconds. Then his tail began to wag and shaking off the tea towel he was on his feet and obviously waiting for some sort of reward.

Quinton stood with his mouth open, his lower lip trembling slightly. 'Oh God!' escaped from his mouth like a sigh. The dog sat now at his feet, begging. Staring straight ahead he reached into his trouser pocket and handed Jethro a dog biscuit.

'I didn't mean to kill her,' he said slowly, his voice trembling. 'She came at me like a maniac, kneed me in the groin, punched me in the stomach. I was winded. I took hold of her neck. I don't know for how long. Then Trudi walked in. I let Carol go. She slumped to the floor. I was in a state of shock but I didn't think I'd killed her. . .'

'And then what?' asked O'Neill.

Quinton didn't answer for a moment. He stared at the kitchen floor as if still seeing her body there. 'Trudi kept crying. I think I cried as well. She wanted me to call the police but I said no. She owed me that. She did. We had been getting on fine until Carol Sykes came along. Then Trudi gave me the brush-off. I came that day trying to persuade her to give me another chance. I'd lost one woman to a younger man, I wasn't prepared to lose Trudi to another woman. I've got my pride, after all. Anyway when we'd both calmed down I said we'd put Carol in the cellar. She helped me carry down the body. We left it there for a couple of hours. Trudi helped me tidy up, the vase of dried flowers got knocked over. . . strange that the vase didn't break. . . then we sort of talked. Trudi was very upset but I thought we'd reached some sort of understanding about our future. We planned to go away together – just as she and Carol had planned. I suggested we could dismember the body and get rid of it just as we'd managed to do with Frank's body. I had an axe in the boot of my car and some sheeting. Trudi covered Carol's face but she couldn't stay in the cellar. I'd just. . . chopped off the arm when I heard a car. I went to investigate. Trudi had gone. I was so angry. I didn't know whether to follow her or stay and deal with the body. I needed a drink then, badly, and suddenly I knew I couldn't continue hacking up the body. I wrapped the arm in newspaper and on my next visit to the college I dumped it.'

'I see,' said O'Neill. 'Why kill Trudi? A woman you professed to want?'

'She ran away, didn't she? She shouldn't have done that. I thought about it – I knew she'd tell someone. Probably her sister. They didn't seem to have any secrets. Mrs Charlesworth told me where she was – her sister Wendy would have definitely shopped me. I had to kill Trudi before her sister got to her.'

'And Frank Melksham?'

'I told you.'

'Did you?' asked O'Neill softly.

Quinton stared for a moment at Jethro who was looking up at him hoping for another biscuit.

'I finished him off, Chief Inspector. He took my woman.'

O'Neill nodded. 'We'll be taking you in now, sir.'

Quinton's shoulders sagged and for the first time his eyes filled with tears.

'Look after my dog, won't you, Inspector? I should have stuck to animals. They stay loyal.'

'Sure I will, sir. We'll be going now.'

It was late in the evening when O'Neill and Fran left the station. O'Neill had just opened his car door when he saw Tom Harrington and Norman Crick approaching the station's front door. 'Look, Fran,' he said indicating with his head. 'Get in the car quick before they see us.'

Fran watched as they entered the police station. 'Shouldn't we go and take statements, boss?'

'We'll be letting someone else have that pleasure, Fran. I think we've done enough for one day. How about that slap-up meal I promised you?'

'What about Steve and Andy? Shouldn't we be arresting them?'

'All in good time, Fran. All in good time. The Two Musketeers have obviously decided to tell us all, well almost all. No doubt they'll keep Sandra out of their little conspiracy, although I think she was in it all along because Andy wouldn't have been able to keep secrets from his mother, she'd be knowing him too well. The night he tried to hang himself, do you remember, I didn't hear a noise, did you?'

Fran shook her head. 'I didn't hear a thing.'

O'Neill smiled. 'That was either the grace of God or a mother's intuition. Now how about that meal?'

Fran looked up at O'Neill and smiled, apologetically. 'Not tonight, boss. I'm shattered. I feel totally drained. I really do just want to go home, wash my hair, have an early night.'

'Tomorrow, then?'

'Maybe,' she said, touching his arm.

At Fran's house he hoped she would change her mind but she didn't.

'Goodnight, Fran,' he said, 'it's been a grand case.'

'Goodnight, Connor. I'll see you tomorrow.'

Watching her go inside he felt a wave of rejection as painful as colic, but unlike colic he knew it would stay with him much longer. Was that how Keith Quinton had felt? he wondered.

He drove then to the Red Lion. And there for a while he drank and talked cricket with an old man who remembered the golden years. And as he drank a final Irish whisky he thought about Fran and how tomorrow is another day. Yes, begorrah! Tomorrow is another day.

KATE CHARLES

Appointed to Die

A clerical mystery

**Death at the Deanery – sudden and unnatural death.
Someone should have seen it coming.**

Even before Stuart Latimer arrives as the new Dean of Malbury
Cathedral shock waves reverberate around the tightly knit
Cathedral Close, heralding sweeping changes in a community
that is not open to change. And the reality is worse than the
expectation. The Dean's naked ambition and ruthless behaviour
alienate everyone in the Chapter: the Canons, gentle John
Kingsley, vague Rupert Greenwood, pompous Philip Thetford,
and Subdean Arthur Bridges-ffrench, a traditionalist who
resists change most strongly of all.

Financial jiggery-pokery, clandestine meetings, malicious
gossip, and several people who see more than they ought to: a
potent mix. But who could foresee that the mistrust and even
hatred within the Cathedral Close would spill over into
violence and death? Canon Kingsley's daughter Lucy draws in
her lover David Middleton-Brown, against his better
judgement, and together they probe the surprising secrets of a
self-contained world where nothing is what it seems.

A selection of bestsellers from Headline

All Headline books are available at your local bookshop or newsagent, or can be ordered direct from the publisher. Just tick the titles you want and fill in the form below. Prices and availability subject to change without notice.

Headline Book Publishing PLC, Cash Sales Department, Bookpoint, 39 Milton Park, Abingdon, OXON, OX14 4TD, UK. If you have a credit card you may order by telephone – 0235 831700.

Please enclose a cheque or postal order made payable to Bookpoint Ltd to the value of the cover price and allow the following for postage and packing:
UK & BFPO: £1.00 for the first book, 50p for the second book and 30p for each additional book ordered up to a maximum charge of £3.00.
OVERSEAS & EIRE: £2.00 for the first book, £1.00 for the second book and 50p for each additional book.

Name ....

Address ....

....

....

If you would prefer to pay by credit card, please complete:
Please debit my Visa/Access/Diner's Card/American Express (delete as applicable) card no:

Signature .... Expiry Date ....